Mayhem at Buffalo Bill's Wild West

This Large Print Book carries the
Seal of Approval of N.A.V.H.

A JEMMY MCBUSTLE MYSTERY

MAYHEM AT BUFFALO BILL'S WILD WEST

FEDORA AMIS

THORNDIKE PRESS
A part of Gale, Cengage Learning

GALE
CENGAGE Learning·

Farmington Hills, Mich • San Francisco • New York • Waterville, Maine
Meriden, Conn • Mason, Ohio • Chicago

Thorndike Press® Large Print Western.
The text of this Large Print edition is unabridged.
Other aspects of the book may vary from the original edition.
Set in 16 pt. Plantin.

LIBRARY OF CONGRESS CATALOGING-IN-PUBLICATION DATA

Names: Amis, Fedora, author.
Title: Mayhem at Buffalo Bill's wild west : a Jemmy Mcbustle mystery / by Fedora Amis.
Description: Large print edition. | Waterville, Maine : Thorndike Press, 2016. | © 2016 | Series: Thorndike Press large print western
Identifiers: LCCN 2016003777| ISBN 9781410488688 (hardcover) | ISBN 1410488683 (hardcover)
Subjects: LCSH: Buffalo Bill's Wild West Show—Fiction. | Missouri—History—19th century—Fiction. | Large type books. | GSAFD: Mystery fiction. | Western stories.
Classification: LCC PS3601.M576 M39 2016b | DDC 813/.6—dc23
LC record available at http://lccn.loc.gov/2016003777

Published in 2017 by arrangement with Fedora Amis

Printed in Mexico
1 2 3 4 5 6 7 21 20 19 18 17

I dedicate this book to Clara Moore,
the woman who has always
been the light of my life and
the gentlest soul in Sedalia.

ACKNOWLEDGMENTS

I tip my fedora to my marvelous critique partners past and present who have steered me aright: Susan McBride, Alexandra Hull, Joanna Campbell Slan, Judy Moresi, Eleanor Sullivan, Sarahlynn Lester, and Claire Applewhite.

In researching *Mayhem at Buffalo Bill's Wild West,* I found these books invaluable: *Life & Times Along Muddy: A Scrapbook History of Early Pettis County and Sedalia, Mo.* by Becky Imhauser and Betty Singer; *Annie Oakley* by Kasper Shirl; *Buffalo Bill Cody, the Man Behind the Legend* by Robert A Carter; *The Colonel and Little Missy: Buffalo Bill, Annie Oakley, and the Beginnings of Super Stardom in America* by Larry McMurtry; *Buffalo Bill and His Wild West: A Pictorial Biography* by Joseph Rosa and Robin May; *Buffalo Bill's Wild West: An American Legend* by R. L. Wilson; *Buffalo*

Bill's Wild West: Celebrity, Memory, and Popular History by Joy Kasson.

Many thanks for Rhonda Chalfont's articles in the Sedalia *Democrat* and the great librarians of the state of Missouri. I am especially indebted to the librarians at the 1901 Sedalia Public Library, the first Carnegie library in the state. Without their 1898 newspapers and their detailed city maps, *Mayhem at Buffalo Bill's Wild West* would have all the color and sweep of a one-straw broom.

AUTHOR'S NOTE

While the key characters and all dialogue and actions are products of my imagination, many of the names in this book represent real people alive in the fall of 1898. My only addition to Buffalo Bill's Wild West was the story's shooting victim, Little Elk. In Sedalia, many characters were genuine — Prentice, the police chief; Sheriff J. C. Williams; the mayor, Dr. Overstreet; and the musician Scott Joplin. The ragtime king studied music composition at George R. Smith College and supported himself by playing piano at the Maple Leaf Club, a saloon over Blocher's Feed Store on Main Street. The music store owner John Stark saw Joplin's brilliance. He published "Maple Leaf Rag," which brought fame to Joplin and riches to Stark.

Descriptions from the 1893 World's Columbian Exposition, better known as the Chicago World's Fair, are genuine — right down to Citizen Train's refusal to shake hands. Also true is the Ferris wheel anecdote about a clever woman calming a crazed passenger by putting her own skirt over his head.

While I take many liberties, I try my best to be true to the spirit of the people and of the age. For example, Professor Gentry's Dog and Pony Show with its baby elephant named Pinto and 150 aristocratic animal actors played Sedalia in September 1898 — though the time was actually after the Wild West left town instead of before the big show.

Buffalo Bill's Wild West and Congress of Rough Riders of the World performed in Hannibal, Missouri, on August 20, 1898, and performed for three nights in Kansas City a month later. The show played Sedalia on Friday, September 23 — without Colonel "Buffalo Bill" Cody — and certainly without his wife, Louisa "Lulu" Cody, who was at home in Platte City during the entire period.

The Cody marriage was as stormy as Annie Oakley's marriage to Frank Butler was harmonious. Buffalo Bill became enamored of actress Katherine Clemmons at the Chicago World's Fair in 1893 — and was caught by Lulu — which landed her the deed to their Nebraska home. However, the dust-up didn't prevent the colonel from engaging in a long-term liaison with Katherine. This indulgence cost him eighty thousand dollars (over twenty million dollars in today's purchasing power.) The affair ended when Katherine married the financier Jay Gould's globetrotting yachtsman son, Harold, on October 12, 1898. Katherine must have been sentimental. Along with six other of the colonel's old girlfriends, she showed up for Bill's funeral in 1917.

Here's one final true event. At the home of Charles Koock Sr., 5th Street at Park in Sedalia, guests really were entertained by a musicale on Wednesday evening, September 21, 1898.

CHAPTER ONE:
TOM SAWYER'S CAVE
HANNIBAL, MISSOURI
SUNDAY, AUGUST 21, 1898

As Lulu raised her hand to catch a drop of water dangling from a stalactite, a bullet whizzed past her outstretched arm. It had to be a bullet.

The sound echoed off the cavern walls in booming thumps. Loose rock clacked down in a hailstorm around her.

Johnny rolled her against the cave wall and pulled her face to his chest until the clicking stopped. Lulu didn't know whether to thank him or scream. Johnny Baker, her husband's employee, took better care of her than did her own husband. But what tenderness could she count on from that famous, handsome, impossible, unfaithful celebrity she had married? What else could she expect from Buffalo Bill Cody?

She fought against the idea that struck her head like a hammer on a carpet tack. It was too horrifying, too hellish to be true. But what if it were true? What if her own husband had just tried to kill her?

He wanted a divorce. She refused. Was he seeking a divorce of the "I may be jailed and damned, but at least I'll be rid of you" kind?

She fought down fear with anger. Pulling back from Johnny's arms, she raised her head into a suffocating cloud of limestone dust. She batted at the haze, but only fanned more in her own nose. Mouth open, she shuddered as the bitter powder descended on her tongue.

Her chest heaved for breath; her brain roiled with unbearable thought. *Where is the famous buffalo hunter? If he wants to shoot me, let him do it in broad daylight — not in some dank cave. Better still, let him execute me right out in public at his precious Wild West and Congress of Rough Riders of the World in front of an audience of ten thousand. Now there's a show to sell tickets. Selling tickets is all he cares about.*

Tears of self-pity filled her eyes. She imagined the tent man's bally. "Come one; come all. See the world famous buffalo killer use his trusty rifle Lucrezia Borgia for the last time. Buffalo Bill's farewell appearance will show the world how the great hero of the Western Plains deals with an unwanted wife."

Then everybody will know what a lecherous old fraud he is. Hero of the Old West? Not in my house, he isn't. Probably scalp me like he did Chief Yellow Hair if he had the chance.

She smiled in grim satisfaction at the thought of her dramatic demise — her bloody head with matron's silver-gray bun torn away to join other scalps on the great buffalo hunter's trophy lance. *After he scalped me in front of thousands, the state of Missouri would hang him.* She said aloud, "I'd buy a ticket to that show myself."

"What?"

In the settling rock dust, Lulu spat lime-stone grit into her handkerchief. "I was thinking out loud." She changed the subject. "Where did it come from — the noise of the bullet? You think it was a bullet, don't you, Johnny?"

His face looked otherworldly in the light cast up from a single lantern on the uneven floor of the cave. Johnny nodded.

In real life, Johnny Baker was the opposite of the hot-tempered shootists he sometimes played in the show. No one in the company was more considerate or reliable. His virtues had earned him the lofty place of second in command to Cody himself.

Lulu could see his eyebrows knitted in puzzlement, and she tried to explain her slip of the tongue. "I was thinking how impressed the audience would be if Bill could re-create the echo sound in his show. It scared me right down to the ground."

"And well it should. You're bleeding." He held up the lantern to cast light on her arm.

Lulu looked down. A red line slashed across the lavender silk of her sleeve. In the faint light, she could see dark ooze turning her forearm black. "I must have thrown my arm up and stabbed myself on the stalactite."

Johnny pulled her hand toward him to examine it. He shook his head. "It's not a puncture. It's a graze from a bullet. I've seen enough of them to know."

Not until that instant did the pain strike. It dashed up her arm in an electric burn. She bit her lip to keep from yelping. She would never give in — not to pain and not to Bill, either.

Johnny wet his handkerchief from a pool of water and laid it over the wound. "Cool water should ease the burn."

Lulu shook her head at the irony. "Cool water. We came to spend a Sunday afternoon in this cave which smells like mildew on old rags so we could escape the heat." She began to shiver.

He spoke in soothing tones. "We should

never have come here. Whatever possessed us to think sights underground would be worth seeing? There are plenty of wonders to see out in the daylight. I could watch the Mississippi River roll by for hours — and we can see Big Ole Muddy from our own hotel windows."

Johnny's voice took on a note of exasperation. "Say, where in tophet is the funny-looking fat man Bill hired to show us the local attractions? Some sightseeing guide. We can't even sight the man himself."

A familiar voice boomed from deep in the cave. "Johnny? Lulu? You two all right?"

Johnny sang out, "Over here. Mrs. Cody is hurt."

A light appeared nearby — too nearby.

With lantern held high, William F. "Buffalo Bill" Cody strode over the rocky cave floor as if he were taking the stage to deliver a monologue. "What happened, Lu? Did you take fright and fall?"

"She's been shot."

"Shot? Not possible. Let me see." He grabbed her arm and held it up under his lantern. "Hold your light higher, Johnny. My eyes aren't what they used to be."

He raised the wet cloth to peer at the wound. "I don't think a bullet caused that nick. Maybe a falling rock."

Johnny felt the bottom of a stalactite for jagged edges, then examined the floor. He shook his head. "No sign of a rock with blood on it."

Bill let the cloth fall back in place. "You can't tell a thing in here. Not enough light. Maybe the tip of the rock rolled off somewhere."

Lulu stared up at her husband. Her eyes narrowed into slits asking a silent question.

His voice took on a defensive edge, "Well, there's nobody here but the three of us and our cave guide. What reason would he have to shoot at Lulu?"

Lulu's gaze traveled down to the pistol that Bill wore low on his hip like an old-time gunslinger.

He pulled it from its holster. "You think I shot at you with this? This pistol shoots nothing but blanks."

He held the barrel up first to Johnny's nose then to Lulu's for the two of them to verify his words. They exchanged looks which bore witness. The barrel was cold and emitted no odor of sulfur.

Cody pointed to the muzzle. "See. It has a bar across the place where the bullets are supposed to come out. I only wear it because people expect Buffalo Bill to wear a sidearm."

Johnny seemed satisfied. "The blank gun hasn't been fired. It wouldn't shoot a real bullet anyway. The bullet we heard was real enough. Probably find it if we set our minds to it."

"I'll have a look-see. Johnny, find the way to the entrance. Take Lulu out of here. Go back into Hannibal. Get a doctor to take care of that arm."

"Aren't you coming with us?"

"I'm going to find our guide. I'm going to give him a piece of my mind for leaving us here. Something about the man seemed wrong, but I can't quite put my finger on it."

"So you think the guide shot at Mrs. Cody?"

"Not necessarily. Maybe at a snake. All kinds of snakes in caves."

Lulu wondered whether she might be married to the biggest snake in the Midwest.

Cody turned on his heel and threw words back over his shoulder, "I'm going to get to the bottom of this. Find out who fired the shot — if it was a shot."

Johnny took her arm, raised his lantern, and turned in the direction of the cave entrance. Lulu picked her way across the slippery cave floor feeling alternately furious and frightened.

Just like the famous Buffalo Bill. Shove his own wife off to Nebraska or palm her off on whoever was handy. Eighty thousand dollars — eighty thousand dollars — he spent promoting the current love of his life, Katherine Clemmons, fancy actress tart with a waist the size of my thumb and ambition enough to last till kingdom come.

Ignore his own family. Why couldn't I marry a simple man — a farmer or a banker?

Folks envy the family of someone famous. If they only knew the truth.

And that time in Chicago. Registered at a hotel as Mr. and Mrs. Cody bold as you please. They were almost as shocked as I was when the real Mrs. Cody — namely me — showed up. Cost him the ranch and the house in North Platte. I made him pay. And that was not the only time. High time, too. He has no idea what I suffer when I see women fawn all over America's heartthrob, Buffalo Bill.

His press agent, Bessie Isbell. I'm not a bit sorry I busted up his love nest in New York City. Hotel made him pay three hundred dollars. I made him sign over another big piece of property to me. Maybe if I make him give me every penny he has, he'll have to come home and stay put. Why should I be the only one to suffer?

20

She bit her lip while her thoughts drifted back to the good times. *How different from the day we met during the War Between the States. I had never heard the name "William Cody." I only knew my cousin had met a boy who rode for the Pony Express in the days before telegraph poles replaced fast horses. Who would have thought my cousin would bring that same boy to our house?*

By the time he was nineteen Bill commandeered everything and everybody as if he owned the big world and every little thing in it. Whatever he wanted simply belonged to him. I was no exception.

I had fallen asleep reading a book. She couldn't help but smile at the memory.

Such nerve. Who else but Buffalo Bill Cody would introduce himself to his future wife by pulling her chair out from under her to wake her up?

The smile twisted into pursed lips. *I should have known from that moment on he would bring me nothing but pain.*

She held her arm above her heart to ease the sting of the gash in her arm. *But how could I not love him — how could anyone not love him? So handsome — so impetuous. Then and there he asked me to marry him. I wanted to say, "Yes — right this minute — this second — whatever you want." But I didn't. I did what a modest, well-brought up young girl should. I told him to come back to St. Louis after the war.*

For a whole year, I spent hours at my window watching for any sign of the 7th Kansas Redlegs. Then one day, he appeared — larger than life and twice as handsome. He had his mind made up to capture the love of the beautiful girl with the dark curls. He wrote in his autobiography that he adored me above any young lady he had ever seen.

Her lip quivered. She felt the full force of injustice settle over her soul. *He said marrying me was the only thing he wanted — needed. But now I'm not the sweet young thing he wed the minute the Great Civil War was over. Now he finds me old and ugly.*

So what if I am past the half-century mark? What reason is that to push me away — to leave me to rot on the plains of Nebraska like a buffalo killed for hide and tongue and the rest cast off like so much garbage? No reason; no cause at all. Excuse — nothing but excuse.

The cause is the man himself. Live up to his own publicity — prove he's still the "King of the Prairiemen." That is the real reason why he wants to bed every female he sees. I bet he was after Victoria Regina herself — only the Queen of England was too smart to let the likes of him get close to her royal bedroom.

Still, I never thought he wanted to rid himself of me enough to . . . kill me.

The pair emerged into the muggy heat of an August day. She shut her eyes against the blinding light and leaned on the rock beside the cave entrance. She shielded her face with her unwounded arm and looked at Johnny.

He brushed limestone dust from his Stetson with his hand then used the hat to swat dirt and rock chips from Lulu's skirts. The results were disappointing. Mud clung to her hem in sodden brown clumps. Lulu wiped the grit from her lips onto her hanky.

Johnny batted dust from his white pants and sky-blue shirt with its button-on fireman's shield front. Lulu wondered to herself. *Does he think Bill shot at me?* Johnny's mild round face and kind gray eyes told her nothing.

As Johnny tried to bring back the shine to his trademark over-the-knee black boots, she tried to pose the question but couldn't find the words. *How do I ask a nice man like Johnny whether he thinks his world-renowned boss is trying to murder his own legal wife?*

Her mind kept falling back to the gunshot in the cave Mark Twain made famous in *Tom Sawyer*. *How fitting. That story was about money and murder, too.*

She wrapped herself in a cocoon of silent grief and said not a word to Johnny on the trip back to Hannibal. Her thoughts tortured her. *Bill said his eyes weren't what they used to be. Maybe I cheated death only because Cody's eyes are getting old.*

Bill was in the right spot and could have fired the shot. The bullet had not come from the blank gun, but he could have others hidden — real pistols with real bullets.

He didn't truly think the guide shot at me. Would he have gone off in search of an armed shooter without at least having his own working firearm? He knew the guide had not shot at me because he did it himself.

After firing the shot, he could have stashed the pistol anywhere in the cave. Maybe he stayed behind so he could go back for it. Maybe next time he would hit his mark. Maybe next time he would put on those spectacles he was too vain to wear in public. Maybe next time, the light would be bright enough.

Maybe next time William Frederick Cody would kill Louisa Maude Frederici Cody.

Chapter Two:

Eighteen-year-old Jemima McBustle pressed
her nose against the window. She couldn't
stop herself from watching the rain-swept
forests flash by in dizzying greens and golds.
She knew she should be studying her sub-
jects, preparing to interview famous people;
but she couldn't resist straining her eyes for
a glimpse of the governor's mansion on the
hills above the river at Jefferson City. The
young lady with auburn hair was riding a
train for the first time in her life. While the
state capitol receded behind her, she sighed
and firmly planted her nose in her book.

Jemmy had set her eyes on a career as a
stunt reporter like her idol Nelly Bly. Suetonius Hamm, her editor at the St. Louis *Illuminator,* had entrusted her with an assignment that should have been a lark and a joy
— to cover the biggest, the most exciting
show in the world.

Her exhilaration would have been higher

than her anticipation at making her debut into society at the Oracle Ball — except for one thing. Jemmy knew Hamm's real motive. He wanted her to fail so he could fire her.

Nothing about being a journalist came easily to Jemmy — nothing except writing the stories. Getting the goods on "The St. Louis Ripper" nearly put her in the morgue. But that wasn't the worst of it. Hamm seemed to take every success Jemmy made as a personal failure for himself.

She managed to survive the six-months trial period the newspaper owner had allotted her — barely. Jemmy had made Mrs. Willmore a rash promise to sell papers. Miraculously she had delivered with a low-down ugly scoop on a private madhouse. Her articles upped circulation by several thousand for a solid month.

In theory, she had risen to become a member of the regular newspaper staff, the staff member Hamm loved to hate. *I know Hamm is sending me to Sedalia to get me out of his hair. At least he would be if he had any hair. Probably wants to plot some way to get me fired. Well, I have absolutely no intention of letting him do it.*

The silver chain of tiny links she wore around her throat had fallen inside her high collar. She tugged it out, then ran her thumb around the charm her father had worn as his watch fob. She didn't need to see it. A shiny bit of silver dangling at the eye level of a ten-year-old girl stuck in her memory far better than her father's face. The *claddagh,* a pair of hands holding a heart wearing a crown for friendship, love, loyalty.

To buck up her courage, she whispered the words in Gaelic. *"Gra dilseacht cairdeas."* Father brought her up to be an independent person — to use the education he gave her, to forge a life of her own. Sometimes being her own woman seemed too much grief, too much work, too much burden for her young shoulders to bear.

Still, what is the alternative? Let Uncle Erwin pick out a rich old grouch of a husband? In weak moments she admitted to herself that marriage to a rich man, even an old one, might not be such a terrible thing. *Maybe older people — more experienced people — would know how to arrange a happy life for a young girl of eighteen.*

The Victorian world proclaimed females too fragile for life outside marriage. Following her family's wishes would be the easiest course. *Maybe I should let my family settle my life and be done with it.*

Left to her own devices, Jemmy had very nearly found herself married to a handsome rotter. Could Uncle Erwin do worse? *No more lazy talk — never be your own woman that way.*

With a start, she realized she had no idea of what happened over the last five pages in her book. *Heaven in a handbag. Keep your mind on your job or you will find yourself married to an old curmudgeon with the gout.* She leafed back through *Adventures of Buffalo Bill from Boyhood to Manhood* until she found a scene she recognized.

To research her assignment, Jemmy had borrowed all the dime novels in her next door neighbor's library of Beadle's Boy's books. Mr. Bappel promised her this particular little orange-covered pamphlet had started the legend of the great buffalo hunter.

She poised her pencil over her notebook and tried to think what to write. *"Mr. Cody, I understand in 1876, only two months after you killed and scalped Yellow Hair, Prentiss Ingraham wrote 'The Right Red Hand; or, Buffalo Bill's First Scalp for Custer.' Since Colonel Ingraham was in New York at the time, I wonder how he came by his information. Did you communicate by telegraph?"*

Jemmy was so immersed in her thoughts that the world inside the coach changed while she wasn't looking. In the rattle and clank, she failed to notice an armed man in the aisle until he growled at Jemmy's traveling companion.

"Put your money and your watches and rings in this here poke." The robber threatened the elderly lady sitting in the seat across from her. Jemmy caught a surprised breath and held it. Tension crackled in the air like lightning down a lamppost. Jemmy's companion did not raise her head.

The train robber held aloft a heavy pistol. Its freshly blued barrel gave off wicked glints and spilled drops of rainwater on Aunt Tilly's crochet work. With the other hand he held out an open muslin flour sack printed with dainty blue forget-me-nots. "Put all your val'ables in this bag."

Aunt Tilly cocked her head to the side and peered at him over her pince-nez. "Not today."

Beads of sweat popped out above the dark blue bandana the robber used to hide his face. He must have thought Auntie deaf. He spoke louder. The strain gave his voice an ever-so-slight quaver. "Place your val-u-a-bles in the sack."

Aunt Tilly said, "Not today. Try again next

week on our return trip. At such time I may be in a more agreeable state of mind."

The robber looked around to see how many people were watching an old lady tell him he had selected an inopportune time for larceny. All eyes focused on him. He paused for a few undecided seconds, then knitted his brow. "Put your val'ables in my poke or there'll be hell to pay."

Aunt Tilly spoke louder, "Are you deaf, sir? I said, 'Not today.' " She twirled white thread around her little finger and recommenced crocheting wee precise loops.

The robber squirmed, then bent over at the waist to stick his face between Aunt Tilly and her doily. His voice became a sharp bark as more water drops tumbled on Auntie's white crochet thread. "Are you deaf, old woman? I said to put your val'ables in my sack."

Aunt Tilly exchanged her crocheting for her umbrella and stood. Aunt Tilly dwarfed the robber by three inches in height and close to a hundred pounds in heft. Jemmy judged he could not have weighed a hundred-and-forty carrying an anvil.

With her formidable bosom Aunt Tilly forced the robber to back up. "Do not shout, sir. It bespeaks ill breeding."

The robber's squirming became jiggling

jumps — the kind little boys make when they need to relieve themselves but can't find a convenient tree. He yelled, "I'm going to shoot you dead if you don't put your val'ables in this bag. That fancy ring and those ear bobs. Put them in here." He shook the bag at her.

She shoved the sack aside with her umbrella. "I believe I have made myself perfectly clear. I do not intend to be robbed today. If my refusal discommodes you, I do apologize."

The robber's voice turned petulant. "You can't treat me like this. It ain't right. When a des-pe-ray-do tells you to put your val'ables in the sack, you're supposed to do it." With twitching hand he started to lower the gun toward Aunt Tilly's broad bosom. "Old woman, are you dead set on making me kill you?"

With dazzling speed, Aunt Tilly slipped her umbrella between his head and his gun arm. She deftly knocked the pistol upward, then used the tip as precisely as if she were inserting one knitting needle behind its partner to purl a stitch.

She flipped up the back of his hat. When the hat fell forward, the brim poured rainwater down his blue denim britches. While he was thus taken by sneak attack, she thwacked him right down the center part of his hair with her umbrella.

His pistol went off with an ear-shattering *whang.* Through the iron filigree of the overhead luggage rack the bullet punctured a medicine hawker's trunk. The hole spouted Dr. Dromgule's Female Bitters over the salesman. In seconds the back of the coach reeked of cheap whiskey and peppermint.

The felon dropped both loot and pistol in order to shield his head against Aunt Tilly's assault, but Auntie was too nimble to deny. She smacked him a good one on the left side of his head and another on the right — then right ear and left ear — then left and right and left and right both high and low while she backed him toward the potbellied stove at the rear of the train car.

At last, another passenger found some gumption. He tripped the backpedaling robber. When the luckless crook lay sprawled on the floor, a swarm of travelers took to pummeling him.

The shot brought others of the gang on the run. The enterprising tripper took charge of the passengers' defense. He ambushed a second robber when the chubby fellow tried to enter from the next car back. Aunt Tilly's champion grabbed the man's loot sack and booted the thief's fat backside clean off the train.

With pounding heart Jemima McBustle picked up the fallen pistol. She hid it in her skirt folds while she slipped toward the front of the car. When she was halfway down the aisle, a member of the gang burst in from the car in front. Jemmy pointed to the robber's skinny partner who was being clobbered with a summer sausage by a savage little boy of seven or eight.

The outlaw's would-be-rescuer raced past Jemmy only to find this "sweet young thing" was more cagey than sweet. Jemmy stopped him cold when she poked his partner's pistol hard against his lower spine. Although her voice trembled, she tried to sound dangerous, "I'm no Annie Oakley, but a blindfolded monkey couldn't miss at this distance."

He surrendered his shotgun. Jemmy turned the robber over to the not-too-tender mercies of the passengers in the front part of the coach. Those passengers had not been able to get close enough to the skinny crook to get in a good kick, pull a hank of hair, or wallop with a sausage. The exercise of pummeling the newcomer cheered them up even more than regaining their purloined property.

By the time the train conductor found his way to Jemmy's coach, loot and owners were reunited, and three well-drubbed crooks had been tossed off the train. Before long the steamy atmosphere of robbery and mayhem returned to the peaceful clack of train wheels counting off the miles. The two ladies who had orchestrated the heroics — one young and one old — returned to their note-taking and crocheting.

Ignoring both soot and rain, the conductor opened a window to let the heady liquor fumes escape. He asked the Dromgule-soaked drummer, "What happened?"

The salesman flopped his sopping handkerchief in the direction of Aunt Tilly. "Ask the lady with the umbrella."

The conductor tipped his cap. "Ma'am, would you be so good as to tell me what went on here?" He nodded toward the Dromgule salesman. "That gentleman says you ought to know."

Aunt Tilly replied, "The passengers decided not to be robbed today. Quite the proper thing. Why, the scrawny one mussed my doily. A remarkably thoughtless act in my opinion. Dampness on the floss makes proper loop size impossible. Besides, only a person of low-breeding would rob a train in the rain. He didn't have the common decency to remove his hat. And, although I usually would not make such a vulgar comment, he smelled like a wet canine."

Naturally, Aunt Tilly did not discuss her own role in the crook's ouster because she was not one to boast or brag. She was not one to approve of flaunting one's own heroic deeds. She was not one to tolerate insensitivity or bad manners.

Among the many things Aunt Tilly was not, one must include she was not Jemmy's real aunt. Gertrude Turaluralura Snodderly was the old maid sister of Jemmy's aunt-by-marriage. Uncle Erwin McBustle's lady wife, Delilah, had no daughters of her own. Hence, she took upon herself the task of preparing her four McBustle nieces for marriage. As the oldest, Jemmy was the first beneficiary of Auntie Dee's generous attention.

Auntie Dee and Tilly-Lilly, the name all the youngsters called the old maid behind her back, were cast from the same mold. Both held definite opinions and refused contradiction or compromise. One trait separated the two. Auntie Dee had oodles and buckets of charm. She could make a rebuke pleasant as a reprieve.

Tilly-Lilly, on the other hand, made a rebuke feel like being dragged by the tongue around the seventh level of Dante's inferno. While Aunt Delilah's sarcastic quips would often tickle the funny bone, Tilly-Lilly was born without a humorous humerus in her body. That was, in fact, her chief talent. Her utter lack of tender sentiment made Aunt Tilly the ideal companion for unmarried young ladies.

No respectable family would permit an unmarried girl, even a gainfully employed one like Jemmy, to travel alone. Besides, Jemmy was fresh from her debut into society, just eighteen and uncommon pretty. The prospect of solo travel for an unmarried girl horrified Auntie Dee. Two hundred miles by train without proper supervision? Such disdain for custom and convention would surely mar Jemmy's marriageability.

Aunt Tilly-Lilly delivered supervision far beyond mere propriety. She dispensed perfection — though she would never be immodest enough to say so.

Aunt Tilly-Lilly may have been too moral to toot her own horn, but Jemima McBustle was not. By the time they reached the Queen City, she planned to pen a rip-roaring train robbery story with herself as heroine to send back to the St. Louis *Illuminator. Print that in your paper, Mr. Editor Suetonius Hamm!* Train robbery tales enthralled readers — especially readers of dime novels — and sold cartloads of newspapers.

When the conductor arrived, Jemmy handed him the robber's confiscated shotgun with a demure, "This rifle has come into my possession. Perhaps you would be so kind as to dispose of it. I detest firearms."

Jemmy was being less than truthful. She knew full well that the lever-action Winchester 1887 ten-gauge was a shotgun. She thought a dab of misdirection would allow her to keep the Smith & Wesson Model Three American .45 caliber revolver she had maneuvered from her skirt folds into her satchel the minute she returned to her seat.

She had already started a weapons collection back home. A fine heavy piece like this one would be a dandy addition. Of course, she thought she probably should learn to shoot first. This assignment might have been custom-made to fill that need. Jemima McBustle was slated to interview the most famous lady shootist who ever lived, Miss Annie Oakley.

Jemmy asked, "Mr. Conductor, do you know the identity of those criminals?"

"No, miss. The passengers threw them off the train before I could get a single look."

"Do you know of any way I might find

out who they are?"

"Well, you might go to the post office when we reach Sedalia. Check the wanted posters."

"Might I prevail upon you in the meantime, if it's not too much trouble? Would you be so kind as to inform me if you should discover the identity of any of the miscreants?"

The conductor tipped his cap. "My pleasure, miss. I'll ask around."

As he left, Jemmy shut her eyes and tried to remember the beat-up robber. She flipped open the red Indian head cover of her tablet and began a list.

Five-feet-five-inches
Hundred and fifteen pounds
Dark brown hair parted in the middle
Dark blue kerchief
Smoked sausage bits on blue shirt

She wrinkled her nose in an effort to recall the color of his eyes. Nothing. She strained to visualize his features. Nothing. *How does a reporter describe a drab outlaw?*

Nose — probably broken
Lower lip split open

She tore the sheet from her tablet and

wadded it into a ball. *How useless to describe a man I will probably never see again. If I do see him, will his bruises still be fresh? Will his shirt still be unwashed?*

Jemmy's photographer, Hal, who had been up front and missed the whole bandit business, burst in from the front of the car. He clumped down the aisle as quickly as anyone could expect from a fellow hampered with camera, tripod, and bag of heavy photographic plates. Breathless, he stopped in the aisle and steadied himself with an elbow on the back of Jemmy's seat.

Harold Dwight Dwyer served as Jemmy's photographer-bodyguard. He asked to be called "Flash" because photography was the most important thing in his world. Jemmy called him "Hal" because she couldn't keep from laughing every time she called him "Flash."

He shifted his camera and said, "Are you all right? Did you actually get robbed?"

"Robbers tried, but all they got for their pains was kicked off the train — thanks to Aunt Tilly, and to me."

Hal knitted his brows in disbelief. "The pair of you — two females — foiled a train robbery?"

"That's right. Don't you believe me?"

Hal sat himself down in the seat next to

39

Jemmy. He took his camera in his lap and began unscrewing the wing nuts to collapse the wooden tripod legs. "Move your foot, please."

Jemmy goaded, "If you had stayed here, you could have taken the greatest pictures of your life."

"I got some good shots of the engine and the trestle over the Gasconade River. I was able to keep the camera still enough when we were moving slow."

"You got a trestle. We got a mob of robbers."

Hal chuckled. "You tell the wildest stories. I know most newspaper reporters gussy up stories to make them more exciting, but I didn't think you would make up such a whopper." Sarcasm gave his words bite. "Stopped bandits from robbing a train? A likely story."

"I'm not making it up. Ask anyone in the car. Ask Aunt Tilly. A lie never darkens her lips. It wouldn't have the nerve."

He leaned toward the lady, "Pardon me, Miss Snodderly. Did Miss McBustle stop a robbery while I was away? Did you two cause all the excitement?"

Aunt Tilly looked up from her crocheting. "I have no idea what young people consider exciting these days. I would call what hap-

40

pened an unconscionable lapse of courtesy on the part of a jumpy little fellow dressed in completely unsuitable wet attire. He shook drops of rain on my crocheting when he attempted to steal our property. Naturally, I refused to be robbed by a person with such an appalling lack of refinement."

Hal gulped and stared wide-eyed. Jemmy winked. Aunt Tilly-Lilly smacked her charge's hand. She glared straight into Jemmy's eyes while she shook a scolding finger. "You are not to engage in such a shameful exhibition ever again. Winking at a male — wicked girl."

Jemmy wanted to scream at being treated like a child. She said, "Yes, Aunt Tilly."

Aunt Tilly turned her attention to Hal. "Mr. Dwyer, are you quite finished putting away your photographical contraptions?"

"Yes, ma'am."

She pointed to the space next to her. "Then, you will be so good as to relocate yourself next to me. Sitting next to Miss McBustle might be considered unseemly. You might inadvertently touch her elbow or her shoe."

Jemmy ducked her head to hide her chuckle as she returned to her notes. Hal sat where Aunt Tilly told him to and opened the new Sears, Roebuck & Co. catalog to

41

the photography pages.

Jemmy stared out the window in hopes something might jog her memory, help her recall a forgotten detail of the skinny robber's appearance. However, she lost her train of thought when she became entranced by the reflection of Hal's remarkable ears.

They stuck out from the sides of his head like lidless sugar bowls of translucent china. The pair served as barometer to Hal's moods because they changed color to reflect his state of mind. Under her heartless teasing, the ears had gone from fear-white to embarrassment-red. Now they eased back to their normal state of baby mouse pink.

Jemmy's boss employed Hal because, like Jemmy, he was a redhead. The fact that Hal resembled Jemmy about as much as a warthog resembles a shoe tree didn't register with the *Illuminator*'s editor. Hal's hair was bright coppery red, not auburn. He was nearly a foot taller and freckled to boot; but the differences didn't dissuade Mr. Hamm from choosing him to play the role of Jemmy's escort and keeper.

By turns, Jemmy abhorred and admired Hal. He meddled in her plans, stopped her headlong rush into uncharted dangers, and generally squashed her stunt-reporter aspirations. On the other hand, he was always around when she needed a shoulder to lean on or a ride home on his ugly chartreuse green tandem bike.

Jemmy should have felt guilty at treating him shabbily, but she didn't. The redheaded duo sparred from the moment they met. They warred the way two ambitious people often do. That was the bad news. It was also the good news. Each knew losing a partner, no matter how vile a partner, would mean losing both jobs at the *Illuminator.*

The traveling party of three absorbed themselves with story-copying and catalog-reading and crochet-hooking until the train pulled in to the Sedalia Missouri Pacific station right on time at 2:45 p.m.

Hal left Aunt Tilly-Lilly to hold her umbrella over the camera and hand luggage while he brought up the trunks. Jemmy went inside to make arrangements to send her story back to St. Louis on the 4:15. She also telegraphed the *Illuminator* to have a messenger pick up the story.

Her telegram read: "*Illuminator* NEWS-WOMAN FOILS TRAIN ROBBERY. SEE 4:15 CONDUCTOR. J. MCBUSTLE."

Jemmy beamed at the Western Union clerk. "Ten words exactly."

To herself, she gloated. *I bet Hamm goes to Union Station in person. He may spout a*

43

little Latin first, but he'll go.

Jemmy folded the second copy of her story in half. "How many newspapers have you in town?"

"Three dailies. The morning paper is the *Capital,* a Republican newspaper. We have two evening papers, the *Bazoo* and the *Sentinel.*"

"Where is the *Capital* located, if I may ask?"

"Take the Ohio streetcar. Four stops, I think. Ask the conductor."

For the first time, Jemmy felt the thrill of being a real reporter. Here she was, Jemima McBustle, sent on a trip to cover the most celebrated and spectacular theatrical production on the planet, Buffalo Bill's Wild West and Congress of Rough Riders of the World.

Sedalia was as far east as Buffalo Bill would travel at the end of the 1898 season. Hamm had sent Jemmy to write several features about the show. He grudgingly noted that Jemmy might be able to do one thing better than a man — interview a reticent female like the Wild West's shooting star, Annie Oakley, "the Rifle Queen." Jemmy might have more success than a man — one uppity female to another.

Jemmy sniffed. So what if his real reason

for sending her off was to get his pesky girl reporter out of his hair for a week — or for good. It was still a peach of an assignment and Jemmy planned to make the most of it. She would write stories to make everyone, including Suetonius Hamm, stand up and salute. Besides, the story she burned to write — an exposé of the Combine — the crooks who ruled the city with their dirty dealings — would still be waiting back in St. Louis.

A bigger obstacle came in the substantial shape of Aunt Tilly-Lilly. True, Aunt Tilly had plopped a rip-snorter of a story right in Jemmy's lap. But the likelihood of Aunt Tilly repeating the feat seemed pretty slim. Supervision by the demanding dame felt like a steel-stayed corset laced tight enough to make a girl's eyes bulge.

After a mere seven hours on the train, Jemmy could see why parents loved Miss Snodderly, the ultimate chaperone, and why her too-well-tended girls loathed her. Jemmy decided her best chance to have her story in tomorrow's local paper would be to duck out on the sly after sending Hamm's telegram at the Western Union office in the depot.

She scribbled a few words, tore the page from her notebook, and folded it. She wrote

"Miss T. Snodderly" on the outside. She handed it and two cents to a porter. The moment she said the words, "Please take this out to Miss Snodderly on the platform," she felt a tap on her shoulder. *What could the tapper be except the tip of Aunt Tilly's umbrella?* She conjured up a smile she did not feel and turned to face the redoubtable umbrella of the doubly redoubtable dame.

Chapter Three:

A little too brightly, Jemmy took back the note and dismissed the porter. "It seems I no longer need you to find Miss Snodderly. She is standing behind me. Of course, you may keep the coins."

Aunt Tilly-Lilly held out her hand for the undelivered message. Jemmy backed up. Aunt Tilly bopped Jemmy's bad ear the same way she had popped the young robber on the train. Jemmy found herself owner of a painful reminder of how dangerous an umbrella could be when plied by skillful hands.

After due deliberation she said, "Ow." She did have enough presence of mind to crumple the note. Aunt Tilly noticed.

Aunt Tilly's umbrella ribs stung the back of Jemmy's hand. Jemmy dropped the note.

Aunt Tilly speared the crumpled paper and lifted it up to read. "I see you were planning a trip to local newspaper offices."

"Yes, Aunt Tilly, I hope —"

Aunt Tilly cut her off. "Quite impossible."

"But Aunt Tilly, it's my job. I work for —"

"Quite so, but first things first."

"You don't understand. I was on the scene for a very exciting —"

"I'm afraid you're the one who lacks understanding."

"Papers across the country will pick up my arti —"

"They shall have to pick up your 'arty,' whatever that might be, after we have been picked up and properly settled at the Koock home as befits guests."

"The whole reason we came here is —"

Aunt Tilly smacked Jemmy sharply atop each shoulder like Queen Victoria bestowing knighthood. But Aunt Tilly-Lilly's umbrella bestowed rain spatter instead of honor. The conversation was at an end. Aunt Tilly-Lilly delivered orders in the voice of a monarch. "You will precede me outside."

On the station platform, the three travelers stood waiting with some degree of impatience for the Sedalia relations to arrive. Well, they weren't exactly Sedalia relations — not of Hal, or Jemima, or even Miss Snodderly.

Aunt Tilly-Lilly had served as chaperone on the European grand tour for the unmarried daughter of Mr. Erwin McBustle's business acquaintance. The daughter then became wife to another business acquaintance, a Mr. Obadiah Koock, who had already outlived two wives and was at that very time shopping for a third. As the young girl's duenna, Aunt Tilly-Lilly paved the pair's bridal path. Result: the duly-wedded Koocks would host the St. Louisans for the upcoming week.

Ordinarily, distance traveled determined length of stay. Travel one hundred miles; stay one week. The party from St. Louis should have planned to stay two weeks in order to make the stay worthwhile and to let the Koocks know their hospitality had been well-appreciated and would be reciprocated at the Koocks' pleasure.

However, Jemmy persuaded Mother that the *Illuminator* couldn't get along without herself and Hal for two whole weeks. Since she believed as much, though for different reasons than she gave Mother, her pleas sounded true and sincere. Fortunately, Mother didn't discuss Jemmy and Hal's value to the newspaper with their boss. Suetonius Hamm placed Jemmy on his likability scale somewhere between cockroaches and death.

The rain eased to a cool mist as two little girls of about three and four came running across the platform. They wore white hair bows and navy blue sailor dresses. White piping and square sailor collars had become all the rage since those horrid Spanish had sunk the *Maine* and started the splendid little war in Cuba.

Trailing the pair was a woman in her mid-twenties who would have been pretty if she could have had a nose replacement. Almost any nose — button, pug, turned-up, even aquiline — would have been an improvement over hers. It resembled a turnip. It ended in a pointy droop — like a wilted tuber.

The woman had gathered her skirts to keep them out of water puddles on the platform. She shuffled to keep up with the tykes while keeping her ankles covered as befits a genteel lady.

Her driver ran past her to corral the little girls before they jumped on people or off the platform — whichever they had in mind. The driver grabbed one, but was too late for the other. The taller of the girls yelled at Hal as she leaped up, "Catch me."

He dropped his Sears-Roebuck catalog in

time to swing her in a circle and park her gently back on terra firma — or at least woodplanka firma.

The other child yelled up to him, "Now me. Now me."

Hal looked to Aunt Tilly for guidance. She dissuaded him with an ever-so-slightly raised eyebrow. The deprived child burst into tears and flopped down on the wet boards.

The mother, who turned out to be Mrs. Obadiah Koock — given name Dorothea — fussed. "Fanny, you're soiling your new white leggings. Stand up now and meet Miss Snodderly."

The child sobbed noisily without producing a single tear. Mrs. Koock pleaded. "Get up now and stop caterwauling."

The child buried her face in Hal's knees and wailed even louder. Hal's face turned so white, his freckles all but disappeared. In stark contrast, his ears turned puce — then crimson — then vermillion. Any minute Jemmy thought they might burst like a thermometer tossed in boiling water.

Aunt Tilly rescued him in the nick of time. Aunt Tilly-Lilly's umbrella came down on Fanny's head. The little girl let go of Hal's legs and turned around in surprise. Before she could recommence bawling, Aunt Tilly's umbrella under her chin persuaded her to move. With a pert prod to the child's backside, Aunt Tilly commanded, "Stand behind your mother. And not another peep."

Fanny did as bidden. Though from time to time she peeked out from behind Dorothea's skirts. The other little girl answered to the name "Sissy." Jemmy never did find out her actual name. Sissy looked terrified. A single glare from Aunt Tilly sent her scurrying to join her sister. Both girls cowered behind their mother's skirts.

Dorothea said, "I can't imagine how you do it. They don't mind me in the least."

Aunt Tilly cocked her head. "I'll see what remedy I can devise."

Dorothea smiled a feeble welcome. "I do hope you'll accept my apologies. We were late on account of the girls. They don't like wearing new clothes. I am mortified to have caused you to stand here in the rain." She turned to her driver, "Jean Max, would you see to their trunks, please?"

Hal broke in. "I sent them on by a drayman. I hope he's careful. My trunks have more than fifty pounds of glass photographic plates."

"Well, then. Do come with me to the carriage. It may be something of a squeeze, but if the young man will ride with Jean Max in the front, I think we can all manage."

Jemmy said, "Mrs. Koock, do you think it would be possible for us to —"

Aunt Tilly pointed her umbrella at her protégé. Jemmy didn't relish the idea of another clip on the ear. She thought better of asking for a side trip to the local newspaper office. She finished her sentence with "take a nap? I know it's gauche of me to ask, but the trip has exhausted me."

Jemmy barely listened to the reply. She was imagining herself slipping away from the house and taking her story to the *Capital.* It would be a snap.

They arrived at the Koock house, a redbrick two-story with a wide front porch. It stood in a handsome location on the corner opposite the main entrance to Liberty Park. Dorothea installed Jemmy and Aunt Tilly-Lilly in the guest room with a park view from its own balcony atop the porte cochére. She packed Hal off to a loft in the carriage house.

Not until past four thirty did Aunt Tilly-Lilly and Jemmy finish tucking their wardrobe in the armoire and their unmentionables in bureau drawers. Dinner was to be at seven o'clock followed by a musicale in the travelers' honor. Jemmy had little time — six o'clock at the latest — to have any chance of her story being run on Wednesday morning.

She hoped to sneak out with the aid of a little subterfuge. "Aunt Tilly, these trunks are in the way. I think I'll ask Mrs. Koock to store them for us."

As she started to drag them into the hall, the driver startled her with, "I take ze trunks, mademoiselle. Madame Koock, she say I put zem down cellar."

With Aunt Tilly hearing every word, Jemmy needed a new escape idea. "I'm famished. I think I'll go downstairs and see if I can find a snack."

Aunt Tilly said, "No need. Dorothea has most thoughtfully provided us with a bowl of fruit. Perhaps you didn't see it."

"Are you sure it isn't wax? Too pretty to eat, isn't it?" Jemmy tried to sound hopeful.

Aunt Tilly handed her a pear. "Now for a nap. I'm sure it will be a relief to get out of your corset. I'll help you unlace." The tiny buttons on Jemmy's shirtwaist seemed to fly open by magic under Aunt Tilly's expert touch. She hung up the bolero jacket and shirtwaist as Jemmy slipped out of her skirt.

Jemmy tried another tactic as Aunt Tilly loosened Jemmy's corset. "Aren't those little girls a terror? Mrs. Koock must be thanking her lucky stars you've come to lend your knack for schooling youngsters."

"This evening will be soon enough. I need to rest from the train trip." Jemmy hoped Aunt Tilly would nap, but had no luck. The chaperone sat in a chair reading *Harper's Magazine* and tut-tutting over the shameless females displayed in the latest fashions.

Jemmy couldn't sleep for fretting about the undelivered story. She became so anxious she even considered asking permission, but couldn't bring herself to say the words. No doubt Aunt Tilly didn't deem a newspaper story as a "first" enough thing to put before a wholesome nap.

She clenched her teeth and stormed inwardly over her imprisonment. Aunt Tilly-Lilly was a born freedom-fighter. She was against it — for females. She could tolerate freedom well enough in men, and she often remarked, "Boys will be boys." But she drew the line at freedom for women. As for girls, they'd best not dare to be anything but modest, silent, and obedient.

Aunt Tilly-Lilly stood ready to do her part in seeing to it that the world functioned in the right and proper way, the biblical way of ancient patriarchs. Without a word of request or bidding, she took upon herself the management of the young girls of whatever home she happened to inhabit. She ruled over her charges with glycerin soap to cleanse mouths of sassy speech and Epsom salts to clean everything else.

At six o'clock, Aunt Tilly announced it was time to dress for dinner. A half hour later, Jemmy stood thoroughly corseted, combed, and curled. Aunt Tilly pointed to the chair at the dressing table. "Practice sitting with your back straight and your hands folded. You have the unfortunate habit of fidgeting. It will not do. I expect you to be seated in exactly the same spot when I return after seeing to the Koock girls."

The instant Aunt Tilly breezed out, Jemmy dashed to the window to see whether she might spy an errand boy to take the story to the *Bazoo* or the *Sentinel*. She had missed the morning deadlines, but perhaps she was not too late for tomorrow's evening edition.

Only street dust greeted her. The Koock house was out in the suburbs, delightfully free from the coal smoke of trains and generators, but distressingly far from the bustling streets downtown — and newspaper offices.

Jemmy resigned herself to the inevitable and tried to situate herself in the precise position she had been ordered to maintain. With a surge of futile anger, she relived the agonizing imprisonment of her seventeenth summer.

She had been a frustrated girl caged in grandmother's sickroom. She felt time nibbling at her precious youth like the Mississippi tearing away bits of soil to be lost forever in the ocean. A year later she found herself trapped by an old woman again. Her chin quivered, but she refused to give in to tears.

At ten minutes until seven exactly, Aunt Tilly returned and scolded Jemmy for moving from her assigned spot. "A girl without self-discipline is like a horse without a rider. Pretty — but it never gets the mail delivered. In consequence of your feeble will, I will expect you to eat two bites of dessert, no more. Beginning the habit of self-denial now will stand you in good stead in later years. I trust you wish to keep your figure."

Jemmy had to bite her lip to keep from sputtering annoyance at receiving advice on weight control from the stout-and-then-some Aunt Tilly.

Jemmy had no choice but to be silent. Could being married be any worse than this? She regretted the thought as soon as it sailed into her head. She knew well enough the power men could wield — all with the full blessing of custom, law, other men — and yes — women, too.

As she followed Aunt Tilly into the hall, the sound of tromping feet and jingling spurs drew Jemmy's gaze over the banister. Coming up the stairs was a tall boy of thirteen under a dark head of curly hair. He dropped his hat on the rail post and reached for the knob of a back bedroom door.

Aunt Tilly stopped him. "Young man, I trust you do not intend to leave the various articles of your apparel hanging about to disorder the house."

As he turned back to claim the hat, he cast a sly grin in Aunt Tilly's direction. "No ma'am. I leave my hat out here, but I generally keep my drawers on."

To his great surprise, Aunt Tilly clipped him a good one atop his head with her cane. She was as skillful with a walking stick as she was with an umbrella. That fact didn't surprise Jemmy, but it came as quite a shock to the insolent young man. He squinted in pain as though he wanted to ease his noggin by rubbing it but had too much pride. He stood with sober expression, hat in hand.

Aunt Tilly said, "If you customarily sit at the children's table, you are too late. They have already dined." She looked him over and scowled. "We will expect you to present yourself in proper attire and good order to escort us to the musicale at eight o'clock, precisely."

"I eat at the main table."

"Indeed. You are in danger of missing dinner with the adults as well."

He tossed his hat into the room and started down the stairs. His lack of manners earned him another crack on the head. "Young man, I am appalled at your actions. Go into your room at once and dress in suitable habiliments for dinner and the musicale. The very idea. Going down to dinner in mud-spattered shirt with no neckpiece and wearing spurs."

She said the word "spurs" as if someone had dropped lye on her tongue. "Completely unacceptable. It will not do."

With a nod to Jemmy, she said, "Come along. We do not wish to tax our hostess's good will by being late."

When Aunt Tilly moved aside, the uncouth young man saw Jemmy. His eyes bulged with unabashed admiration. He evaporated behind his door but didn't shut it all the way.

Jemmy suppressed a chuckle when she stared back. Her eyes met one of his as he peeped through the crack. He reminded her of her sister Miranda peeking out from the covers on Christmas morning. Randy had to wait until the room was light enough to risk dashing downstairs. She couldn't sleep at all because she was too eager to see whether Saint Nicholas had left her a palomino Shetland pony and a diamond tiara.

Aunt Tilly marched down the stairs with Jemmy in her wake. Dorothea met them at the landing and escorted them into the dining room where the table had been set for six. Dorothea took her place at the end of the table nearest the kitchen door. She pointed to the chairs on either side of her own. Aunt Tilly paused. "Are you sure you wish us to sit there? Are the other two places for female guests as well?"

Dorothea's eyes brimmed with tears. "No. The other places are for Mr. Koock's two sons. But I never know when they will come. I find it best not to count upon them."

Aunt Tilly prompted, "And Mr. Koock? Will he be dining with us?"

"He's frightfully busy at the shops. You know railroad cars must be built and painted and repaired. I always lay a place for him, but he seldom fills it."

Jemmy's heart went out to this shy girl with the turnip nose. Poor Dorothea must have eaten countless meals alone in this properly elegant dining room with its dark red wallpaper, the color most suitable for proper digestion.

Dorothea motioned to the chair on her right. "Please do sit down. Cook has made a very special dinner to welcome you."

Aunt Tilly said, "Are you accustomed to wait for . . . ?" The three ladies exchanged glances at each other as they heard the young man clomping down the stairs. His speed almost matched his transformation from muddy horseman to dapper gent. He entered the room plastering down his hair with a more-or-less clean hand. The boy reeked of bay rum and Macassar oil.

The Koock son started to take the chair by Jemmy until Aunt Tilly's meaningful look told him to sit next to her instead. He stood behind the chair where her arrow eyes pointed him to go.

To his credit, he made no motion to sit down before the ladies. To his discredit, he simply smiled and gawked at Jemmy instead of seating the ladies until Dorothea said, "Miss Snodderly, Miss McBustle, this young man is my stepson Lilburn Boggs Koock. Lilburn, this is Miss Snodderly and her niece, Miss McBustle. Miss Snodderly graciously attended me on my grand tour of Europe."

Lilburn said, "I am happy to make your

acquaintance, Miss Snodderly, Miss Mc-Bustle. I hope you enjoy your stay in Sedalia."

Aunt Tilly's lips said, "I'm sure we shall savor it, Mr. Koock." Aunt Tilly's eyes said, "Give me a month, and I'll turn you from sow's ear to silk purse — or at least to a sow's ear with decent manners."

Jemmy murmured, "I'm pleased to meet you, Mr. Koock."

"Please call me 'Burnie.' Mr. Koock is my father." He showed a mouthful of white teeth in a Cheshire cat grin.

Jemmy smiled but did not extend an offer to let Burnie call her by her first name.

With introductions made, the obvious next step was to sit down, but nobody did. Dorothea had to remind the uncultured lad, "Lilburn, Miss Snodderly's chair."

He snapped to and seated them in proper order by age and status — Dorothea after Miss Snodderly and Jemmy last. Dorothea said grace and dipped her spoon into a cold and creamy vichyssoise, the signal for all to commence.

Tasty dishes followed — shrimp in aspic, watermelon ice, roast capon with baked squash, sliced tomato and cucumber salad — each course served with an appropriate wine. Jemmy had never felt as grown up, as sophisticated.

Mother allowed no spirituous liquors of any kind in her house. The only time Jemmy had ever tasted wine was at the Oracle Ball when she made her debut. The less said about how her introduction to society turned out, the better.

Jemmy's eyes crossed. Her head seemed to float above the table. She felt so good she very nearly forgot how much she hated being hemmed in by family, society, laws, and tradition.

She sobered up a little when she reminded herself what this trip meant to her future. She had to succeed. If she failed, Hamm would have proof that Jemmy was no newspaperwoman — that she had landed her job on a fluke and was keeping it by luck. She had little to gain, but everything to lose, including her one and only chance to be her own woman.

When Dorothea rang a tinkly glass bell, the maid produced coffee in a silver service to accompany *marron glacés* over ice cream. Jemmy longed to eat every bit of the syrupy chestnuts and cream, but dutifully put down her spoon after her allocated two bites.

Jemmy had not expected such continental culinary flair on the prairie. She tried not to slur her words. "Mrs. Koock, I marvel at the dinner. However do you manage?"

For the first time, Dorothea's face registered pleasure. "I am blessed to have a fine cook. She learned French cuisine in Haiti. A correspondent of mine who once lived there sent her to me when her employers returned to Paris. They couldn't take Pélagie back to France with them, but they feared for her life on the island. The revolutions, you see. So Pélagie came to me."

Aunt Tilly pontificated, "Such turmoil in such a small place. The smaller the place and the larger the number of inhabitants, the greater the need for self-discipline."

Jemmy tried to bring the conversation back to a happy point for her hostess, "This feast is in every way comparable to the food in Tony Faust's famous restaurant in St. Louis."

Dorothea blushed. "Pélagie works wonders in the kitchen, and Jean Max works wonders in the garden. I don't know what I would do without them. Perhaps you'd like to meet her? You've already met Jean Max. He tends our animals and drives our carriage."

She started to ring for the maid to bring out the cook but stopped with the bell in midair. Aunt Tilly's eyes put her on notice not to perform such an improper act. Treating a mere servant like a human being was not something Aunt Tilly would endure, much less endorse.

When Dorothea obeyed the silent order, Aunt Tilly gave the lady a reward. "My dear, the dinner was indeed most delicious." Then she promptly took it back. "Such a shame Mr. Koock had to miss it."

Dorothea rose above the slur as she described her plans for entertaining her guests beginning with Tuesday night's musicale at the home of Mr. Koock's brother Charles. Before she could list anything for Wednesday, the front door slammed with a bang

Red-faced, Dorothea dropped her head nearly into her dinner plate. "That must be Mr. Koock's other son, Marmaduke."

Chapter Four:

Louisa Cody rose from her seat on the eastbound train into Kansas City. Traveling made her bones stiff and achy. Still, trains were infinitely faster and more comfortable than farm wagons. How well she recalled a dashing young Bill Cody introducing his wife to the "Great American West" of Nebraska.

She remembered her awe at seeing endless plains overarched by a sky so blue, so close, she couldn't help but smile. Her hand reached out of its own accord to pull down a patch of that lustrous cloth from the heavens.

It seemed silly, now, to think how frightened she had been of the emptiness — and how thrilled to be mistress of something so pristine — so primeval and ancient. She half-longed to return to St. Louis, family, and civilization. She half-longed to put down roots and grow for centuries like a

66

seasoned oak tree — ever in the same place and ever giving shade and nourishment to all creatures.

She smoothed her skirts and walked to the exit. Without the rolling of the coach, the world seemed somehow less kindly, less familiar.

On the platform she waved her trunk claim check. A porter took it as he tipped his cap and shoved his trolley toward the baggage car. She stood awaiting his return, wondering why she had come. *What foolish hope brought me here? Why should I believe I can change Bill when I've tried and failed for more than a quarter century?*

She looked back at the train with longing — as if it had been a refuge. Perhaps it was the last barrier — the last buffer between herself and her husband.

Now it was gone. What she had determined to do lay before her. She raised her parasol against the sun and took a deep breath. Her plan would need all her courage and all her cunning.

She looked back yet again. *I don't have to do this. I could get on the next train home and no one would be the wiser.*

But then, nothing would change. Perhaps I could just talk to him. Talk? I've done nothing but talk. Time to do something — no matter what the cost. Time to act.

The last of the Grand Review of Buffalo Bill's Wild West and Congress of Rough Riders of the World trotted from the arena to the strains of "The Star-Spangled Banner." Frank Butler set props for the first act on the playbill. Who else would the colonel trust to win the hearts of the crowd but his shooting star, Annie Oakley?

Frank closed his eyes when the spotlight hit him full force. His arm flung wide to send the spotlight slowly drawing all eyes to the end of the arena. The moment the canvas parted for the woman he took pride in calling his wife, the audience set up a din of applause that shook the grandstand.

The little Quaker girl from Darke County, Ohio, commanded every eye to watch her and every heart to idolize her. No one could woo and win a crowd faster — not even the great showman himself, Colonel William Frederick Cody.

Every inch the coquette, Annie wore her hair in long girlish curls. Yet, she radiated a far more potent appeal. Close-fitting buckskin showed off her tiny waist. Despite the fact that she revealed not so much as ankle or nape of neck, she gleamed with feminine allure. Under her scandalously short skirts, she wore pearl-buttoned leggings sewn by her own hands.

Something else, too — danger flowed from the bullets sent into the world by her clear eye and steady hand. Little Sure Shot embodied polar opposites — luscious ladylike vulnerability and seductive death-dealing power. Who could keep from falling in love with her?

No one could resist, certainly not Frank Butler. For Annie, he gave up his title as the greatest sharpshooter in the United States. For Annie, he left his wife and children. For Annie, he gave up the adulation of the ladies who admired his Broadway-star good looks.

He had given up even his masculine pride, but never regretted his choice for a single minute. Frank lost a shooting match to the tiny lass who could drill a squirrel through the head with a .22 and won the greatest prize a man can have, the partner of his heart.

On the day Phoebe Ann Mozee married him, the heavens smiled on Frank. Ever since, his brain produced no single thought without her in it. On this Tuesday — and all other days of the week — his heart beat faster with anticipation simply because he was about to see her again.

Waiting for her entrance, he held his

69

breath. He could not help thinking back to the first time they met. His newspaper ads dubbed him "Greatest Rifle Shot in the U.S." He challenged all comers to pay a fifty-dollar fee and try their skill. He bragged he could "outshoot anything then living." How amazing a little girl, just fifteen and barely five feet tall, proved him wrong.

He missed only once, but Annie shot a perfect twenty-five of twenty-five targets to win the purse.

Even more incredible, Frank suffered no pangs of envy when she toppled him from his perch as champion marksman. To become her shadow — her assistant in the arena — he cast away his fame without a backward glance. He wanted nothing more in life than to please her, to protect her, to hold her close to him.

As Annie's fanfare swelled from Sweeney's Cowboy Band, Frank beamed with the pure pleasure of seeing her once more. What an entrance she made. She didn't walk or run. She didn't splash in waving a hat from atop a white horse like Buffalo Bill. She skipped into the arena looking far more virginal than her thirty-eight years of life and twenty-two years of marriage said any woman should.

In silver-starred hat, starched collar and cuffs, Annie turned her charms upon the good folk of Kansas City. Her every move dazzled them.

Annie lay on her back on a bearskin and gave the signal. Frank threw six glass balls in the air at once. She used three double-barrel shotguns — six shells exactly — to break all six targets before they reached the ground.

She shot backward over her shoulder using a hand mirror. She shot while riding a bicycle. She shot an apple off the head of her fearless dog. When she finished a feat, she beamed as she gave a pert tilt of her head and flirty back kick of triumph.

Frank held a playing card edgewise. She sliced it in half. He tossed coins in the air. She shot holes in them. On the rare occasions when she missed, she pouted with index finger to the corner of her mouth like a winsome six-year-old. The crowd folded her into their hearts.

As he held her horse for her to mount, he winked and grinned. The show of confidence was all make-believe. His fear for her clamped his chest. Like a blacksmith's rusty vice, the agony wouldn't release him until she was safely back outside the arena. Years of practice had taught him to manage props and still keep his eyes riveted on Annie.

After shooting from a galloping horse, she

performed her last trick and brought the house to its feet in awe and amazement. Frank muttered a prayer to himself.

She lay stretched full length on her galloping horse's back with a single foot in a stirrup. She seemed suspended in midair, jolting over the ground as she lowered herself to untie a handkerchief from the horse's hind leg. The crowd went wild with applause. Fear clamped Frank's heart in a painful ache.

The horse stumbled and gave an odd little buck with both rear feet in the air at the same time. Annie hovered a mere two feet from death. An unexpected lurch could send her to the ground to be trampled by eleven hundred pounds of horse wearing iron shoes on heavy hooves. Frank's throat gurgled as terror sent stomach acid burning into his throat.

No, Annie didn't fall. She tucked herself into the horse's side and stayed there a bit longer than usual before pulling herself back into the saddle. The crowd hadn't seemed to notice. Frank exhaled in a wheeze like the sound from a collapsing concertina.

As she made her exit, Annie blew kisses amidst a racket almost louder than the boom of her guns. Everyone in the audience would have sworn her publicity was true. Any one of them would have gladly taken the bet Annie could "scramble eggs in midair."

Frank finished loading the cart with props and drove outside. Annie took a victory lap as she waved and blew kisses to adoring thousands.

Outside the arena, Frank climbed down from the cart to greet her with praise for another brilliant performance as he always did. But tonight, they both knew something was off kilter. Her face did not show its usual flush of excitement from her success or the golden glow of love flowing from the crowd.

She frowned as she slipped from her horse. "Something is wrong. Tiffin stumbled or bucked. Thank heavens I wasn't shooting at the time. I might have injured someone. I thought Tiff was too well-trained to get spooked."

Frank pointed to the horse's rump where blood oozed from a dark blotch. "Something hit your horse — a bullet I think — and no more than a foot above your head when you were untying the handkerchief."

"A what?" Annie scrutinized the slash, then nodded. Between them, the pair had seen three-quarters of a century's worth of the work of bullets.

Frank turned his nose away from the pungent smells of horse sweat and blood. "Could it have happened during the Grand Review?"

She shook her head. "In the Review everyone uses blanks — including me. Anyway, I would have noticed. It's on the left side. I would have seen the blood when I climbed up during my act."

"Could a stray bullet from one of the six hundred Rough Riders . . . ?"

"You know full well only Johnny Baker and I ever use live ammunition. Everyone else uses blanks — even the colonel. He rarely does any real shooting anymore."

"Is it possible that Johnny . . . ?"

"No, it's not possible. Johnny and I check our guns together before the Grand Review. Blanks only."

"Could you have . . . ?"

Annie's raised eyebrow said he should know better. "Tiffin stays near the arena opening. I always shoot toward the canvas at the far end. Even if I miss, there's no way I would hit anyone in the stands on either side. Nor is there any way I could hit my own horse standing by the arena entrance. I shoot in the opposite direction."

"Then what could it be?"

Annie's jaw set in a hard line. "I under-

74

stand Lillian Smith is working in Kansas City."

"You can't mean it. Surely, she wouldn't hold a grudge after all this time."

"I believe Lillian Smith is capable of anything — except outshooting Annie Oakley."

"Let's not leap to conclusions. We'll have the animal doctor examine Tiffin. Maybe he can tell what happened. It may not even be a bullet wound."

"It is a bullet all right. Look there." Annie's finger hovered over the congealing lines of blood on Tiffin's flank. A bean-sized lump bulged just under the horse's thin skin.

Frank put his arm around Annie. He felt more helpless than he had ever felt in his life. *What if someone were trying to silence the singing of his little Phoebe bird with the eagle eye? What if sharpshooting rival Lillian Smith hated Annie as much as Annie still loathed Lillian?* He would have to find out. He would have to stop it.

He knew beyond doubt the death of Phoebe Ann Mozee would spell the doom of Frank Butler, too.

CHAPTER FIVE:

A pair of jangle-spurred boots tromped down the hall.

A brown-haired boy of about sixteen stopped in the dining room doorway to take in the scene. He couldn't have looked less like his slim, smooth-faced brother. He stood about Jemmy's height but had the shape of a wooden fireplug. His straight hair flopped down the side of his face to partly obscure his beard stubble and acne. He knocked his head back to point at Jemmy and Aunt Tilly with his chin as he sneered. "Damn me, what are they doing here?"

Clomping into the dining room, Meredith Marmaduke Koock stopped short when Aunt Tilly rose and impaled him on her stare. "Young man, only the ill-bred would interrupt the peaceful repast of the members of his home by uttering profanity. Intolerable at any time, but particularly reprehensible when one's family is entertaining

76

guests. It won't do."

The rude boy pulled his lips into a thin line but made no reply.

She surveyed him up and down. "If you'll forgive the effrontery, I might suggest you see to your toilette since we shall need to leave for the musicale quite soon."

The boy cocked his head like a pigeon on a ledge. He said, "I'm hungry."

"If you'll pardon the presumption, a gentleman must learn to anticipate his needs and arrive in time to satisfy them without discommoding others. Failing such foresight, I fear you shall have to do without dinner."

Confusion crossed his face, then defiance. "I'm not going to any pantywaist musicale."

"If you'll excuse the impertinence, perhaps you are aware your father sets great store by my judgment?"

"So what if he does?"

"If I recommend you be sent to a place which is certain to develop proper comportment and praiseworthy manners, I predict you will find yourself in Lexington at Wentworth Military Academy in less than a week."

He said nothing more but turned on his heel and walked off — still jingling, but no longer tromping.

Dorothea hung her head. Jemmy tried to think of some word of comfort, some way to soothe — but nothing came.

Burnie broke the silence. "Duke's not my brother — well, not really. We had different mothers. He and my mother never got along. Maybe that's why he . . ."

Aunt Tilly was not one to let a boorish boy spoil her digestion. "We shall see whether he responds to persuasion as satisfactorily as young Mr. Lilburn." She nodded toward Burnie with something akin to a smile.

"If not, other measures might be required. Might I suggest you save eggshells from each morning's breakfast to give to young Marmaduke. The membrane inside is a capital remedy for facial eruptions. Place them in a container with an egg white and store them in the ice box to keep them cool and soft."

Dorothea tucked the little girls in bed and left them in the maid's care. The three ladies, escorted by Master Lilburn Boggs Koock, set off to be entertained at a musicale especially arranged for their visit at the home of another Koock.

Upon arrival, Dorothea blushed and apologized for the absence of her husband. No one said a word about the absence of

Duke. In fact, Jemmy noticed Mrs. Charles Koock's smile became genuine only after she learned that the young hooligan's boots were wiping mud somewhere other than on her Aubusson carpet.

After installing Aunt Tilly and Jemmy in the place of honor on an ornately carved sofa with three blue brocade tufted ovals in the seat back, the hostess introduced the first performer. A screechy soprano sang an aria from the not-entirely-respectable new opera, *La Bohéme.* Everyone applauded politely, even Aunt Tilly; though Jemmy could see disapproval lurking behind her chaperone's pince-nez.

Next came the high point of Jemmy's evening, a surprisingly delightful rendition of "Listen to the Mockingbird" whistled by a most talented lady whistler. Jemmy envied the woman's volume of sound, which could undoubtedly summon a cabbie or a cop over any amount of street noise right up to a steam calliope. Of course, a real lady would never do such an outlandish thing — or ever whistle in public. Perhaps Sedalia was more tolerant, or more musical than St. Louis.

Other acts followed — violin, flute, one particularly boring fugue on two cellos. Even Aunt Tilly, the paragon of politeness, stifled a yawn. Each number became more tiresome than the last until the musicale was about to come to a close.

To the surprise of all, Burnie requested permission to sing. Mrs. Charles Koock raised her eyebrows to ask Dorothea for guidance. Dorothea nodded a nearly imperceptible affirmative. Mrs. Charles looked doubtful, but consented. Young Burnie unfolded sheet music from his back pocket and handed it to the pianist at the upright.

Jemmy was surprised at how pleasant his voice — and how annoying his actions. He sang the lilting "The Band Played On." He sang it straight to Jemmy. She was not blond. Her hair was upswept, not in curls. But the smirks on audience faces and the cat-in-the-cream-jar expression on Burnie's face told everyone Jemmy's hair was strawberry enough to load his poor little brain until "it nearly exploded."

By the time he reached the line, "Such kissing in the corner and such whisp'ring in the hall," every set of eyes in the room had sneaked at least two glances at Jemmy.

On the line, "And telling tales of love behind the stairs," Jemmy hiccupped. This ill-timed infraction of unwritten rules reduced the entire room to telltale tittering and furious fanning. She vowed she would never again drink three different wines at one meal. She hiccupped again. She vowed she would absolutely never drink a glass of wine ever again — well, no more than one — two at the most.

Giggles of glee broke out from all points of the compass. When she realized what people must be thinking, Jemmy promised herself not to blush. Result — a flush creeping up her face like mercury on a sunporch thermometer. She reddened first with embarrassment, then with anger. She vowed to do something about this smitten boy whom Cupid had so conspicuously skewered on a love arrow.

After the performances, wine betrayed Jemmy yet again. Luckily, this time she didn't have to pay a price. She waited until Aunt Tilly's back was turned, then crammed into her mouth a whole petit four with a sugared violet on top. She chomped in Aunt Tilly's direction as long as Aunt Tilly's back was turned. Jemmy whirled toward the refreshment table when Aunt Tilly's head began to come about. Auntie didn't seem to notice Jemmy's mutiny against her dessert orders. Jemmy congratulated herself on knowing the old lady was near-sighted.

After chitchat about the multitude of thrilling events to be held in Sedalia over the next week and copious thank-yous to Mrs. Charles Koock, the guests of honor wended their way home.

Jemmy took care to sit by Aunt Tilly — not "Li'l Lil" as she mentally dubbed Lilburn Boggs Koock. His bay rum and Macassar oil fumes made her gag when he leaned near. To his face she continued to call him "Mr. Koock." He continued to urge her to call him "Burnie."

On the way home, Li'l Lil panted in Jemmy's direction. He fawned over her like a newly housebroken puppy itching for a scratch on the belly. Jemmy gave him looks fit to clabber milk.

Dorothea said, "I'm more than pleased, Lilburn, that you offered to sing for the first time in public. I've so admired your voice ever since it stopped cracking."

"Thank you, Mrs. Koock — Stepmother — Mother." He groped for the right words. "For the first time, I had something to sing about. Isn't it wonderful to have an important — not to mention beautiful — lady journalist all the way from St. Louis right here in Sedalia?"

Jemmy could see moonlight dancing off his eyes as he turned to her. "Did my singing please you, Miss McBustle?"

Jemmy wanted to scream he was wasting

his time and his voice. He had not a snow-ball's chance in Baton Rouge on a broiling August day of winning her approval. She said, "Yes, Mr. Koock."

"Please call me 'Burnie.' " The longing in his voice made Jemmy cringe. A refusal would bring him to the brink of suicide or, at very least, a plunge into an ice-water bath.

"Yes, Burnie." Jemmy recognized her mistake the instant she let the words slip from her lips. The rest of the way home, he beamed his Cheshire-cat smile at the reluctant object of his affections.

That night, Jemmy set the Li'l Lil Boggs boondoggle aside. She lay in bed trying to tune out Aunt Tilly's snores and snorts while she considered the best way to get her rewrite printed in the local paper.

She had to find some way to get out from under Aunt Tilly's thumb. Auntie's maddening interference could mean the end of every hope Jemmy held dear. *My articles simply must sell enough* Illuminators *to make up for the cost of this trip to Sedalia.*

And she had expenses of her own. She still owed Jaccard & Co. a week's pay on the cut glass and silver decanter she had given Dorothea as hostess gift. Aunt Tilly would surely expect some expensive token of appreciation when they returned to the city.

That familiar trapped feeling returned with a vengeance. The mind-numbing depression she had slogged through while tending her irascible old grandmother gripped her by the throat. The black cloud of her seventeenth year descended on her soul to chill her hopes and shackle her ambitions.

Once again she felt her precious youth ebbing away in the great ocean of society's expectations. The specters of her grandmother — her mother — Aunt Delilah — appeared like giant parasites to suck away her spirit.

Yes, she loved her family and would never deliberately hurt them; but why would they not understand? Her desperate need to be her own person — to live the life she chose — ached in the pit of her heart like a leech growing fat on her blood and thinning it to water at the same time.

In the depths of her own personal Slough of Despond, she heard echoes from another soul in misery.

A sound from the nursery pierced through Jemmy's woe and Aunt Tilly's snoring. Was it weeping? She slipped out of bed and put her good ear against the wall. Sounds of sobbing convinced her something was amiss.

She pulled on her wrapper and opened

the bedroom door. Moonlight through the round stairwell window gave light enough to see by.

In the hall, a creaky board betrayed her presence. In seconds, Dorothea appeared in the nursery door. She asked in a hushed voice, "Miss McBustle, what's wrong? You're not even wearing slippers. Is Miss Snodderly unwell?"

"Everything's fine — at least with Miss Snodderly and me."

Dorothea paused, then whispered, "Come in." She closed the nursery door and led Jemmy to her own room with its clean smell of geraniums and lemon verbena.

Inside, she turned up a gas jet and motioned for Jemmy to sit on the settee. She brought a shawl to warm her visitor's feet.

She dabbed her eyes with a substantial man's handkerchief. "I usually bear up better than this. I know I shouldn't burden you, but I have the feeling you might be the one person I could trust to understand."

Jemmy made no reply, just offered a wan smile.

Dorothea looked down. "I can't think why you should be kindly disposed toward a stranger, but I am desperately unhappy. I have no one close to my own age to confide in."

Jemmy nodded a bit of encouragement.

"Perhaps I feel close to you because you're from St. Louis. I had many friends in St. Louis, but I can't seem to find a single one here. Oh, I suppose it's my own fault. I'm embarrassed by . . . Well, I'm afraid the girls will misbehave or the boys will be rude."

Dorothea shook her head as she mopped away a few more tears. She sat on the settee and spoke in a quiet voice.

"When I saw you today — so lovely, so self-assured — I grew miserable enough to consider doing away with myself. That frightened me, Miss McBustle — frightened me to the marrow of my bones."

Dorothea looked straight into Jemmy's eyes. "I fear if things stay as they are, I shall surely die. I do not wish to die, Miss Mc-Bustle. I don't want to be just another of Mr. Koock's wives who was too frail for this world."

Dorothea leaned closer. "You seem so full of life, so daring and so confident of success. Perhaps you can help me see the way of things. Why, you've already accomplished more with Lilburn in five hours than I have in five years. I need someone to give me courage, Miss McBustle. Without it, I don't see how I can go on."

Jemmy took Dorothea's hand in hers and

squeezed it. They sat just so for some time while Dorothea filled two more handkerchiefs with tears of self-pity.

At length, Dorothea seemed ready to talk again. Jemmy prompted, "Tell me how I can help."

"I don't know, Miss McBustle."

"Jemmy."

"Jemmy. I can't seem to make friends here, and the children are a cross to bear instead of a joy. Lilburn is going the way of Marmaduke. Marmaduke frightens me. He will speak of nothing except his idols, the outlaws Frank and Jessie James. Even my own daughters don't obey me."

"And Mr. Koock?"

"Mr. Koock is hardly ever here. When he is, he is in such ill humor no one can please him."

"Doesn't he insist the boys respect you?"

Dorothea's answer caught a sob in her throat. "He does — when he is here. And that makes everything worse. He whips the boys; then they hate me even more."

"Does he also strike the girls?"

Dorothea shook her head in the negative.

"Or — I know I've no right to ask you this, but has he ever struck you?"

"No, he never has. Perhaps that's why he stays away — so he won't be tempted."

"If you think you and your daughters are in danger in any way . . ."

"Not from Mr. Koock, never from him. Perhaps from Marmaduke, but Obadiah's not rough. In fact, in many ways he's generous. When Pélagie arrived and brought along a husband and a sister I didn't even know existed, Obadiah welcomed them as if he'd known they were coming all along. He never objects to the money I spend or tells me whom to see or what to do with my time."

"What then?"

"It's just — he's distant, not here even when he's here."

At last, Dorothea seemed to be all cried out. She sighed as she recalled the early days. "I had such high hopes in the beginning. We had the loveliest honeymoon in Chicago. We spent more than a month in the summer of ninety-three during the Columbian Exposition."

"Yes, the big World's Fair to honor Columbus's discovery of America. I would give anything to have been there. What did you like best?"

"The gigantic Ferris wheel — the first one ever built — thirty-six cars — each one big as a day coach on a train."

"I've heard the ride makes you giddy."

"The lightheadedness of floating into the sky could drive a person quite insane." Dorothea warmed to her story. "In fact, while we were riding up with our stomachs queasy from the height, a fellow named Wherritt went completely berserk. He started throwing himself at the walls hard enough to crack the heavy glass. He even bent the iron."

"Heavens in a handbag, weren't you scared?"

"The car swayed until I thought it would break and send us all crashing to the earth more than two hundred feet. When we were on the way down — and still alive, he became himself again. He even talked quite sensibly — said he had fought the beast and slain the dragon. We thought everything would be fine."

"Wasn't it?"

"No, we started to go up again and he went crazy — even wilder than before. How could we possibly bear another ten minutes of his hurling himself against the walls? No matter how hard the men tried to hold him, he would break away and fling himself against the opposite end of the car."

"How did you make it down alive?"

"Finally, a woman unfastened her skirt, stepped out of it, and stood in her petticoats. Can you believe it? Undressed right there in public. She threw her skirt over his head and held it tight around him. Until the wheel stopped, she kept stroking his head through the skirt and saying, 'There, there. Nothing to be afraid of any more. I'll take care of you.' The fellow became quiet as an ostrich with his head in the sand."

"Who was she?"

"I never knew her name, but she saved a man's life — perhaps the lives of everyone in the Ferris wheel car."

"What a story."

"You should have seen the way Mr. Koock looked at her — admired her. How I wished he would look that way at me. I still wish it." Dorothea's eyelids batted back her tears. She sniffed and put on a resolutely cheerful face.

Jemmy hurried the conversation back to the fair. "I heard you could see amazing things everywhere at the Chicago World's Fair. What else did you see?"

"Such wonders — a map of the United States all done in pickles, a knight on horseback made entirely out of prunes, real cannibals with sharpened teeth from Da-homey in Africa."

"Weren't you scared of ending up in a cannibal pot?"

Dorothea shook her head. "I had Obadiah to protect me."

"Tell me more."

"The buildings in the grand Court of Honor made us feel the size of fleas. Immense structures — hundreds of feet tall — covering acres. We had to wear glasses with blue lenses so our eyes could stand the glare from the white staff — a sort of plaster surface on the buildings. The *Lady of the Republic* statue was completely covered in gold leaf. Blinding — like looking at the sun itself."

Memories of magic from the past slipped onto Dorothea's face to crinkle her eyes. "The Fourth of July fireworks lit up the lake with a portrait of George Washington in colors of fire. Thousands sang 'Home Sweet Home' and wept. I felt so close to Obadiah then, so wanted, so beautiful."

"You make me feel as if I had been there myself."

Dorothea sniffled and then giggled. "We did naughty things, too. He took me to the Ball of the Midway Freaks. Its official name was the 'Midway Ball.' I had never seen anything like it in my life. I don't think anyone else had, either.

" 'Citizen' Train played the grand host at the head of the receiving line. But he wouldn't shake hands with anybody."

She fluttered her fingers in front of Jemmy's face to imitate a snobbish wave. Her eyes grew wide as she mocked the fabled George Francis Train. "Shaking hands might let some of his psychic electricity ooze away. You should have seen him all decked out in a white suit with red sash and Turkish fez."

"Citizen Train — I've heard of him. Wasn't he the one Jules Verne used as his model for Phileas Fogg in *Around the World in Eighty Days*?"

Dorothea laughed out loud as she nodded. "You'll never believe the menu — 'roast missionary à la Dahomey,' 'monkey stew à la Hagenbeck,' fried snowballs, sandwiches prepared by the *leather* exhibit. I have no idea what was actually in the food. I hope the Methodists didn't find themselves short a few missionaries."

Dorothea's gusto as she relished her glad memories sparked gaiety in Jemmy. "How wondrous it must have been to attend the great fair."

Dorothea turned coy. "The costumes at the Midway Ball were bizarre and scandalous. Even my costume was — well, I'd never let my mother see me in it."

"Tell me."

"Obadiah first. He dressed as an Arab sheik in a flowing white robe and turban with egret feathers and a huge paste ruby in front. He wore dark greasepaint and sandals. When a fellow bumped into him on the dance floor, he would flash his eyes and put his hand on his dagger hilt."

"And you, what costume did you wear?"

"I'll show you if you promise not to report me for public indecency."

"Trust me. As a female journalist I've been places I wouldn't tell my mother — and I've worn clothes in front of strangers I wouldn't care to have her see."

Dorothea placed a chair by the armoire and climbed up. From the top she took down a parcel wrapped in brown paper tied with purple ribbon. She knelt before the settee as she untied the bow and spread the paper. The costume spilled out in whispers of silk chiffon. Golden coins winked in the gaslight.

Dorothea giggled as she held a veil trimmed with gold spangles over her nose. "Can you imagine me in this?" She picked up harem trousers and spun in a circle. The red silk ballooned as the bells tinkled like icicles falling off a roof in a thaw.

Jemmy picked up a bit of purple silk and said, "Where does this go?"

"That's the blouse."

Jemmy held it up to the light. It had the shape of a blouse, but with very short sleeves and a much-too-short torso. "Why this would only come down to . . ." Her eyes opened wider. "This bodice wouldn't even cover your stomach."

"Remember your promise not to report me."

"It would show your corset."

"I didn't wear a corset."

Jemmy fell back on the bed muffling her laughter with one hand while she draped the blouse over her own upper body to see where it would fall.

Dorothea clicked together the bottoms of soft red leather shoes with an odd curl at the toes. "We even went to see Little Egypt — the original hoochie-coochie dancer. I've been practicing ever since."

"You haven't."

Dorothea nodded. "I have. Want to see?"

Jemmy nodded. "Wouldn't miss it for the world — not even the World's Fair."

Dorothea snatched up the costume and ducked behind a screen painted with a pastoral scene of sheep and dancing shepherdesses. As she changed, she asked, "What did you mean when you said you'd been places you wouldn't tell your mother?"

Jemmy thought for a moment. Was it wise to entrust a secret to a stranger, even one who'd shared so many of her own?

"Of course, if you don't want to . . ."

"No, no. I'm trying to think how to tell you without giving the wrong impression. I worked as an errand boy in a house for ladies of the evening."

"You did what?"

"I mean that literally. I worked as an errand boy. I dressed like a boy. I ran errands, nothing else." Jemmy hoped she wouldn't regret telling a stranger a secret of such a shameful nature.

"You do astound me, Jemmy. And I am grateful for your confidence." Dorothea jingled as she emerged from behind the screen, "I'm ready now. Will you supply the music?"

"I have a bad ear, but I'll try. What tune would you like?"

"There's only one for the *danse du ventre* — the snake charmer song."

Jemmy lah-dahed the tune as best she could. Dorothea twirled to the center of the room. She kept the beat with metallic clashes on miniature cymbals, which she wore on thumb and forefinger of both hands.

Dorothea swayed a few steps to each side

then stopped for the centerpiece of the dance. She heaved her bare midriff in rapid waves like the undulation of choppy seas.

To her amazement, Jemmy found herself delighted and not a bit embarrassed. Mrs. Nanny had considered this dance too ribald for her girls to perform at her middle-class bordello in St. Louis. But to Jemmy, the scandalous belly dance looked like no more than healthy exercise for the tummy.

Dorothea positively glowed in the soft gaslight. Despite two daughters and a French cook, she had a fine figure. What's more, the veil did a splendid job of hiding her horrid proboscis. Dorothea looked downright attractive.

Suddenly, she stopped and pulled off her veil. Jemmy said, "Don't stop. You dance wonderfully."

"This is silly. I'm silly. I keep practicing in hopes someday I will have the courage to dance for him. I saw how Obadiah watched Little Egypt when she danced. That selfsame moment told me I could never measure up — never be the kind of wife Obadiah needs. He should have married someone important like her or like you or like the woman on the Ferris wheel."

"But you're a good dancer. You danced

for me. Surely you can dance for one person."

"Strange, isn't it? I could dance for a room full of people, but not for my own husband."

"Why not?"

"I guess I'm afraid to try. If I fail — if he disapproves — I think there can be no further hope."

Jemmy spoke gently. "Would that be so very much worse than the way things are now?"

Just then, they heard the front door open. Dorothea put her finger to her mouth as she tiptoed to turn off the gas jet. Footsteps came up the stairs and into the next bedroom. After everything was silent next door, Dorothea whispered, "You'd best go back to your room."

Jemmy took Dorothea's hand. "Leave the children to Aunt Tilly. She'll set them right or bust her bustle trying. I confess to having a purely selfish reason, too. I can't hope to do my job unless I find a way to get her off my back. Keeping her occupied with the children will give me freedom. With a push in the right direction, Aunt Tilly might solve all your problems with the children. As for me, I don't know whether I can be of any help at all. I know less than nothing about husbands. But there is one thing I can do."

She took Dorothea's other hand. "I know what it's like to be without a friend. When my grandmother was ill, all the people I thought were my friends deserted me. Loneliness taught me to value real friendship. Please, I'd like to be your friend."

CHAPTER SIX:

SEDALIA
WEDNESDAY, SEPTEMBER 21, 1898

Wednesday dawned as perfect a day as one would ever want. Not too hot, not too cold — soaked in sunshine. Jemmy scarcely noticed.

She pretended to sleep until Aunt Tilly left. Jemmy heard her pad off to perform her morning ablutions down the hall. Jemmy yanked on her clothes and was still buttoning her shoes when she heard the trolley bell. She had very nearly pulled herself together without help, despite the fact that she had quite a ferocious tussle to fasten her corset hooks.

Thank heavens in a handbag the trolley line ends at the park entrance. The driver had to unhitch the horse from the west end of the car and re-hitch it to the east end of the car. She needed every one of those precious minutes to grab her hat and gloves and race out to meet the bright yellow streetcar.

Rewritten story in hand, she boarded the

Third Street trolley and asked which evening newspaper office might be nearest. The conductor let her off at Lamine Street and pointed in the direction of the *Evening Sentinel.*

After a brisk two-block walk, she opened the door. A bell announced her presence to the only person in the front room of the establishment. A man in felt sleeve protectors, which had once been green but were now nearly black with printers' ink, rose from his desk.

He walked to the counter hitching up his sleeve protectors. "We have a special offer this month for new subscribers." Buzzing, whangs and clanks announced the presence of a printing press in the room beyond.

He pointed to a banner over the door to a back room. The banner read, "All the news you want to know."

"May I speak to the news editor, please?"

His smile faded in a snivel of disappointment. "I have the misfortune to merit said title. How may I help you?"

She handed him her sheaf of papers. "I have a most stimulating story to sell. The foiled robbery on yesterday afternoon's train from St. Louis."

"Too late. I already have the story."

"Is your story an eyewitness account written by a participant who happens to be a professional journalist?"

"Professional? Yes. I wrote it myself."

"Might I inquire as to your source of information?"

"I interviewed the conductor."

"Then you had no eyewitness account."

"The conductor was on the train, wasn't he?"

"Yes, but the conductor didn't see what happened. He wasn't present in the car."

"But this professional journalist was there at the time?"

Jemmy nodded.

"What's his name — this professional journalist who saw the attempted robbery?"

"Foiled robbery." Jemmy braced herself. Telling people her pen name made Jemmy tremble. Her nom de plume had become a pretend brick she carried in an imaginary gunny sack weighting down her neck. She took a deep breath and stood up as tall as she was able. "The byline name is 'Ann O'Nimity.' "

The editor snorted. "So who put you up to this little joke? Dave over at the *Bazoo* — am I right?"

A second imaginary brick added its choking weight to the first. "This is no joke. If you read good newspapers — any papers

101

other than your own rag — any decent papers — like the St. Louis *Illuminator,* you would certainly remember the byline, 'Ann O'Nimity.' I know for a fact because it's mine. You will see 'Ann O'Nimity' below the headline of some of the most stirring news stories you've ever read."

He laughed out loud. "Not a chance. Those stories are written by a fellow who's afraid to get beat up, so he hides behind a woman's name — an obviously made-up woman's name."

Jemmy snatched back her story and flounced out the door — at least as fast as anyone could flounce with a gunny sack of three imaginary bricks around her neck.

Still chuckling, the *Sentinel* editor called after her. "You tell old Dave he can't fool me. Tell him I said Ann O'Nimity is a man. I know him personally. I call him 'Nimwit' for short."

Jemmy's dander rose higher every time she remembered Hamm's deceit. Her boss had tricked her into signing herself as "Ann O'Nimity." She raged inside over the way she had acquired that farcical moniker. Her original plan was to follow in her idol Nelly Bly's footsteps — to use a name from a popular song, like "Annie Rooney" or "Rosie O'Grady." Hamm said she shouldn't be a copycat.

Besides, those names didn't do what a pen name was supposed to do — intrigue the reader. But "Ann O'Nimity" — now that had mystery to it.

Jemmy recalled Hamm embraced this particular pseudonym with unusual alacrity. In fact, he was the one who thought up "Ann O'Nimity" in the first place. That should have set her wise. How foolish she'd been not to put two and two together and come up with the startling word "anonymity."

When she got back to the city, she would have it out with Hamm and get that horrid pen name changed.

Once she managed to choke down her anger at Hamm for putting one over on her, she chafed at being dismissed like a trinket by the *Sentinel* editor. Jemmy regretted her fit of temper. If he had only read the story, he would have liked it.

But no — I had to go and grab it out of his hands before he had time to read a single word. She vowed to be a better saleslady at her next stop and her last hope, the offices of the Sedalia *Bazoo*.

In a coffee shop she fortified herself with toast, cocoa, and directions to the newspaper. Over wild plum preserves, she planned the exact words to use. She resolved to stay calm regardless of all provocation — and never, ever, to let her temper get the better of her. Unfortunately, the best-laid plans of mice and men offer equal opportunity for "ganging agley" to lady mice and wo-men.

At the *Bazoo* another newsman in ink-smudged sleeve protectors stood to serve her. Jemmy had gained wisdom through her earlier trial. This time she asked for the main man himself. "May I speak to the managing editor, please?"

"Our managing editor is too busy to see anyone," the clerk replied. "May I help you?"

She handed him her story. "Surely your editor would not mind being interrupted for a story which would sell papers — a piece both exciting and timely. The foiled robbery on yesterday afternoon's train from St. Louis. A professional journalist saw everything and indeed participated in thwarting the robbers' intentions."

The clerk nodded. "For a humdinger of a story, I'll risk interrupting him. If he recognizes the newsman's name, he might be willing to read the story. Who wrote it?"

Jemmy braced herself for the reaction she had come to dread. "Ann O'Nimity."

The man chortled and slapped his knee. "Ann O'Nimity. That's a slick one. Dave at the *Sentinel* — am I right? You go back and tell that other good old Dave this good old Dave has no time for his practical jokes." The man shook his head and chuckled.

A fourth brick plopped into her gunnysack necklace. The fact that it was imaginary did nothing to reduce its weight, or its power to strangle Jemmy.

Her luck had gone south. A second wiseacre named Dave had popped up to bedevil her. "I assure you, Dave did not send me and this is no joke. I report the news for the St. Louis *Illuminator.* The byline 'Ann O'Nimity' follows the headline of some of the most compelling news stories coming out of St. Louis today — the Ripper story — the madhouse series."

He laughed out loud. "You're good. I'll give Dave credit. Where did he get you? Are you an actress?"

"You have no call to insult me by calling me an actress."

The clerk ignored Jemmy's wounded feelings. "I bet you're in the new melodrama over at the Liberty The-ate-r. That's it, isn't it?"

Jemmy reined in her temper. "Please, please, if you'll read the story, you'll see I'm

105

telling the truth."

"Fine, fine. I'm sure Dave has cooked up something clever. I'll read it right after supper tonight. Then I'll think of some suitable answer for good old *Sentinel* Dave. But right now, if you'll excuse me, I have work to do."

Jemmy's temper turned to anguished plea. "But tonight will be too late. You have to run the story in today's paper while it's still news."

He backed up as he said, "I'd love to spend all morning gabbing with a lovely young lady like you, but you'll have to excuse me. I have a pile of work on my desk."

Jemmy all but wailed, "Please, I beg you. Just read it."

"You're an excellent actress. You've convinced me to see the play this weekend."

The dam on Jemmy's temper burst. "Read today's *Illuminator*. You'll see that story — on the front page — my story. Only the version you have in your hand is better because I had time to rewrite."

"You can tell Dave for me he isn't paying you enough. If it weren't so far-fetched — a woman journalist — I'd believe every word you said. You sound powerful sincere."

Jemmy's vow to herself not to lose her temper washed out in a flood of clipped words. "Don't you dare print my story without paying for it. I'll sue your socks and spectacles off."

Fighting back tears of frustration, she flounced out the door. "How did I get to be so unlucky? Two newspaperman named Dave in the same town who make a hobby of playing jokes on each other."

One good thing did happen. Her anger vanquished her pen name dread and made those imaginary bricks disappear. As she calmed, she mulled over the real cause of the problem. *What do I have to do to get men to take me seriously? Those two newspaper Daves are typical — too pigheaded even to read my story. First thing I do when I am back in St. Louis is give Suetonius Hamm an earful. I will shoot him dead if he doesn't agree to change that hideous name!*

On the Third Street trolley, Jemmy tried to put the morning behind her. She was a guest in the Koock home. She had already behaved in a most unbecoming way by sneaking out of the house without a word to anyone. Well, she had left a note under Dorothea's door saying she would not be present at breakfast. She hoped Dorothea would understand.

Back at the house, Jemmy half expected Aunt Tilly to send her to her room without lunch, but Aunt Tilly was far too pre-occupied with the little girls to chastise Jemmy for her bad manners. In fact, Auntie didn't make an appearance. She took her noon meal with Fanny and Sissy in the nursery.

When she saw the hurt in Dorothea's eyes, Jemmy tried to apologize. "I beg you to forgive my sneaking out this morning. It was frightfully rude. The only excuse I have is my desperation to sell my story to the local papers. I am a horrid guest who doesn't deserve a tenth of your generosity."

Dorothea patted Jemmy's shoulder and offered a feeble smile. "I understand wanting something so badly nothing else can claim even a small piece of your mind."

Dorothea's eyes said she meant what she said. Jemmy felt so relieved she gave her hostess an awkward hug. "Thank you for giving me much more understanding than I deserve or can ever repay."

Dorothea changed the subject. "I have no reason for complaint this morning. The house has been blissfully quiet. Only twice did the girls scream and throw things — and not even one item smashed to smithereens."

Before lunch, Jemmy asked after Hal's whereabouts. The maid said he had borrowed Mr. Lilburn's bicycle and set off with his camera.

Only three sat at table for luncheon — Jemmy, Dorothea, and moony-eyed Burnie. He was even more Macassar-oiled and bay-rummed than the day before. He and Jean Max had spent the whole morning cleaning and oiling guns and loading shotgun shells with birdshot. He announced his blueprint for the afternoon.

The boy could barely keep his enthusiasm under control as he invited the ladies. "I have made plans which I very much hope will bring you pleasure, Miss McBustle." As an afterthought, he added, "And of course, for you too, Mrs. Koock — Mother — Mother Koock. You must accompany us, naturally."

The possibility that Dorothea might refuse to go along flashed across the boy's face in alarm. Dorothea had to come. Without her, all three knew Jemmy would not be able to be seen in public with a young male acquaintance alone — not even in the daytime.

For her part, Dorothea beamed over the boy's suddenly civilized behavior. Since Aunt Tilly had things more than under control in the nursery, the lady of the house said, "I would relish an outing to the country on this superb day."

Jemmy would do whatever her hostess suggested as a matter of course. In this case, she was genuinely happy to agree for reasons of her own. She wanted to learn how to defend herself.

She aimed to land a dangerous assignment when she returned to St. Louis. Hamm had given her fair warning. The power behind everything in the city, "the Combine," forced its will on St. Louis with every trick in the book and every weapon in the arsenal.

The Combine used lethal force like a scalpel to lance boils that now and then cropped up in the guise of civic betterment. Fewer than fifty men decided the fate for the half-million souls who lived in the fourth-largest city in the United States. Hamm said the Combine wouldn't hesitate to slay her if she crossed them — even though she was female, and therefore not considered much of a threat.

Firearms were great equalizers — the best hope for people too small for fisticuffs and too squeamish for knife-fighting. However, St. Louis officials frowned against shooting inside city limits. How could Jemmy learn to shoot? Li'l Lil dropped the perfect opportunity right in the lap of her gray linen skirt.

Jean Max had the pony cart waiting with

guns in gun cases under the front seat. A bulging burlap bag rolled and rattled in the middle of the cart. The clinks told Jemmy the bag held empty bottles and cans. Pélagie tucked a covered basket under Jemmy's feet and waved as the trio set off at a sprightly trot.

Just outside of town, they stopped to admire a hoarding, a tall billboard fence with a mammoth poster in garish colors advertising Buffalo Bill's Wild West and Congress of Rough Riders of the World.

Jemmy was quite touched when Burnie handed her a nosegay made of a pale pink roses surrounded by dusty miller and tied with a pink ribbon. She was even more touched because he gave one to Dorothea as well. She soon learned the flower gift was more practical than romantic.

On the Georgetown Road, Dorothea motioned for Jemmy to plunge her nose into the roses. "I think the city fathers put the stench of the sanitary system along this road expressly to annoy the folks out Georgetown way north of town. You know General Smith snatched the county seat from Georgetown when he built the railroad several miles to the south. That little trick stirred up considerable resentment on both sides. Of course that was before the Civil

War, but folks around here have long memories."

Burnie rushed to change the subject, "Father owns a farm a few miles out — far beyond the smell. We provide the land and the seed. Our sharecroppers provide the machinery and labor. They grow corn, wheat, hay, and the like. They sell milk and cream in town, butter and eggs, too. And they make cheese."

Dorothea added, "The cream for last night's dessert came from Mr. Koock's farm."

At the farmstead, Burnie rounded up the lady of the house to welcome Jemmy and Dorothea. The farmer's wife said something in German that Jemmy couldn't quite follow. Jemmy was no linguist; but she had learned *Guten Tag* from Gerta, the boardinghouse cook back home.

Hearing "good day" in her native language put a smile on the hausfrau's lips. The woman looked enough like Gerta to be her sister — right down to florid complexion and dark braids wrapped around her head.

The farmer's wife said *"Ja, ja,"* to Burnie's attempts to explain what he wanted to do. She gave him half a peck of grain to put in the empty burlap bag. She even lent him a retriever, a spotted mutt with a tail perma-

112

nently a-point. But she did waggle her finger at Burnie while she said something about *Milchkine.*

Burnie turned the pony cart back to the main road and down a hill to the bottom land at Muddy Creek. He watered the pony, then tied him to a wild plum tree.

He took the bag of cracked corn well out into the corn stubble and split it open. Back at the cart, he removed guns from their cases and began giving Jemmy lessons.

She concluded that putting his arms around her was his primary reason for engineering this little trip. He took much too much time turning her left and right to line up the sights.

Jemmy considered training those gun sights on him, but she held steady and shut her nose to the bay rum. She needed to learn to shoot.

Burnie buckled a piece of thick tanned leather over her right shoulder. "So the recoil of the shotgun won't break your shoulder."

Jemmy knew guns were dangerous on the barrel end, but it had never occurred to her they might be dangerous to the shooter as well. Burnie must have seen her alarm, and misunderstood it. "Don't worry. The gun won't blow up. Jean Max and I packed the shells this morning. And every gun is whistle-clean. I promise."

Burnie edged behind Jemmy to brace her right arm with his. He stood so close his hot breath on her neck sent shivers down her back. "Line up the piece of metal sticking up from the far end of the barrel so it sits exactly in the V right up here."

As she gazed down the barrel, Jemmy noticed the crows, dozens of them, flying down to peck at the corn. Burnie said, "Aim low. The gun will kick up. When the gun kicks up, you'll shoot high. Aim about two feet in front of the crows."

"I thought we were shooting bottles." Jemmy had never personally killed anything — well, nothing bigger than a wasp. She knew people eat animals, which necessitates mass murder of certain creatures. Nearly every week she helped Gerta pluck chickens after Gerta had wrung their necks. The boardinghouse cook grabbed them by the head and twirled them until the heavy bodies parted from the necks. The headless poultry flopped around the backyard until the creatures were truly dead.

Once the corpses stopped trying to fly, Jemmy and her sisters held the birds by their feet and dunked them in scalding water to loosen the feathers. The girls learned to shut their nostrils to the vile smell, but that odor was fresh-baked cookies compared to the stench produced by the next step.

Over open gas flames at the stove, Gerta singed off pinfeathers that were too short to pick by hand. The kitchen smelled like a mixture of hot tar and burning hair. They did their best to rid the kitchen of the fumes. No matter how cold the weather, Gerta stationed one of the girls at the back door to flap the stench away with an apron. Sometimes Mother dumped used coffee grounds on a shovel and lighted them. Burnt coffee smelled heavenly compared to singeing feathers.

Jemmy had never before supposed anyone would kill an animal without intending to eat it. On the scale of un-eatable-ness, crows were in the same category as porcupines.

Burnie answered Jemmy's startled look: "We will shoot bottles — later on, with rifles. For now we're going to do local farmers a favor. Kill some crows for them."

Dorothea nodded in agreement as she stood ready to shoot. "This time of year crows steal bushels of corn. A farmer needs his crops so he can pay his mortgage. We're performing a service."

Jemmy straightened her back. She might

have to kill something sometime. She might as well begin by doing a good deed.

Burnie instructed, "Aim low, take a breath, and hold it. Then squeeze the trigger."

Jemmy followed every order to the letter. The shotgun blast exploded. The gun butt slammed into her leather protector. Jemmy lurched against Burnie, and both of them tumbled backward onto the old army blanket he had most conveniently spread behind them — to catch spent shells as he said. Later, Jemmy took care to notice where shell casings ended up. They landed to the side and in front of the shooters — not behind them.

Dorothea looked annoyed at Burnie's shenanigans, but said nothing. Jemmy tried to regain her feet without putting her hands on the boy.

Burnie apologized profusely as he scrambled to help her off him and on her feet. He batted at her skirt to dust it off. "Miss McBustle, I'm terribly sorry. I clean forgot to show you the proper stance — leaning forward with your right foot advanced. Here, let me show you now."

Dorothea said, "Perhaps I should take over Miss McBustle's lessons."

Jemmy said through clenched teeth, "Don't trouble yourself, Mrs. Koock. I think I know what I did wrong."

Jemmy lifted the shotgun, twisted her shoulders to free them from Burnie, aimed, and fired. The recoil mule-kicked her shoulder, but she held her stance rock solid.

Burnie praised her. "Excellent job, Miss McBustle."

Dorothea reproached her, "Next time you might wait until the crows have returned. You very nearly killed the dog."

The mutt raced back to the trio with a crow in its mouth. He dropped the flapping bird at her feet and awaited approval. Burnie scratched behind the dog's ears before he grabbed the bird by its feet. He ended the crow's misery by stepping on its head and pulling off its body.

Jemmy was beginning to feel queasy, but she kept on firing deafening blast after deafening blast. The three continued shooting until they had killed four or five dozen crows and exhausted their supply of shotgun shells. Sulfur fumes burned Jemmy's nose and stung her eyes until they watered.

After a snack of limeade and oatmeal cookies, Burnie set up bottles on a log. The shooting party took turns with rifles. First Jemmy, then Burnie, then Dorothea, who was clearly the best shot of the three. Whatever the other two missed, she unfailingly destroyed.

After a time, Jemmy became skillful enough or lucky enough to hit her target a time or two. She decided rifles were more to her liking than shotguns — and they sure didn't hurt the shoulder as much.

When all the bottles had been broken, Dorothea asked Burnie to toss up tin cans. When she missed just one out of twenty, the corners of her mouth turned down in disappointment; but Jemmy was impressed. "Where did you learn to shoot so well?"

Dorothea smiled a wistful smile. "Mr. Koock taught me — on the Midway Plaisance at the World's Fair."

On the trip back to Sedalia, the three ignored popular songs of the day in favor of old-fashioned tunes like "Oh Susanna" and "Polly Wolly Doodle." Jemmy rated her afternoon as somewhat better than her morning. She felt confident the evening would be better still. But in a new town and in unfamiliar surroundings, it's best not to be overconfident.

Chapter Seven:

Louisa Cody didn't know whether to be delighted or disgusted. She attended her husband's show the night before in perfect anonymity. Very good for her plan — very bad for her self-respect. She wore lavender, a color everyone knew to be her favorite. Not a single Wild West worker paid the slightest bit of attention to a well-dressed matron of a certain age, a bit on the plump side.

No one noticed. That hurt. No one recognized her — the wife of the man everyone came to see. She had become inconsequential, invisible, worthless.

I will not be ignored — treated like a worn-out shoe tossed in the street for dogs to tear apart. One corner of Louisa's mouth turned up in a sardonic smile. *I've already taken the first step.*

Frank Butler rode across Kansas City to the

seedy music hall where Lillian Smith worked. She performed in vaudeville. No longer a Wild West star, she wore brown greasepaint and called herself Indian Princess Wenona.

The backstage doorman, a wizened old fellow with a face as gray as his nondescript sweater, refused to let Frank in. "The first show goes on in twenty minutes. She has makeup to do and costumes to get in to."

Frank adopted a chummy camaraderie he did not feel. "But Pops, Miss Smith and I go back more than ten years. When she was a headliner in Buffalo Bill's Wild West, I was there, too. Let me go in, huh? Surprise an old friend."

"My boss the manager don't care much for surprises sprang on the females 'round here. He's had to kick out a few chaps with his own boot toes if you get my drift."

"This is nothing like that. Miss Smith was a nice young girl — a roly-poly kid if you get my drift. I'm in town this week and have a few minutes to look up an old friend. Come on, now. She'll blame you if she finds out I was here, but you wouldn't let me in."

"Well, I'll go see. No surprises though. Theater's no place for surprises. What you 'spect me to say?"

"Tell her Frank Butler wants to see her."

Pops issued a low whistle. "Horse holder to the great Annie Oakley — no insult intended, Mr. Butler. Well, I'll tell Missy Smith."

He shuffled off backstage. His hand riffled the black curtains known as legs until they billowed like storm clouds. Pops disappeared past the counterweights on the rail. Ropes knotted around belaying pins held heavy scenery aloft on battens above the stage floor. Frank knew how quickly an artificial sky could fall upon your head in the theater.

Forget bad omens. Frank muttered to himself the words he'd come to say. He inhaled the musty smell of old stage curtains as he walked under sandbags tied to overhead ropes.

In his old hothead days he would never have allowed anyone to suggest Frank Butler was an errand boy, a pitiable lackey fit to hold a playing card while his brilliant wife shot it in half.

He seldom admitted as much to himself — very seldom, and only when he drank more than one schooner of beer. His line of work demanded a hand as steady as the shootist's. He valued his fingers well enough to keep them free from hangover shakes. He treasured his head enough to never let it be woozy from booze. *Wish I had a shot of whiskey right now.*

In a few seconds, the doorman motioned for Frank to come with him. "Mind you pick up your feet and don't touch the prop carts."

Pops showed him into a cubicle about the size of a jail cell. The stuffy room reeked of liniment and rose oil.

Lillian Smith was setting her greasepaint with rice powder. The too-light powder caked in hard lines on her face. She was twenty-eight, but she looked twice as old. The cloud of white dust gave her the ashy pallor of a Native American — recently deceased.

"You look most fetching as an Indian princess." Frank started on a positive note to put her at ease, though it didn't come out quite right. "It's a fakery worthy of Barnum himself."

Lillian shot back. "It's not a fake. At least no more than Sitting Bull calling your wife Whatchamacallit."

"Watanyacicilla."

"At least my Indian name is easy to pronounce, and just as real as hers. I've been properly adopted into the Sioux tribe by their greatest fighting chief, Crazy Snake — a man who knows shooting talent when he sees it."

Frank's attempt at jollity had received something less than the welcome he had hoped for.

She glared at him in the mirror but didn't turn around. She picked up the handle of a baby's hair brush and started whisking away excess powder. "After all these years what brings Frank Butler to see the Greatest Shot in the World? Looking for a replacement meal ticket?"

Her snide suggestion stoked Frank's internal turmoil. He tried to shrug it off. "Just came to say hello. I don't have much time for seeing old friends, but we're in Kansas City for a few days. I thought I'd look you up."

"Well, you're looking. What do you want? Not to see an old friend. We were never friends."

"I always considered you a friend, a valued colleague. It was Annie who . . ." He made another stab at softening this woman's hard memories of the past. "And understand she didn't hate you. I think she was afraid of the competition. That's why she acted so —"

"Don't bother explaining your vicious wife to me, Frank Butler. I have little time and no interest." She dabbed powder on a spot

123

she had missed. "You never do anything without a purpose. Why did you come?"

"No reason to get your back up, especially not if you really are the best shot in the world." The minute he said it, Frank hated himself for slipping in an insult. Somehow, he couldn't bring himself to like the bitter woman this once bubbly girl had become — or to control his tongue, either.

Lillian slammed down the brush with a thwack. "I was the best shot in the world and the fastest rifle shot the world has ever seen. You could throw up a glass ball and I could fire four times — three times into the air and break the glass with my final shot. I could break four hundred ninety-five balls out of five hundred. I could break twenty in twenty seconds."

Frank thought a good wheedle might work. He put on an injured look. "Didn't I try to advise you to be more ladylike? Back on Staten Island, wasn't I the one who warned you not to wear such racy clothes and that bright yellow sash or silly plug hat?"

When her hand refused to remain steady, Lillian threw down her thin bristled makeup brush. Red and black Indian "war paint" splatted on the dressing table to congeal there like the blood of a squashed tick.

Her voice quivered. "Annie wore short skirts. She still does. Why should Annie Oakley get away with wearing little girl clothes when Lillian Smith can't?"

"Annie is small, and she looks like . . ." Frank saw the error of his ways too late.

On the verge of tears, she let go the pent up resentment of ten years in exile. "And Lillian Smith looks like a great sow. Always has. Even when I really was a little girl."

A tear made a pasty rivulet as it furrowed through the greasepaint down her cheek. A sob caught in her throat as the hurt poured out. "I was just fifteen when I joined the Wild West. Fifteen. Annie was twenty-five — ten years older."

Frank couldn't help feeling guilty. He adopted a soothing voice. "I did try to help you. That time in England when the shooting club fined you. Didn't I tell you to go back with a lighter weapon and prove you could shoot as well as they could — better even. But you didn't go back."

"How could I go back? I didn't even know the name of the man who invited us."

"You could have asked Nate. And the fine. What possessed you not to pay the fine?"

"I thought we were shooting for exhibition. Nobody said anything about bets or money."

"The club thought you were dodging the fine. The rest of us thought the same."

She sneered. "Wasn't it nice of you to explain to me the errors of my ways after the club blackened my name all across England."

"What did you think the newspapers would say about a female who tried to shoot with the big boys but couldn't measure up? Then she went off in a schoolgirl huff after she broke all the rules?"

"Oh, yes, I remember how helpful you were." She waxed more sarcastic. "I remember how eager you were to keep me from making a fool of myself at Wimbledon."

She leaned forward to stare at him in the mirror. "You should have told me about the mechanical deer. Who ever heard of such stupid rules? Rules I didn't know then. Oh, I know them now all right. I know the rules now." She counted them off on her fingers. "Don't aim for the tin head — you'd spoil the trophy if the deer were real. You must shoot their piece of tin in the place where a real deer's heart is supposed to be. Most important of all, never hit the stupid piece of tin anywhere else or you'll get fined. Hitting a deer — even a tin deer — without killing it means you have to chase it down to kill it. That would be much too exhausting for their exalted British lordships."

Her annoyance blared out with ever-increasing volume. "How was I supposed to know shooting a piece of tin in the butt was worse than missing altogether? How was I to know the club would fine me for wounding a deer that wasn't a deer at all? For the love of all that's holy, their mechanical deer was nothing but a piece of metal on a greased track." By now, she was on the verge of yelling.

"I didn't know, either. I swear. Not until afterwards."

She rounded on him with the stored spite of twelve years' injustice. "It's your simpering little Annie who was jealous of me. Your truthful little Annie — butter wouldn't melt in her mouth — pretended she was six years younger just to compete with me. Annie Oakley will always be ten years older than Lillian Smith."

Mumbling, she turned her back to the mirror. "Did everything she could to destroy me. Smeared me in the newspapers. Accused me of cheating. Told people I used a smooth bore shotgun instead of a rifle."

She shook her finger at his reflection in the mirror. "She's the one with the smooth bore, not me. I know she got me fired. She left the show because she couldn't stand the competition — didn't dare let me stay. I might get even better. Lillian Smith might outshine the great Annie Oakley."

A demonic gleam came into Lillian's eye. "She blackmailed Cody, didn't she? She made the colonel fire me. She refused to come back to the show if he didn't. Tell the truth. That's what happened. It is, isn't it?"

Frank swallowed hard. "I'll tell the truth about our return to the show if you'll tell me the truth about something."

Sarcasm dripped from her lips. "Exactly what truth does Annie's errand boy Frank want from Lillian Smith?"

Frank had made a mess of the visit. His mind went blank. He could think of nothing better than to ask a direct question. "Last night we found a bullet in her horse's back, right under the skin — right about the place where her head would have been a split second earlier. Did you fire it?"

"If I had been aiming for Annie's head, she'd be dead."

"So you deny shooting at Annie?"

"I was nowhere near your precious Annie last night. I was right here. I know you don't believe me. Ask anybody."

Frank turned to leave. She stopped him. "One thing I would be interested in is your wife's obituary notice. I'd give a thousand dollars to the one who caused it. No, make that a hundred dollars. She's not worth a thousand."

Frank had to fight to keep his temper in check as he strode out the door and into a crowd gathered by the harsh words flying from Lillian Smith's dressing room. Between clenched teeth, he asked, "Is one of you the owner here?"

A balding fellow in mutton-chop whiskers said, "I'm the manager. I'll escort you out personally." To the cluster of vaudevillians he said, "Everybody back to your business. Show starts in five."

Out in the alley by the theater, Frank asked, "Was Miss Smith here for all the shows yesterday?"

"Indeed she was — all six."

"How long is her act?"

The manager squinted as he emerged into the sunlight. "Nine minutes."

"How long is each show?"

"One hour and fifty-five minutes."

"Did she go out of the building when she wasn't onstage?"

"Of course. They all go out sometimes."

"Does she go on at the same time every show?"

"Sure. Twenty-two minutes past the start." The manager hitched up his pants and leaned toward Frank. "I've got to get back inside so let's understand each other. As a favor to you, I've answered your questions." He poked a determined finger hard enough in Frank's chest to drive home the point. "Mind you, I was not obliged to tell you anything."

The manager looped one thumb in the pocket of his striped vest. With his free hand he pulled out his watch to check the time. "I don't expect ever to see you again — unless of course, you buy a ticket and sit out front." He turned on his heel and strode back through the artiste's entrance.

Frank walked around to the front of the theater and bought a ticket. He studied the program order as he waited to see whether one-time teenage prodigy Lillian Smith could still shoot straight.

Chapter Eight:

SEDALIA
WEDNESDAY EVENING,
SEPTEMBER 21, 1898

Dorothea planned a quiet dinner at home. But then, things don't always go exactly as planned. It all started off well enough. The master of the house deigned to put in an appearance. It would seem Aunt Tilly had put him on a leash only a little longer than the ones she snapped on Fanny and Sissy.

Obadiah Koock was a handsome man with gray sideburns and a little brush of a gray mustache. He was past forty but not gone to fat, not even around his midsection. Jemmy thought he would be equally at home at a senator's desk or a poker table.

A gold charm of a railroad boxcar with "MKT" — for Missouri, Kansas, Texas — spelled out in rubies dangled from his watch chain. He looked well-oiled and well-heeled as he presided over pre-dinner sherry in the front parlor.

The portiere drapes of green velvet, pulled back and tied with gold tassels, provided a stage for Aunt Tilly to display the talents of her new charges. With the little girls in front and the maid trailing behind, the quartet stood framed like an oil painting under gold web and fringes. She pushed the young ladies forward to make awkward curtsies first to Dorothea, then to their father, and last to Jemmy.

Dorothea beamed. Obadiah nodded as though he expected salaams as daily routine in the Koock household. At the touch of Aunt Tilly's hand on her shoulder, Fanny dutifully recited, "Goodnight, Mother dear, Father, Miss McBustle. I wish you all a pleasant dinner."

Sissy recited her well-rehearsed lines. "Goodnight. I wish you all a pleasant evening." They curtsied again and allowed themselves to be escorted upstairs by the maid without the slightest fuss.

When they had disappeared from sight, Dorothea couldn't hold back a tear or two. "How wonderful! Going to bed — and already fed. Oh, Aunt Tilly, how will I ever thank you?"

"You may thank me best by following my teaching. Tomorrow, I will allow you to observe in the nursery — provided you do as I say. You must not interfere or even say a single word unless I speak to you first. Have

I your promise?"

Dorothea raised her chin as she dabbed her eyes. "Yes, Aunt Tilly."

"Remember, a parent must have backbone to raise children properly. Since you don't have one, I mean to provide you with a few artificial ones — corset stays of steel — if you'll pardon the indelicate comparison."

Obadiah rang the bell. To Jemmy's amazement, the server was none other than her own photographer-bodyguard, Hal. In answer to Jemmy's wide-eyed stare, Hal flicked his head in the direction of Aunt Tilly. It would seem Aunt Tilly didn't think Hal was pulling his weight; so she put him on her leash along with everyone else in the household. Hal had become temporary butler.

If Obadiah noticed a new face among the minions of his household staff, he registered no surprise — just glanced at his watch and queried, "Is cook ready to serve?"

Hal answered. "Dinner will be delayed a few minutes while the gardener brings in fresh tomatoes. The young man threw the others at the stove."

Obadiah's words came clipped and cold as a northern gale. "Which young man?"

"Young Marmaduke, Mr. Koock."

"Do you know why he would take such

idiotic action?"

"Perhaps he can tell you himself better than —"

Obadiah cut in. "I expect straight answers from a person in my employ."

Hal's ears reddened. "Mr. Koock, sir, Mr. Marmaduke did not explain his actions to me."

Obadiah spoke to the ladies in eerily soft tones. "Please go in to dinner as soon as it is ready. I may be somewhat delayed."

In silence all watched him walk with firm step up the stairs. Burnie flattened himself against the wall under the portrait of some ancestral Koock to let his father pass. Mr. Koock didn't even acknowledge his younger son's presence on the steps. Burnie hastened down and turned to gawk with his hand on the newel post.

Aunt Tilly shooed Dorothea and Jemmy in the direction of the dining room. When she couldn't catch Burnie's eye, she grabbed him by the shirt collar and pulled him down the hall. She closed the dining room door behind her and announced, "I expect everyone to be deaf until I give permission to regain hearing."

Jemmy knew what Auntie meant. Victorian homes forbade family quarrels when guests were present. For a guest to show the slightest knowledge of such familial disharmony was even more taboo.

Aunt Tilly tried to initiate conversation. "I wonder, Dorothea, as to the significance of the boys' names. Certainly I am aware both came from notable governors of Missouri. But why did Mr. Koock choose these two particular governors?"

A sprinkling of white powder from the plaster rosette around the chandelier followed a loud thump from upstairs.

Dorothea tried to ignore it. "Mr. Koock is a believer in rugged individualism and personal achievement. He greatly admires Governor Meredith Miles Marmaduke's staunchness during the Civil War. The governor stood up for the Union against his own children. All ten of them were rebels, you know."

If Aunt Tilly noted a similarity to the rebel children of Mr. Koock, she refrained from mentioning it. "I understand Governor Marmaduke began the fight for a state-sponsored insane asylum."

"Yes, and he presided over the first state fair. You know, we Sedalians have hopes for building the state fairgrounds here — if we should fail in our campaign to move the state capitol here from Jefferson City."

"Sedalia would be an excellent choice for

the state fairgrounds. It is centrally located and convenient to rail transportation from every corner of the state. Even if the capitol building should burn to the ground, I would not approve of rebuilding anywhere except Jefferson City."

(Thump, thump.) Demanding sounds from overhead boomed down.

Aunt Tilly soldiered on. "And you, young Lilburn, what is the significance of your name?"

"I was named for Governor Lilburn Boggs. He stood up against the United States government. He said he would never let Congress take one inch of Missouri soil. That was in the Honey War of 1839 over the boundary between Missouri and Iowa."

(Whump, smack, thump.) The sounds from upstairs grew louder.

The diners needed masterful self-control to keep from jumping at the turmoil overhead. Jemmy couldn't. She could find no way to shut her good ear to Obadiah's booming baritone. Reverberations from above grew louder until the demand, "Unlock this door" came through clear as thunder on the wind. Then came two loud thuds and the wrenching grate of splintering wood. Dorothea bit her lip and pulled her hanky from her sleeve to dab at her eyes.

Jemmy wished she could be almost any-where else. Even scouring pots on a muggy summer day back home would be better. Who could pretend to be deaf when the patriarch was tearing down the doors? Duke's unseemly behavior brought punish-ment to everyone and everything on the premises.

Thundering feet down the stairs followed by the slamming of the front door left a silence more deafening than the sounds of fury. No words had come from the pair descending the stairs. No words came from the group in the dining room.

Hal broke the tension by excusing himself and escaping to the kitchen, but not before Aunt Tilly asked him the question he had twice refused to answer. "Mr. Dwyer, I ap-preciate your sense of honor and discretion in allowing young Marmaduke to speak for himself. However, the rest of the Koock family and I would be in a much better position to proceed with civility if you were willing to tell us what you know."

Hal examined the faces around the table before he gave in. "The cook yelled at him for not wiping the horse sh — manure off his boots before he walked through her kitchen. He lobbed tomatoes at her. She ducked. The tomatoes hit the stove."

Aunt Tilly dismissed him with a nod and took control in the dining room. "Since we're in the dining room, we may as well be seated."

Jemmy wiggled her jaw from side to side to unclamp it. She had heard family quarrels. When her father came stumbling home late, her mother's voice often penetrated to the bedrooms above. But never had she heard anyone break down a door.

Hal appeared from the kitchen to announce, "Dinner is ready."

Dorothea gave a sideways glance to the hall door before she said, "Please ask Pélagie to keep it warm." Hal disappeared again.

This evening, Burnie needed no prodding to seat the ladies according to rank. Aunt Tilly endeavored to keep the conversational ball rolling. Actually, not rolling — deflating by slow leak. "Dorothea, I understand you took Jemima and Lilburn on an outing this afternoon."

"The outing was Lilburn's idea. He imagined Miss McBustle might have little opportunity to practice shooting in the city. He thought she might enjoy rustic sport."

Aunt Tilly turned to Jemmy. "And did you find the experience to your liking?"

"Indeed, Auntie. I found it most instructive."

138

"Please tell me what you learned."

"To wear shoulder protection, to lean with one foot forward in a firm stance, to aim low." She glared at Burnie. "To go shooting only with people I trust."

Burnie fired back, "And to avoid shooting the dog."

Dorothea scowled. "Lilburn, apologize. Had Miss McBustle actually shot the dog, the fault would have been yours."

"Please forgive me, Miss McBustle. My attempt to make a joke was ill-considered."

Jemmy nodded toward him, then tactfully changed the subject. "Mrs. Koock is a superb shot, Sedalia's own Annie Oakley."

Aunt Tilly surprised Jemmy with a declaration of her own. "Indeed. I once was a passable shot myself. If you plan another outing, I would be pleased to be included."

Dorothea apologized. "Oh, of course, Aunt Tilly. How could we be so thoughtless?"

"No matter. I could not have accompanied you today in any case. Attending to the girls demanded my full energies."

The sound of the front door closing and boots clomping stopped all idle chatter.

The diners braced for whatever calamity was approaching from the hall. The door swung open. Mr. Koock entered behind his eldest son. Duke's acne glowed orange and angry like coal embers stuck in a glob of bread dough.

Mr. Koock's jaw set in hard angles. With hands on the boy's shoulders, he escorted his son to the table.

A clap on the shoulder told Duke to recite his speech. "I am sorry to have inconvenienced everyone. It was most ill-mannered of me. I regret my actions most deeply." His words sounded sincere, but clenched fists betrayed his resentment.

Obadiah's anger, Duke's sullenness, and the electric tension between father and son sat like a dark unholy cloud over the table. No one felt like eating despite the heavenly aroma from Pélagie's dishes. The only relief from the poisoned atmosphere came from Hal's less-than-stellar debut in domestic service.

With every course he chalked up another faux pas — each one worse than the last. He was hopelessly inept at serving oysters with two spoons pincer-fashion. He trembled so around the formidable Mr. Koock that he dropped a half dozen oysters in his host's lap. Mr. Koock took it in stride — which is to say he kicked the fallen oysters rattling across the wooden floor boards. Dorothea insisted her husband should eat her oysters since she had never cared for them anyway.

Hal spilled pumpkin soup on Jemmy's skirt. Dorothea promised to have the maid clean the spots that very night. Jemmy lied, "I wasn't planning to wear this after today anyway."

When lemon sorbet intended for Burnie's gullet slid down the back of his collar, he yipped. "You great awful . . ." He stopped short of uttering words that would have earned him his own trip to the woodshed.

Is Hal trying to be an equal opportunity slob? Jemmy began to think no one could be so clumsy except on purpose. An unexpected lamb chop landed atop Duke's head. Hal removed it, but the damage was done. Three tablespoons of mint sauce added to Duke's oily locks made him look like a leprechaun with chicken pox wearing a green tam-o'-shanter.

Dorothea cringed when Hal brought in salad. She ended up wearing a spinach corsage.

The worst mishap of all came with the pièce de résistance. For dessert, Pélagie had created a magnificent bombe. Homemade peach ice cream frozen in a half-football shape atop a white cake base, then slathered in whipped cream and dotted with brandied sugar cubes.

Hal bore it in on a silver tray. Eyes shining with her triumph, Pélagie herself lit the sugar cubes with a flourish. Jemmy searched the faces around the table. All smiled — even Mr. Koock — even Duke. Dorothea beamed. This magnificent dessert might save this night from full-blown disaster.

Whether it was alcohol fumes from the burning sugar, uncontrollable muscle tic, or yet one more caprice of fate, triumph turned to ruination. Hal lost his grip on the tray at just the wrong moment. Fingers of flame teetered above Aunt Tilly's head and poised on air for a tantalizing moment. Then the bombe slewed forward and skittered off the tray to land atop Aunt Tilly's topknot like a flamboyant summer hat ignited by sparks from fireworks.

In tears, Pélagie ran through the kitchen door. Hal stood statue-still as if shocked from his senses. Mr. Koock had the presence of mind to rise and give assistance. He spooned out the flaming sugar lumps and dumped them on his plate. With a flourish, he doused the flames with water from his goblet.

Aunt Tilly stood with the rest of the bombe balanced regally upon her head and turned toward the dumbstruck Hal. How she managed without tipping the ice cream from her head mystified all who watched. Golden rivulets of peach trickled down her brow as she faced the guilty freckle-face.

Jemmy concluded Aunt Tilly was right about one thing — breeding tells. The bombe stayed in perfect equilibrium until a discreet ducking of her head plopped it onto Hal's outstretched tray. Burnie clamped his lips shut as he raced around the table to open the door for Auntie. A snicker or giggle might have been fatal.

Hal disappeared into the kitchen with the ruined dessert. Aunt Tilly swept majestically into the hall and upstairs, no doubt to reclaim her coiffure. Her composure she never lost — not for a single second.

From that moment on, Hal maintained melting ice cream as the slipperiest substance known to man. His exact words were "Slipperier than snot." Jemmy didn't dare let a chuckle escape.

Later Aunt Tilly confided to Dorothea and Jemmy her belief the "accidents" at table were evidence of Hal's bad breeding. *Did he use food as a weapon to vent his spite at being coerced into butling. Surely he isn't vicious enough to dump dessert on Aunt Tilly's head on purpose — or is he?*

Mr. Koock made the devastation complete

by decamping even before coffee. He excused himself to attend to "urgent business." He towered over Duke. "Consider what I've said. Do not leave the house this evening. When I return, we shall discuss your future."

With her plans for the lovely evening ruined, Dorothea went to her room — probably to weep. Still sticky from the lemon ice, Burnie was off to change his shirt; and Duke was just off. Jemmy's conscience pulled her in two directions. She knew she should go upstairs to comfort Dorothea. Her hostess must be in a state of despair. No one could have done more to ensure her family and her guests would have a splendid evening. The debacle was none of her doing, but the weight of it fell on her slender shoulders.

Jemmy pushed aside her guilt and promised herself to console Dorothea as soon as might be, but first she had to see Hal. She walked into the kitchen where Pélagie was banging pans and clucking over the waste wrought by Hal's incompetence. The cook hollered at the would-be butler in French. He took the abuse in a resigned way, as though he recognized the music even if he couldn't follow the lyrics.

Jemmy stifled her laughter behind her

hand while she and Hal slipped out the kitchen door into the backyard. "How did you get to be butler?"

"Aunt Tilly — Miss Snodderly — says Dorothea doesn't have enough help. She must hire a nanny and a butler at the very least. Dorothea asked me to take the job notices to the newspapers. It seemed like a good idea. Why shouldn't I buttle — whatever that means — as long as I'm here? At least until they find somebody permanent."

He sighed. "Miss Snodderly said until they find 'suitable' candidates, she guessed I would have to do."

"She guessed wrong."

"I never thought anybody but a bank would have so much silver as the Koocks, and I polished it all. How can people keep straight in their heads about which fork goes with what dish and where the bread plate goes? So many courses. At home we don't have courses. We have food — all at once — just plain food."

Jemmy patted his arm in sympathy.

Hal gave a sad, puzzled shake of his head. "Who would have thought it would be so hard to do a simple thing like put food on the table?"

"You mean, besides the millions who don't have enough to eat?"

"Don't try to make me feel better." He waved off her arm and hung his head. "I was never meant to dish up lamb chops with two spoons. My mother sets the platter down in the middle of the table, and we spear the meat with our forks. If I had used a fork, I wouldn't have dropped the chop on Duke's head."

"I'm sure forks would have saved my skirt and Aunt Tilly's hair, too."

His head sagged even lower. "That's right. Rub it in."

"I'm trying to cheer you up. I can't imagine anyone would want you to serve up another calamity like this one. I expect you're glad to get out from under."

"Yes and no. I'm not one to turn down making a few bucks on the side. I don't have a rich family to support me."

Jemmy stepped back with a little cough of disbelief. "If you're implying my family is rich, you're crazier than I thought. My mother runs a boardinghouse. You call that rich?"

"To people from Kerry Patch, yes."

She dismissed the argument with an impatient wave of her hand. "Enough of this. Tell me about your pictures. Do any of them warrant a story?"

"Maybe, maybe not. I don't know what to

look for."

"What have you been doing when you're not bombing Aunt Tilly's head?"

"Finding out about the wrong side of the tracks."

Jemmy cocked her head to the side and waited.

Hal backed away. "Not anything I want to tell you about, but I will say this. There's a fellow down at the Maple Leaf Club plays piano like you never heard. Name of Scott Joplin."

"Perhaps you could take me there."

"Not a chance. Your mother would skin me alive — not that I would be alive once Aunt Tilly found out."

"Killjoy."

"Some joys deserve killing."

"I wanted to see you because we have to get some real work done tomorrow. Prove to Hamm we are worth the money he's spending on us."

"What's the plan?"

"Burnie says the day before the Wild West comes to town is a big holiday. Lots of country folks come in to see the show, and lots of out-of-town dudes and slickers come in to relieve country folks of their spending cash."

"Is that news?"

"When will you learn that you and I must find big stories? Sensational stories sell papers. So far we've been producing them. That's the only reason Hamm doesn't fire us." Jemmy shook her head. "Just take pictures when I tell you to. We have to earn our keep."

Hal nodded. "What time?"

"Right after breakfast." As she walked back toward the house, she called over her shoulder, "And sharpen up your nose for news. Maybe there's a story in that piano player Joplin fellow."

Burnie nearly ran her over as he burst out the back door buttoning his clean shirt. He mumbled an apology as he swept past Jemmy in his rush to get to Hal. "Do you know where he's going?"

"Your father?"

"Duke."

"Duke?"

Burnie nodded. "I tried to stop him. I told him Father would probably beat him half to death."

"What makes you think I know where he's going?"

Burnie jiggled with impatience. "Don't play stupid. I know he took you around town last night."

Hal drew up his chin in indecision, then

relented. "I know where he planned to go tonight, but what's the problem?"

"He stole a bottle of Jack Daniels."

"He wouldn't be the first young buck to get drunk and sleep it off at some place other than his home."

Burnie lowered his voice and tugged Hal toward the back door with Jemmy trailing behind. "He also took a gun."

"I thought the guns were locked up in the gun case in the study."

"He broke the glass. I don't like him much, but he's the closest thing to a brother I have."

"What does he want with a gun?"

"I think he means to kill Father."

"You think so because — ?"

"Because that's what he said. He said he was going to kill Father."

Jemmy offered, "Maybe you misunderstood. What were his exact words?"

Burnie thought a while then repeated slowly, "He said, 'I'm going to kill that monster. I won't let anybody ruin my life.' "

Considering the recent broken doors and forced apologies, Mr. Koock seemed the logical target for Duke's anger.

Still, something in the back of Jemmy's head said the boy might resent the interference of women who had changed everything in his world in the space of a single day. *Maybe to him "monster" meant Aunt Tilly, or Dorothea, or Jemmy herself.*

Inside the stable Burnie stood with his hands on his hips. "How are we going to catch him? Both the saddle horses are gone."

Hal pointed toward the tack room. "We'll have to take the carriage. Not as fast as horseback, but faster than walking."

The commotion drew Jean Max down from his lodgings above the stable. He helped with the traces. Meantime, Jemmy installed herself in the carriage.

Hal must have forgotten about her because when he opened the door, he looked surprised. "Get out. I don't have time to mollycoddle you."

"Get in. I require no mollycoddling, thank you."

Hal stuck his face up to hers. "Get out. Sometimes bystanders get hurt when guns are involved."

"Get in. Sometimes bystanders write news stories like our employers expect us to do."

"Get out. We're going to the dangerous part of town."

"Get in. You're my bodyguard. Protect me."

"Get out. I guard you when we're on a

150

story, not when we're on personal business."

"Get in. We are on a story."

"Get out. We're not."

"Get out. We are, too."

"Get in. We are not."

"I'm already in, thank you."

A how-did-that-happen frown came over Hal's face as he realized he'd been tricked.

Burnie climbed in and took advantage of the quarrel to sit by Jemmy. "How much time are you two going to waste griping at each other? If she stays in the carriage, she won't get hurt."

Still grumbling, Hal clambered in and hollered out to Jean Max, "Main Street, the Maple Leaf Club."

CHAPTER NINE:

SEDALIA
WEDNESDAY, SEPTEMBER 21, 1898

Sedalia, Missouri was a prosperous city of some fifteen thousand souls. Like other towns spawned by the railroad, Sedalia had tracks with a right side and a wrong side.

A visitor stepped off a train at the Missouri Pacific Depot on the wrong side of the tracks. Few lingered, but most took a gander at the backside of the right side while crossing the railroad tracks. Chugging into town gave the visitor a clear view of Midwestern ways in the good old days.

Stretching as far to the west as the eye could see, a line of two- and three-story warehouses backed to their own track spurs. The sidings allowed commerce to flow smoothly from railroad cars to loading docks or from loading docks to railroad cars with no more fuss than slapping down a pair of wooden planks to connect the two.

Everything from John Deere threshers to Belgian lace came in from freight cars through the back and went out into horse-drawn wagons through the business fronts along Main Street. Oddly enough, Main Street was not the main street in Sedalia — at least not the main street of banks, well-lighted drug stores and the Pettis County Courthouse. That honor went to Ohio Street.

But if one judges the "main-ness" of a street by sheer volume of life, Main Street deserved its name. In the daytime, haberdashers argued over the wholesale price of English wool yardgoods; and green grocers disputed the high cost of South American bananas. Wagons clogging the street raised a choking haze to grate the throat raw despite frequent trips by sprinkler wagons to keep down the dust.

Main Street was the place of meeting and merging by day — for business. Main Street was the place of meeting and merging by night — for pleasure.

Main Street was not a line of demarcation so much as a line where the wrong side of the tracks bled over into the right side to the profit and amusement of both. That evening the trio hunting for Duke stayed on the right side of the tracks, but just barely.

East of the intersection of Main and Ohio, the primitive beat of the city's heart poured from the doors of its clubs and saloons. On this warm September evening, Jemmy heard laughter and music spilling into the streets, music the like of which she had never heard before.

Jean Max pulled up in front of the Maple Leaf Club. The roar of a train thwarted all attempts at hearable speech. After the train rumbled by, Hal sent Jean Max to speak to the other drivers. He asked Jean Max to discover whether any of them had seen Duke.

Hal's words to Jemmy were, "Stay in the carriage. Don't so much as poke your head out. We can't do what we came here to do if we have to worry about you." He followed Burnie into the saloon with one backward glance of warning.

Jemmy strained to hear the rollicking piano. Somehow one instrument managed to sound like an entire band. The piano player captured the beat of drums in the bass, a catchy tune in the middle register, and a tinkly descant in the upper keys. All the parts conjoined in a broken romp of a rhythm to banish Jemmy's inhibitions. Of their own volition, her fingers started drumming on the carriage door.

The music so beguiled her that she stuck her head out the carriage window without realizing what she had done. As she turned to listen with her good ear, a voice said, "Isn't that the toe-tappin'est music you've ever come across in all your put-together?"

Jemmy swung her head around to see a skinny fellow standing in the shadows. He smiled a crooked smile as he nodded in the direction of the saloon. "Come on out."

An unnerved Jemmy sank out of sight behind the carriage curtain and said, "I don't dare. I'm expected to stay here."

He peered in the door and wheedled. "Just up to the front to get an earful of music. No need to go inside."

"I really must stay here. I would be in trouble deep if anyone recognized me. I left without a hat or even a scarf to cover my face."

He handed her the kerchief from round his neck. "Use my bandana."

With a start, Jemmy realized she had seen this bit of blue cloth before — or its twin — on the skinny train robber. She hesitated. *A lady would stay in the carriage. But what would a journalist do?*

The fellow coaxed, "Are you coming out? I promise you'll be safe with me."

Jemmy asked herself what Nelly Bly would do. The plucky Pink Cochrane would undoubtedly pump the criminal for information. At very least, she would find out his name.

Jemmy covered her bright hair with the bandana then tied the tails in a knot under her chin. In hopes the material would obscure her face, she kept her head down and unlatched the door.

She took the boy's hand and stepped out into the street. He smelled faintly of apples and tobacco smoke.

A sudden chill shook her frame. *What if he recognizes me from the train? How could he not? When he first spoke, I had my head stuck clean out the window.*

Jemmy prayed either the gaslight was too dim — or he was. After all, every step took her farther away from the refuge of the carriage. At that moment she recognized her own vulnerability. She saw his face clearly. Though he stood inches taller than she remembered, he was surely the same fellow Aunt Tilly had lowered her umbrella on.

He started toward the front door of the Maple Leaf Club, then abruptly switched direction and yanked her toward the side of the building. Jemmy had no time to grasp the meaning of what was happening.

He dragged her down the alley toward a wagon with the words KICKAPOO SAGWA spelled out in letters two feet high. A wave of panic hit Jemmy. A known criminal was carting her off in the dark for who-knows-what dire purpose.

She tried to jerk her hand away. He put his free index finger to his lips, then pointed toward an open window high above them on the second floor. He braced one nonchalant shoe sole back against the bricks. As he leaned against Blocher's Feed Store, he dropped her hand. She was free to go if she liked, but Jemmy stayed.

Maybe he didn't recognize her after all. She bucked up her courage and reminded herself why she had left the safety of the carriage in the first place.

She couldn't resist flirting a little. "I'm sorry I acted silly when you pulled me down the alley. I should thank you for bringing me to such a good listening spot. I have a bad ear from scarlet fever when I was three. But how can I thank you? I don't even know your name."

"John."

"John what?"

"You first."

Jemmy popped out the first lie which came into her head. "Mac." It wasn't really a lie. After all, her last name was "McBustle."

John chuckled. "Mac? Mac's no name for

a pretty girl like you."

Jemmy held her head high. "I think it suits me. I'm no sissified female."

"Well, Mac, I'm pleased to make your acquaintance. I'm John . . ."

Jemmy couldn't hear the all-important last name. The boom-crack of gunshot exploded from inside the Maple Leaf Club. Screams of women and scuffling of chairs filled the air.

John and Jemmy raced back to Main Street in time to see Hal and Burnie wrestle Duke into the carriage. Jean Max stood on the sidewalk with the pistol muzzle pointed skyward. He pushed out the cylinder with his thumb and rotated it to drop three bullets onto the ground. He picked up the fallen bullets and handed them to a bystander as proof that Duke's abductors meant no further harm. The demonstration calmed the crowd.

The music started up again. Revelers meandered back inside. A few stood around to see whether the altercation might provide still more fun. It did.

Hal hopped down from the carriage step. His eyes searched the crowd until they lighted on Jemmy. He strode to her and grabbed her elbow. He said nothing at all as he clamped her arm in an iron grasp and shoved her in ungentlemanly fashion toward the carriage.

John grabbed Hal's wrist and leaped to her defense, "You've no call to treat a lady so rough — or Duke, either, come to that."

Hal turned on the skinny fellow and taught him a quick lesson in minding his own business. He belted John in the solar plexus then laid him out flat with a left cross to the jaw. He stood over the prone would-be rescuer and said, "Don't meddle." John probably didn't hear. The unconscious seldom do.

Hal grabbed Jemmy's arm and jerked her into the carriage. She huddled in the corner and tried to make herself as small as possible. Burnie scooted across to sit beside her. Hal clambered in to sit by Duke and rapped twice on the door to signal Jean Max all were aboard. Jemmy couldn't see Duke's face because he had his head between his knees.

Through clenched teeth Hal said, "This is not a safe section of town. Why didn't you stay put? And what's that rag you've got on your head?"

Jemmy snatched off the bandana and wadded it into a ball. "I was trying to get a story. For your information, getting stories is what reporters do."

"What story? The story of Duke Koock shooting at me when his brother and I were trying to haul him out of a Main Street dive? Wouldn't Aunt Tilly and our hosts love to read all about that in the papers?"

Jemmy sat with back straight as a duchess. "Do you have the slightest idea of the identity of the fellow you slugged? No, of course, you don't. You were somewhere else when a gang of thieves tried to rob our train."

"I suppose you were going to get him to confess?"

Jemmy stuck out her chin. "I suppose I was trying to find out his name. Trying to gain information that might help police round up a bunch of train robbers. Trying to get us a story."

"And did you?"

"Part of it. His name is John."

Mock astonishment made Hal's voice crack. "That narrows it down. Only half the men in Missouri call themselves 'John.' "

Jemmy shoved her face up to Hal's. "He told me his last name, too. But on account of a certain gunshot ruckus, I couldn't hear what he said."

Hal sputtered, "So you think it's my fault a drunk shot at me?"

Burnie threw in, "Miss McBustle, Duke

wasn't trying to shoot Mr. Dwyer. He was after Father. Mr. Dwyer probably saved Father's life."

Jemmy's voice suddenly dropped in volume. "Do you mean . . . ? Mr. Koock was at the Maple Leaf Club — not out on business?"

Burnie backpedaled. "We didn't actually see him . . ."

Hal broke in, "The elder Mr. Koock wasn't in the club. He may have been out back." Hal sent Burnie an apologetic look Jemmy didn't quite understand.

Burnie sounded hurt. "Mr. Dwyer, I hardly think Miss McBustle should be subjected to knowledge of the goings on behind the Maple Leaf Club."

"Calm down, Burnie. We have no good reason to believe your father was back there, either."

Hal explained to Jemmy, "We didn't see Mr. Koock or have any idea where he might have gone. When we arrived, Duke was threatening to shoot the saloonkeeper unless the man told his father's whereabouts."

Jemmy reddened when she realized what Hal and Burnie were up to. In their clumsy way, they were shielding her from an ugly possibility — that Mr. Koock might be visiting a woman of the streets. Her heart ached

161

for Dorothea. Not only did Dorothea suffer from loneliness, her husband didn't.

Except for an occasional moan from Duke, a sullen silence reigned until they reached the Koock house. While Jean Max led the horses to water, Hal and Burnie performed the same service for Duke. They dunked his head in the horse trough over and over until Jemmy felt certain they had drowning on their minds. At last, Duke came up coughing and promptly relieved himself of the biggest part of the stolen bottle of booze.

Hal and Burnie towed Duke between them toward the house. Wearing a white wrapper, Dorothea appeared like an apparition on the back steps.

At that unlikely moment, the songster in Duke burst into a loudly off-key rendition of "The Blue Tail Fly." He belted out, "When I was young I used to wait . . . on Master and give him his plate . . . and pass the bottle when he got dry . . ."

Jemmy stopped Duke's mouth by stuffing it with the skinny robber's bandana. Duke didn't seem to notice. He kept trying to sing, though not much sound escaped. Dorothea held open the doors. The boys dragged Duke up to his room. All the way Jemmy backed up the stairs with her hand over Duke's mouth to keep him from spitting out the bandana.

While Burnie and Hal tucked Duke into bed, the ladies slipped into Dorothea's bedroom. Jemmy told the gunshot story, but left out the part about Duke threatening the saloonkeeper with death if he failed to divulge the elder Mr. Koock's whereabouts. She also did not mention Hal and Burnie's belief that Mr. Koock might be indulging in unseemly behavior behind the Maple Leaf Club.

Dorothea looked relieved to have the wayward Duke at home. Still, the night had been less than satisfactory. She gently rebuked Jemmy. "I wish you had told me you were going. I've been frantic."

"I couldn't. They would have left me behind. I'm sorry you worried."

Dorothea confessed, "I would have done the same thing. When my life is not unbearably miserable, it is so boring I'd do anything for a bit of excitement. I'm not a journalist like you. I'm not daring."

With a start, Jemmy thought about her chaperone. "Heavens in a handbag. I forgot all about Aunt Tilly. Where is she? Please don't tell me she's out hunting for me."

"She's asleep in the guest room, like always."

Jemmy looked at Dorothea with new respect. "How on earth did you manage?"

"I put on your nightclothes and pretended to be you. I'm only a little taller."

Jemmy nodded her approval. "Tell me — and start from the beginning."

"I was in my room when I heard glass breaking. I went downstairs to see what had happened. Then I had to get the maid to clean up the mess at the gun case before someone got cut on the broken glass. By the time I finished in the study, everyone had left the house except Aunt Tilly. I can't tell you how I dreaded facing her when I walked into the nursery. But an angel smiled. The girls were asleep and Auntie was snoring in the rocking chair."

Jemmy edged closer and giggled. "Tell me. How did you get her in bed when I wasn't here?"

"I can be sneaky when I need to. I put on your nightgown and changed the clock in the guest room. I even dabbed on your perfume — which I adore by the way. Jasmine, isn't it?"

Jemmy nodded. "Please, tell me more."

"Then, with the gas jets turned way down, I led her to the bedroom and helped her change. She gave me a few anxious moments, I can tell you. I didn't dare breathe until I heard her start snoring again."

Jemmy rolled her eyes and chuckled. "I can't imagine what Aunt Tilly-Lilly would say if she ever found out."

"Well, I can. I spent six whole months with her, remember? She was my chaperone on my grand European tour."

Just then, thudding sounds came from down the hall. Dorothea opened the bedroom door, then closed it in a hurry.

"Aunt Tilly is headed for the necessary." Dorothea's voice became a mumble as she pulled Jemmy's nightgown over her head. "Get out of your clothes and put on your own nightie."

Jemmy fumbled so clumsily over the scores of tiny buttons on her nightdress she yanked one clean off.

The quick change left both breathless and red-faced, but ready to brave Aunt Tilly. The conspirators tiptoed through the door to the nursery adjoining Dorothea's room.

They emerged into the hall from the nursery while Aunt Tilly was returning to the guest room. She paused and said, "I wondered where you were, Jemima."

Jemmy kept her voice low. "I heard a noise in the nursery. I thought I'd see about it without waking Mrs. Koock, but she was already there. Fanny lost her china head doll."

Aunt Tilly yawned. "Since we're all awake, we may as well dress. It's nearly time for rising, I believe."

Dorothea poked Jemmy and hissed into her ear — her good ear, "The clock."

Aunt Tilly yawned again. "What's that, my dear?"

Dorothea shoved Jemmy toward the guest room door as she said, "It's not near dawn. The clock hasn't even chimed midnight, Aunt Tilly. You must be mistaken."

"Nonsense, I am never up at midnight. My routine won't allow it."

"Still, Aunt Tilly . . ."

Jemmy heard no more as she raced through the guest room to grab the sides of a cherrywood veneered Seth Thomas. Holding the pendulum, she clutched the clock in her arms and dived under the blanket to muffle the hour chimes as she reset the hands.

She emerged from the bedclothes when Aunt Tilly walked in — and straight to the mantel. She stared at the space where the clock should be, turned without saying a word and walked to the nightstand.

With clock tucked behind her back, Jemmy edged to the mantel and re-settled the clock in its home. When Aunt Tilly returned to the mantel with candle in one hand and pince-nez in the other, the clock began clanging off the twelve chimes of midnight.

Although shock was an emotion Aunt Tilly would never confess, she did allow herself a minor moment of surprise as she cleared her throat. "*Hrumph.* I don't know what I would do without my spectacles. I didn't see the clock at all."

Aunt Tilly peered at the Roman numerals on the face and pursed her lips. "A housekeeper who can't keep the clocks wound and set to the proper time is doomed. Poor management is the chief difficulty I see in this household. No one knows what time it is."

Chapter Ten:

BUFFALO BILL'S WILD WEST
KANSAS CITY
WEDNESDAY, SEPTEMBER 21, 1898

Louisa Cody fingered the .22 pistol in her reticule. Before the show she had ample time to lose herself in the past. How ironic that Bill Cody himself had taught her to shoot — purely for self-protection, of course. There never had been the slightest suggestion that she might come on the road with him. Perhaps if he had ever wanted her to come along . . . to be with him . . .

At eight fifteen in the evening the biggest show on earth unleashed excitement on Sedalia. From their little iron room atop the center of the grandstand, Heerman and Bailey focused their spotlights on the ends of the arena. A square hole opened in the middle of an immense canvas mural painted with waterfalls, pine trees, and craggy snow-capped mountains. Through it, Buffalo Bill's buckskin-clad arm emerged waving his white sombrero. When his flowing white locks appeared, the stands went wild with cheering.

The twenty-seven musicians of Buffalo Bill's Wild West Cowboy Band stood in their wide-brimmed hats, chaps, boots, and steel-studded gun holsters to play Handel's "See, the Conquering Hero Comes."

When the band played a cornet fanfare to heighten the drama, Bailey scrolled his spotlight to the other end of the arena. Canvas flaps parted for the Grand Parade of the Wild West and Congress of Rough Riders of the World.

A uniformed color guard of veterans from the Spanish-American War marched into the arena. Dignified Indians followed on foot. Behind them Vincente Orapeza led *vaqueros* twirling *riatas* or leaping in and out of loops of rope.

The bandmaster, William Sweeney, launched his men into "The Star-Spangled Banner" as the canvas parted a second time. Buffalo Bill rode his snowy white horse, Isham, at an easy gallop to make a star's entrance.

William F. Cody lived up to his publicity posters in every way. Resplendent in cream-colored buckskin with fringed seams, he pulled his jacket open to better display his crimson shirt. He looked every inch the bold hunter and gallant sportsman of the plains.

He stopped in the center of the grandstand directly in front of the governor's box. Sombrero held high, he announced, "Ladies and gentlemen, permit me to introduce to you the Rough Riders of the World."

Ladies came first — a bevy of beautiful equestriennes — frontier girls waving to the crowd. South American gauchos twirled bolas overhead; Cossacks in fur hats carried whips in their teeth; Arabs in striped robes rode high-stepping horses with elegantly shaped heads. Syrian horsemen in black turbans sat erect on exotic saddles of red leather. Mexican vaqueros in sheepskin chaps and Texas cowboys in tooled leather whistled at imaginary cattle. Indians in full eagle-feather head-dresses whooped war cries as they perched on blankets atop paint ponies.

Then came Cody's tribute to the Spanish-American War. With cannoneers hanging on like possums on a tree, six horses raced two cannon down the field at full gallop. At the far end of the arena cannoneers fired a deafening salvo. Gun smoke from the color guard joined cannon fumes. Together they puffed yellow clouds overhead to fill nose and mouth with acrid sulfur. A brown haze watered eyes as it settled over spectators and performers alike.

As Buffalo Bill led the Rough Riders in a thrilling lap of the arena with blanks blazing from more than one hundred guns, an Indian slumped over his horse. That wasn't supposed to happen. Indians always rode proud and upright even when they had consumed excessive amounts of stump liquor.

Cody motioned to Johnny Baker to get the man off the field. The colonel distracted the crowd by waving his hat and circling the arena in another lap. He stopped to pose for photographers and shake hands with patrons sitting in the front row.

When the grand parade cleared the field, the colonel returned to the front of the governor's box. He announced through a brass megaphone, "I am proud to present —" He paused to heighten the import of his words. "Miss Annie Oakley, adopted daughter of the legendary Sitting Bull. The chief called her Mochin Chilla Wytonys Cecilia, which means 'little sure shot.' She will amaze and delight you with her dexterity in the use of firearms. Ladies and gentlemen, Miss Annie Oakley."

With thunderous gunfire and more sulfurous smoke, the Butlers performed their show. As soon as they left the arena, Annie lay down in her tent to soothe her gunsmoke-irritated eyes with a cold compress.

Frank entered the cook tent on his usual mission of taking a cold drink to Annie. Not until he had picked up a tin dipper to ladle lemonade from the crock did he see a knot of show people standing around a trestle table.

He walked to the group and saw Marm Whittaker cradling the head of a man wrapped in a soldier's gray wool blanket. She pressed a tin dipper to his lips and urged him to drink a sip of lemonade.

Frank shook his head. "Dead drunk is he? The colonel won't like that. Cody's the only one allowed to —"

Johnny Baker turned a scowl in his direction. "Not dead drunk, but pretty close to dead."

Alarms went off inside Frank's head. "But how?" He dropped in a squat to open the blanket.

Johnny pointed to a trickle of blood from the man's chest. "Small caliber, probably a twenty-two. Most likely hit a rib."

"How come he's still here? The man needs a hospital."

Johnny scowled. "Doctor's on his way."

"I sent for the staff Pinkertons, too. They should be here soon."

The muscles in Frank's belly tightened. He realized evil had come to the Wild West. He looked up at Johnny. "Did you see anything?"

Johnny shook his head. "The colonel pointed to him and motioned for me to get him out of the arena. We 'bout had to pry him off his horse."

Marm Whittaker mopped dribble from the wounded man's chin. "Aren't they amazing? Indians, I mean. Staying on a horse bareback no matter what happens. I guess they're trained from little kids to wrap their legs around a horse so tight they won't fall off — not in sleep or even when they've been shot."

Frank stood to face Johnny and took his arm to draw him away from the injured man. "Do you know where he rides in the parade?"

"Right behind the colonel."

Frank fought to master the dread churning in his chest. "Right behind the colonel means he was right in front of Annie."

"What exactly do you mean?"

Frank drew his lips taut with self-control. "The shooter was aiming at Annie."

A puzzled expression flashed across Johnny's face. "Why do you think the shot was meant for Annie? Why not the colonel, or even Little Elk himself? I mean, he is the one bleeding from a bullet."

Frank confessed his fear in a husky whisper. "This week, someone tried to shoot Annie."

"This is the first I heard of it."

Telling Johnny eased Frank's panic enough for his words to tumble out. "Someone shot at her yesterday. Hit the horse. Bullet lodged just under the skin."

Johnny's baby face reddened. He spoke loud enough to turn heads their way. "And you didn't tell anybody?"

Frank pulled Johnny closer as he made a feeble attempt to explain. "The animal doctor didn't remove the bullet until late this afternoon. Before then I wasn't sure. Didn't see the point —"

"No doubt your failure to see the point will be a great comfort to Little-Stepped-on-by-an-Elk's wife and three children."

Johnny's sarcasm burst the dam of Frank's pain. "Don't get nasty with me. No one wants — needs — to find out who did this as much as I do."

Johnny flinched as if Butler's words had been body blows.

Frank's mind began to function. *I must*

take charge of myself. I must have self-discipline if I'm to protect Annie. Stay calm and rational. "I went to see Lillian Smith today. She denied being here last night, but she might have lied."

"You think Lillian Smith shot Little Elk by mistake? Do you think she would shoot at Annie?"

Frank raised his eyebrows. "Could be."

Johnny shook his head. "Lillian is incapable of shooting a person by mistake. I never knew her to aim at anything the size of a person and fail to hit it. She still makes a living shooting, doesn't she?"

"She's on the stage. Her show is pure vaudeville — boxes of nothing but blanks in her dressing room."

Johnny clicked his tongue. "I still don't think the bullets were necessarily meant for Annie, but tell me what I can do to help."

Frank scowled in exasperation. "It's plain as day — plainer even. The bullets were meant for Annie."

"I have reason to think otherwise."

When Johnny paused, Frank exploded in anger. "Now who's the one keeping secrets?"

"I didn't tell you because it has nothing to do with you or Annie." He paused again.

Frank drew back a fist as if he were about

to throw a punch. Johnny held up both hands as he took a step back. "In August, the Sunday after we played Hannibal, the colonel and I took Mrs. Cody sightseeing to Tom Sawyer's Cave. You know, the one in Mark Twain's book.

"The guide and the colonel went off somewhere. While they were gone, a bullet grazed Lulu's arm. It wasn't too bad, just enough to hurt like the dickens and to scar. Happened more than a month ago. I all but forgot it. Nothing bad has happened since — leastways nothing I knew about until now."

"So just what are you saying?"

"Most likely the colonel is the target."

Frank snorted. "Then the shooter is plum stupid. Anyone who knows the colonel would know he'd not shed many tears over Lulu's final goodbye."

Johnny's eyes blazed. "I was standing right next to her. Maybe he was shooting at me and missed. Did you think of that?"

Frank put a hand to Johnny's shoulder. "I'm sorry. Maybe the target is the colonel, or the show. Maybe someone is out to close the show."

"You're not making a lick of sense."

Frank bit his tongue to keep from saying something he'd regret.

Johnny patted Frank on the shoulder, "Don't get your hat caught in your boot. We'll scope it all out."

Frank turned in a circle as he scanned the grounds. "Why aren't the Pinkertons here yet? Maybe they've gone to get the Kansas City police."

Johnny rubbed his forehead. "At least I won't have to face Little Elk's wife. I don't envy the colonel that job."

Frank massaged his chin thoughtfully. "You were near Little Elk. Where did the bullet come from? Could you find the bullet casing?"

"I could try, I guess. Look in the stands. Tomorrow when it's light out. What can we do now? I mean once tonight's show is over? Can't see much in the dark."

Frank took a furtive look behind him before he pulled Johnny farther away from the murmurs of the crowd around Little Elk. "Doesn't look like anyone aimed to do him in. Twenty-two has to be at close range to kill. Inside a person's skull a twenty-two ricochets around and does more damage than a through-and-through forty-five. But Little Elk took the bullet in his chest."

Johnny jerked his head up with a sour expression on his face. "I guess you're saying if anyone was trying to kill him, the shooter had lousy aim."

"Annie rides close to Little Elk — and on a smaller horse."

"If I'm hearing you right, you're thinking one of us in the show did it."

"No. I don't mean that. I don't know what to think, except we have to find the shooter before someone else gets hit." Frank picked at the headband inside his hat.

"Where you think we ought to start?"

"Poke around to see if anyone has live twenty-two ammunition who shouldn't."

Johnny nodded and spoke soothing words. "Maybe no one is after Annie. Maybe the shooter really was after Little Elk. You and I both know that nutty Indian told anybody who would listen he was with Crazy Horse at the Little Big Horn. Only a fool would believe him. He was too young to have been in a battle twenty-odd years ago. He's genuine Oglala Sioux, though. That part's true enough.

"Don't let anyone know I said this, because it's wrong to speak ill of a wounded man." Johnny put a reassuring hand on Frank's shoulder. "Think about it, though. The way he goes around bragging about the Indians scalping Custer. He talks high and mighty even when he's cold-stone sober. Lots of folks don't like such brass, especially from a red man."

"Not many would put a bullet in a fellow's chest just because they don't like a man's politics — not unless the man is the president, anyhow."

"Someone famous is an easy target. That may be reason enough." Johnny sighed. "I know how you feel. I'm just saying let's not go off half-cocked. Don't accuse Lillian Smith or anyone else without good reason."

Frank turned to leave but wheeled back, "At the end of the show, be around front. Try to spot Lillian." He added, "Or anyone else who might want something bad to happen to Annie, or Little Elk, or whomsoever."

Johnny called after him, "Pawnee Bill is here; Mae, too — come to see their main rivals, I'd say. The colonel gave the Lillies passes. I saw them in the governor's box."

"Pretty hard to hide a shot from the governor's box." Frank doubted his own words the minute they escaped from his mouth. Galloping horses, shouting performers, noise, and smoke fill the field even when the audience is dead silent. A .22 pistol held between a couple might escape all notice. Little Elk was on the opposite side of the arena when he slumped over. Even famous sharpshooters might miss the mark from thirty yards away.

Even if Pawnee Bill and Mae would resort to murder to sabotage the Wild West, they couldn't hope to succeed by killing Little Elk. Only through the loss of a star like Annie or the colonel himself could they hope to destroy the show.

Frank felt a pang of guilt for suspecting such nice people as Bill and Mae. The Lillies were successful enough and sensible people to boot. *Pawnee Bill would never commit murder and risk hanging. Would he?*

CHAPTER ELEVEN:

SEDALIA
THURSDAY MORNING,
SEPTEMBER 22, 1898

On Thursday morning, Aunt Tilly insisted Burnie attend school. She reprimanded Dorothea for allowing him to play hooky the day before.

After breakfast Auntie spirited the lady of the house up to the nursery and laid down severe instructions to spend the day in silent observation of Sissy and Fanny's re-training.

Left blissfully free to do the job they came to do, Jemmy and Hal set off on a mission. They sallied forth to cover pre-event festivities. When the Wild West blew into town, each and every village, burg, and city celebrated. City fathers congratulated themselves for bringing in the show and for bringing in free-spending showgoers.

On the Third Street trolley, Hal told Jemmy about his photo excursion of the day before. He had ridden Burnie's bicycle west on Broadway toward Kansas City to photograph one of the huge posters pasted on the side of a barn.

"An old man fixing fence told me Cody's advance men held a bill-posting contest one Saturday about six weeks ago."

Jemmy jotted down the specifics in her notebook.

"The winning team could put up a thirty-two-sheet poster in ten minutes flat. He said a feller working alone would take at least a half hour to unfold and paste-up, and another half hour to paper a billboard. Each one of those big posters costs four dollars — and Buffalo Bill bought a thousand for this season alone."

"Four thousand dollars on nothing but paper." Hal shook his head at Colonel Cody's spendthrift ways.

He drew a rectangle in the air to show Jemmy the size of a single lithograph. "That's the size of each one of those poster pieces — two and a half feet by three and a half feet. The fence feller seemed to know all about them. He owned the barn you see, so he had the right to know everything about the pictures.

"He said printers had to lay them down just perfect four times — one for each color. He said Buffalo Bill spent a hundred thousand dollars on posters every year. Can you imagine? Enough money to buy twenty grand mansions in St. Louis."

Hal gushed out information too fast for Jemmy to write down. Her usually neat letters now sprawled big and loopy in her notebook.

"If I could take some really good pictures, do you think Cody would use them on some posters? I'd be famous. I'd have enough work so I wouldn't have to put up with you."

Jemmy stuck out her tongue.

"Just wanted to see if you were listening."

"I'm listening. Go on."

"The man said two train cars of advance men came in town a couple of weeks ago to rent advertising space and to stick up thousands of smaller posters. They also had to get parade permits and order food for the workers and the livestock and such."

Jemmy had stopped taking notes.

Hal's voice burst with impatience. "Say, are you listening to a single thing I'm saying?"

She surreptitiously snapped off her pencil point, then held it up. "My pencil lead broke." She handed the yellow stick to him as she balanced her satchel on her knee to unfasten a strap. "I'll see if I can find another. Whittle this one with your pocket knife, will you?"

"You might say 'Please.' "

Jemmy could tell Hal intended to be touchy.

She batted her eyelashes at him, "Will you please sharpen my pencil, Mr. Dwyer? I would be eternally in your debt."

Hal gave a disgusted sigh, but dutifully opened his pocket knife. "Why don't you get one of them mechanical pencils — the kind you stick more lead in if it breaks."

Jemmy could be touchy, too. "I'm so grateful for the advice. It's the very first thing I'll buy with the million dollars I'll soon make writing articles for the *Illuminator*. A mechanical pencil — solid gold — on a lon-n-ng gold chain to wear around my neck."

In silence, Hal sent gouges of yellow paint, wood, and graphite into the street. Jemmy could see this was apt to be a trying day. He handed her a pencil sharpened to a fare-thee-well, but barely half as long as when she gave it to him.

By the time they reached Ohio Street, the pair had calmed down. Neither apologized. Jemmy tried to get her bearings while Hal checked his wooden case for broken plates.

Hal hoisted the tripod to his shoulder with the camera head sticking over his back. "Where to?"

"I'll tell you in a minute."

Hal set the tripod back on the board sidewalk and put one impatient hand on one impatient hip. Jemmy lifted her head and sauntered into the druggist shop without gracing Hal with so much as a backward glance.

The shop smelled pleasantly of camphor and vinegar. Jemmy assumed folks would gather at the courthouse. She asked the druggist where to find it.

He chuckled. "Cain't miss it. Big-time Missouri senator out speechifyin' today. Walk out the door and follow your nose to the right. You must be blind, you poor thang. 'Taint more than a block away. You can see it from the front winder, but you got to open your eyes first."

As red crept up her cheeks, she half lied and half told the truth, "Thank you, kind sir. Being nearsighted as well as deaf in one ear is such a burden. I hope you never suffer similar disabilities."

The man cast his eyes down in a suitably contrite gesture.

Jemmy brushed out the door past Hal, who hastened to take up his burdens. After walking a short block past storefronts, they paused to survey Courthouse Square from across Ohio Street.

Pettis County's civic pride rose aloft in

the midst of green lawn and white graveled walkways. Its lantern tower soared twenty feet or more above the second story. The building loomed altogether more prepossessing than Jemmy had expected.

The two St. Louisans were properly impressed by the Courthouse, a handsome Italianate edifice of gray limestone with columned porticoes between pavilions at each corner.

With elections six weeks away, a bombastic politician gesticulated wildly from the west steps as he stumped to win office.

Jemmy could hear a few words as he harangued a crowd.

"I promise you if I am elected . . ."

Jemmy had a good idea of what the politician meant. He made campaign promises he would forget as soon as the vote count became final.

Hal set up his camera to memorialize the scene. Before he could get a plate from his trunk, commotion broke out in the politician's audience. Reporter and photographer dashed across the street to capture the action.

They narrowly missed being run down by the Ohio streetcar. The conductor clanged his warning bell and shook his fist. Hal returned a shrug for the conductor's pains.

Jemmy tried to make sense of the melee. Apparently, some disgruntled soul had lobbed a brown missile — perhaps a clod of dirt or a batch of something even less fragrant — at the speaker. The crowd made little attempt to contain its snickers and guffaws. Pale-skinned ladies under wide-brimmed hats and lace parasols hid their giggles behind white-gloved hands.

The speaker sputtered as his face turned red. He evidently failed to see humor in the event. He sicced his ward-heelers on the knee slappers. Naturally, they protected themselves. The onrush of the politician's henchmen led to a brawl. The set-to sent ladies scattering like cottonwood fluff. They hid behind trees surrounding the square.

Seeing females flee waved a red flag at every red-blooded man within shouting distance. They came a-running and quite happily joined the fracas until the whole west lawn became a boxing ring.

Hal set up his camera in record time. He was so intent on capturing the action, he trod on Jemmy's foot without offering a single word of apology.

Something else caught Jemmy's eye. A show wagon had drawn a crowd to the street behind the courthouse. She tugged at Hal's sleeve to tell him where she planned to go.

He brushed her hand away as if it were a pesky mosquito.

Jemmy left the courthouse lawn with a single backward glance. Hal's head and shoulders disappeared under the black cloth flap of the camera.

She examined the scene in the street behind the courthouse as she walked.

A tall man with skin the color of an oak table stood behind a plank on two sawhorses. He peddled brown bottles of Kickapoo joy juice to the masses.

Jemmy knew those bottles were more likely to give the user a hangover than a cure. Here was just another of the many tricksters who found a semirespectable way to sell liquor to rubes.

Emblazoned on the wagon's side, a placid Indian sat cross-legged on a painted blanket. The painted Indian smoked a sacred pipe by the orange flames of a painted campfire. Arching over his head were the words ELIXIR OF THE RED MAN — KICKAPOO SAGWA — TO PURIFY THE BLOOD.

On a drop-leaf stage in front of the canvas sat a real live Indian maiden. She wore a beaded headband with a feather in it. Multicolored beads depicting corn stalks decorated her fringed buckskin dress.

The plump dark girl sat cross-legged on a

pile of animal furs. She looked heavenward as she plaited her dark straight hair in fat pigtails and tied them with buckskin thongs.

A banner hanging from the stage boasted the legend CURES ALL DISEASES OF STOMACH, LIVER & KIDNEYS, and in smaller letters, SALMASIUS SCALAGER, ESQ. PROP.

Naturally, when a better show erupted in front of the courthouse, the hawker lost his audience. With a bang of his fist on the plank where he displayed his wares, Salmasius Scalager, Esq. pulled the Indian girl to her feet in mid-braid. The pair left an assistant to guard the merchandise while they disappeared behind the canvas into the wagon.

The assistant interested Jemmy. The fellow had an uncommonly swarthy face, but something in his slender frame seemed familiar. As she walked toward him, she became more and more convinced she had seen this same person at the Maple Leaf Club and on the train.

The story she sought might be locked inside a person counting bottles on a board not ten feet away.

She struck up a conversation. "If you want to go on the minstrel stage, I recommend burnt cork. I understand professionals use cork to blacken their faces."

When he jerked his head up, Jemmy had to bite her lip to keep from laughing. His face was the color of acorns with globs of other colors added. It looked as though someone had chewed tobacco and used his face for a spittoon several dozen times.

In spite of nervous flutters of his eyes, he put up a good front. He gave her a quizzical stare and said, "Ho mo mo jo."

Jemmy laughed. " 'Homomojo' to you, too. Do you really think some brown muck on your face is going to fool anybody into thinking you're an Indian — a blue-eyed Indian?"

He wavered, then turned to go inside the wagon.

Jemmy raised her voice. "I would stay here and talk to me if I were a train robber who had been found out by a St. Louis journalist."

He appeared more curious than frightened when he turned back to talk to her. "How could you tell it was me?"

Jemmy folded her arms and produced a sarcastic grin. "Let me think. Who would choose to look the way you do? Would it be a handsome young man seeking a pretty companion during the excitement of the Wild West show coming to town? No, I think it would be a low-down miserable excuse for a crook hiding his bruises under a thick coat of whatever it is you have on your face." She tapped her jaw with an index finger. "That's what I think."

"Did I ever harm you? I tried to be nice to you — took you to hear Scott Joplin play."

"After you tried to rob me."

"You think I tried to rob you?"

"You tried to rob Aunt Tilly. You would have robbed me next. The only reason you didn't rob me was an old lady stopped you before you had the chance."

"You don't know what you're talking about. I never planned to rob you."

"I suppose you were going to propose marriage to me."

"No, but I planned to kiss you."

Jemmy batted her eyes in disbelief. "Kiss me?"

His injured tone said she must have hit a sore spot. "I don't think that's funny. You've heard of Black Bart, the Gentleman Bandit of California. I don't see why I couldn't be the Kissing Bandit of Missouri."

"Oh, you're the infamous Bussing Bandit." She put the back of her hand to her forehead like a frail heroine in a melodrama. "Shall I swoon now or later?"

"Are you going to turn me in?"

"Why don't you turn yourself in? You're

in the right place for it."

She pointed to a redbrick building behind the show wagon. In bold letters the sign over the front door read PETTIS COUNTY JAIL. Underneath in smaller letters were the words J. C. WILLIAMS, SHERIFF.

The skinny crook opened his eyes wide. His pupils bulged like robins' eggs stuck in a loaf of pumpernickel bread.

Jemmy stopped her banter as the expression on the boy's face told her the show wagon's location behind the courthouse was no accident. Scalager had parked in front of the jail not for business business, but for monkey business. She stood stock still in thought.

He urged between clenched teeth, "Well?"

"I might turn you in . . . unless . . ."

"Unless what? What do you want?"

"Your story."

"My story?"

"Why a nice boy, probably from a nice family of Missouri farmers, would become a dastardly outlaw."

"Who says I'm a dastard?"

"I do."

"I'll have you know my mother and father were married in the Baptist Church in Sweet Springs."

Jemmy giggled as she said, "The word you

think I meant starts with a B. The word 'dastard' —"

A voice interrupted from behind. "Damn me. You're a cheeky piece. Calling a fellow names right to his face."

She whirled around to see the acne-scabbed face of Marmaduke Koock.

"You might at least wait until he's out of earshot. I shudder to think what you might be saying about me behind my back."

She stood on tiptoe so she could be eye level with the disgusting fellow. "Mr. Koock, I wouldn't bother talking behind your back. What I have to say to you I would say right out on the courthouse steps. I might even put it in the paper."

As she turned on her heel and marched off, Jemmy muttered, "Why of all people did the Koock boy have to butt in when I was about to —"

A new realization stopped her in her tracks. *Why, indeed? Why would he take it into his ugly head to speak to me? After all, he must know I was with Hal and Burnie when they dragged his sorry carcass out of the Maple Leaf Club.*

Duke Koock had no reason at all to seek Jemmy's company. In fact he had every reason to avoid it. She turned back. Both boys had disappeared. She scanned the street to discover their whereabouts. They had no time to go anywhere but behind the wagon or inside it.

She pondered the meaning of it all. *Why does Duke hobnob with crooks? Why did criminals set up a medicine show wagon in the most unlikely place — right in front of the county jail?*

Lost in thought, she walked toward the nearly deserted front steps of the courthouse. As she ambled toward the columns, she realized she had not seen Hal. She trudged up the steps to the portico and turned to survey the scene. Hal was gone. Gone were camera on tripod with black flap waving off the back. Gone was Hal's wooden box full of glass plates.

Hands on hips, she tapped her toe in impatience. Where did that impossible freckle-face go?

CHAPTER TWELVE:

SEDALIA
THURSDAY MORNING,
SEPTEMBER 22, 1898

Jemmy stood on the west portico of the courthouse as her feelings caromed back and forth between anger and hurt. *How could my bodyguard be so irresponsible? Leave me stranded without saying a single word?* She wrung her hands. *Please, Hal, come back to me.*

Anger charged up her torso like fire up a haystack. *How dare he have so little regard for the fair sex as to leave a young girl unescorted in a strange city. To have any chance at forgiveness, that — that — that man will have to make good account of why he ran off.*

She muttered aloud, "He'd better have some prize-winning pictures. Nothing else could make his bad manners and thoughtlessness excusable."

She stood bouncing between two horrors for what felt like an eternity, but was in fact seventeen minutes by Grandma's brooch watch. Jemmy checked the dial a hundred times or more. Twice she put the watch to her good ear to see if the timepiece ticked. Each time she opened the watch, the pin made new puckers in her fashionable dead-leaf-colored linen jacket.

She ignored the men who stared at her, their mustaches twitching like tomcats eying a jug of sweet cream. When one man sauntered up the steps toward her, she realized she could stay put no longer. As he removed his hat and started to speak, she stuck her nose in the air and swished past him down the stairs.

She swooshed across Ohio Street back to the drugstore. She marched to the counter and forced a smile, "Sir, has a young man with a camera come in recently?"

"You mean the tall young feller with you — the one with the red hair?"

"So, you have seen him." Jemmy felt Hal's betrayal quiver her jaw.

"I saw him, yes. He didn't come in though."

"Do you remember which direction he took?"

"Same direction you took. He was with you."

Jemmy's voice neared screeching because of the man's stupidity. "I don't mean when we left for the courthouse square together. I mean later. Did you see him alone?"

"No."

Jemmy felt dizzy and began to teeter, but the man didn't offer smelling salts or even seem to notice. "Pardon me, miss, but I'd be greatly obliged if you would step outside."

Jemmy blinked her eyes. Was this man callously booting from his shop a young lady on the verge of fainting?

The man had taken off his white jacket and was holding down his cuff with his middle fingers as he ran his hand into the arm of a gray suit jacket. "I have to close the store and go upstairs to get my children. I promised to take them to the dog and pony show this afternoon."

"Dog and pony show?"

"Yes, that one."

He smiled as he nodded toward a newspaper open to a full page advertisement. "My little girl wanted to be sure I didn't forget so she brought me the *Democrat* with the page already turned."

A line drawing of a little wagon pulled by two big dogs accompanied an ad that read:

The only moral exhibition in the world
under canvas.
An educational festival patronized and

endorsed by the elite of the land.
Fourth and Quincy Sts.
Afternoon and Evening.
Prof. Gentry's Famous Dog and Pony
Show.
150 ~ Aristocratic ~ Animal Actors.
See Pinto today — the world's best
trained baby elephant.
Watch for the Grand Free Street Parade
at 11 a.m.
Admission
Children 15¢ Adults 25¢

The drugstore man hustled her out and locked the door behind her. The last she saw was a hand through the glass door turning the OPEN sign to CLOSED.

Along Ohio Street, crowds were gathering three or four deep. Little boys in argyle stockings and brown knickers jumped into the street to be the first to see Professor Gentry's red silk banner fluttering its gold fringe. The faint music of fife, drum, and banjo set a bouncy rhythm as the crowd joined in singing "Oh Susanna."

Little girls wearing dresses printed with tiny pink or yellow roses peeked around parental skirts. Jemmy craned her neck to get a better view of the people waiting for the parade — and maybe glimpse her missing photographer. One little boy picked his nose and wiped the result on his mother's sleeve.

Despite hostile glares, Jemmy elbowed to the front to scan the crowd. *No tripod. No boxy camera. No tall redheaded young man seeking some photogenic character to remain in one place long enough for him to take a picture.*

Suddenly, the parade was upon her. She backed up onto the boardwalk and stepped on the little nose-picker's toes. The tot screeched a note that set off howls and yowls among all 150 aristocratic animals parading up Ohio Street. Heads turned in his direction.

His mother hastened to comfort him — an action that yielded an unanticipated outcome. When she bent over, her protruding posterior bumped the cane of the gentleman standing behind her.

He lost his balance and tried to regain it by grasping the nearest available article that might be used for stabilization — namely, the protruding derriere. The mother, distracted from the sniveling little boy who now really did need a handkerchief, rounded on the gentleman with the cane.

Her eyes popped wide when she recognized the assailer of her chaste person.

"Reverend Polkinghome, well I never!"

The reverend blushed an indescribable color combination of puce mixed with chartreuse. "Madam, I assure you, I had no intention of —"

"I've heard about the goings on in the Methodist Church. Besides dancing, what other outrages do you permit?"

It was the reverend's turn for eye-popping. His face turned crimson red with a touch of pond-scum green.

"Madam, you wrong me most terribly. I was leaning on my cane because I am victim of a painful bout of the gout in my right leg. When you leaned over, you knocked my cane and my balance with it. I apologize for the result, but surely you must see I was not entirely to blame."

"Gout caused, no doubt, from dancing." Her tone suggested she considered dancing only slightly less immoral than blasphemy — probably in the same category as gouging the eyes out of sheep.

The minister knew when he was out-manned. He leaned heavily on his cane and tilted his head in a pitiful plea. "I beg you to forgive me. I ask it most humbly and sincerely."

The mother pulled her chin up. "A real gentleman would have broken both lower limbs rather than touch a lady in an improper manner."

The minister's head sank still lower. "I wish I had two broken legs — pardon me — lower extremities — to redeem myself — but what is one to do in the face of nature itself? I had no thought to touch you in an improper manner. My arms reached out of their own accord. Please, I beg you to forgive me."

The lady was still deliberating when Jemmy threaded her way north as the parade traveled up the street. She thought to herself how little the lady knew about gout. *Rich food and strong drink cause gout — not dancing. Surely Reverend Polkinghome knows as much. Perhaps he was wise not to mention it.*

The episode gave her only a brief rest from her harping brain. She hit upon a shred of hope. *Maybe Hal had sought a corner where crowds were thinner.*

As she walked down Ohio Street, she barely noticed dogs on pedestals in their multicolored plumes and sequined costumes riding in wagons. A brigade of monkeys dressed as firemen on a pony-drawn pumper held her attention for a single moment. Petite Roman chariots pulled by miniature horses received but a glance.

She took care not to trample additional toes as she peeked between shoulders or over the heads of children. *Where is that Irish lout of a cameraman?*

A sinister thought popped in her head. *What if Hal did not disappear just to make me miserable?*

Hal could be annoying, but she had never known him to shirk his responsibilities. *What if he wants to be on the job with me, but can't?*

But why? Police don't arrest people for taking pictures, do they?

Jemmy clicked her tongue when a new idea took shape. *Why didn't I think of it before? Maybe Hal got himself embroiled in the fight on the courthouse lawn. Maybe he's been arrested for fighting or disturbing the peace. Maybe he is sitting in the Pettis County Jail this very minute.*

Jemmy decided to go back to the jailhouse as soon as she could cross Ohio Street.

She walked all the way to Main Street without finding a break in the array of "aristocratic" animals or catching a glimpse of anyone who remotely resembled Hal.

The parade had cordoned off Main Street all the way down to the Missouri Pacific railroad tracks. The professor's roustabouts were still unloading barrels and hay bales from boxcars bearing the label GENTRY'S

EQUINE AND CANINE PARADOX. She had no way to reach the other side.

As she jostled her way back up Ohio Street, her boots pinched her toes. Her stays jabbed her ribs even when she took breaths so shallow she had to keep her mouth open to pant.

Frustration mounted as she trudged block after block. She began to loathe dappled gray ponies with pink ribbons tied in their manes. By the time she reached the drugstore, she wished she would never set eyes on another feisty ankle-high dog with a starched red ruff around its neck.

Her dry tongue stuck to the roof of her mouth as she muttered, "One hundred and fifty aristocratic animals? Seems more like one hundred and fifty thousand. Is it possible for animals to multiply on parade?"

At last, the final wagon came into view: not a miniature, but a full-sized Conestoga. Jemmy shook her head at the insolence. Buffalo Bill's advance men had pirated Gentry's parade to advertise their own show. Painted canvas featured roping and shooting. Banners in four-foot-high letters urged parade viewers to WAIT FOR THE ONE-HUNDRED-AND-FIFTY-THOUSAND. BIGGEST SHOW ON EARTH TOMORROW NIGHT BY THE MKT YARDS.

Jemmy fumed when she arrived back at courthouse corner. She had placed herself permanently on the wrong side of the festivities. The parade turned the corner as it marched west on Fourth Street toward Quincy. She tapped her foot in impatience while the crowd closed in to promenade behind the baby elephant.

At last Jemmy could cross the street. She dodged steamy piles of droppings as she marched to the jail. She sashayed into the office and demanded, "May I speak to Sheriff Williams, please."

An angular man in a striped shirt sat with his feet up. The battered desk must have hosted his boots and hundreds of others for a good many years. He was smoking a pipe with one hand. With the other he held a ball-on-a-string attached to a bell-shaped cup on a handle. He tossed the ball up and made a half-hearted attempt to catch it in the cup. He yipped when the ball whacked his thumb.

Caught playing cup-and-ball on county time, he dropped the game to the floor. It rumbled along the pine boards until it rolled out of sight behind a spittoon. He covered the noise by landing his chair legs on the floor with a creak and a bump. "You'll have to make do with me, miss. I'm Deputy

Sheriff Futcher. The sheriff done gone to lunch." He made no move to put out the pipe.

"Perhaps you'd be so good as to let me see a young fellow who was arrested in the brawl on the courthouse lawn this morning."

The deputy's embarrassment turned to amazement. "No brawl at the courthouse this morning I know of."

"But of course there was. The political speaker was assaulted with . . ." When she couldn't think of a more genteel way of putting it, she whispered, "Offal."

"Oh, that. A good dose of dung is exactly what he should expect seeing as how he wants the country on the gold standard. Folks around here are for free silver."

Jemmy knew farming folks favored William Jennings Bryan's plan to get rid of the gold standard. Legal tender backed by silver would mean more money — more money for folks to borrow — money farmers needed to borrow every year so they could plant crops in the spring.

But she didn't care to discuss the ins and outs of national economics. "Do you mean to say no one was arrested?"

"I meant to opine no one should have been arrested."

"So you didn't arrest anyone?"

"Me, myself? No. I wasn't on duty at the time."

"Sir, would you be so kind as to speak plainly. Was anyone arrested this morning?"

"I wouldn't know. I wasn't here."

"You are being extremely rude. May I see the prisoners you have in jail? Perhaps the man I seek is among them."

"They're a rough bunch, miss. I hate to think what they might say to a pretty young girl."

"I believe I'd prefer their rudeness to yours."

"All right, but remember I warned you." He made great show of unlocking a door. Jemmy thought it strange the key ratcheted the door locked and then ratcheted again to unlock it. He opened the door and motioned her through. Inside the bars, a single cell spanned the back of the entire building.

Jemmy stood on tiptoe to peer at the upper bunks. She examined the rows of neatly tucked gray wool blankets for dents. No sign of occupants. The whole cell was empty as a cistern in a seven-year drought.

She stamped her foot as she turned to the deputy. "You might have told me the jail was empty."

Futcher sported a wide grin. "I thought

you'd rather see for yourself."

"I should report your rudeness to the sheriff. You had no reason to wrong me with your spiteful jokes."

"I'm sorry, miss. I couldn't help myself. You seem such a serious little thing. Pretty girls shouldn't worry themselves about brawlers. Worry will turn you old before your time — 'specially worry over brawlers. No greater worry has a young woman than when she takes a brawler to be her lord and master. Them's true words. You'd do well to remember them."

Jemmy stomped toward the door. "One more thing, miss. You're looking in the wrong jail. This here's the county jail. City police would take care of any disturbance happens in the city."

Jemmy closed her eyes and gritted her teeth as she replied, "Where, might I ask, is the city jail, then?"

"I'm not going to tell you. Believe me, miss. Forget him. It's for your own good."

There it was again. Yet another person telling her something was "for her own good." The nerve of him to think he knew whom she was trying to find or why! She flounced out of the office with her jaw set and banged the door shut.

When her anger boiled over like baking

soda in vinegar, she turned on her heel. She wheeled back to give Deputy Futcher a piece of her mind.

Jemmy opened the door and marched back inside. What she saw gave her such a start she clean forgot to be furious. The pudgy woman from the Kickapoo Sagwa wagon stood talking to Deputy Futcher with her back to Jemmy. Both stopped talking.

Where did that Indian girl come from? Was a few seconds enough time for her to come through the back door? Maybe she was hiding in the cell all along.

In an overloud voice the deputy ordered the woman into the cell. "We have ordinances in this town. You think Pettis County is some uncivilized mining camp up in Alaska?"

To Jemmy he said, "This one set up a medicine show right out there behind the courthouse. Drew a crowd and no permit. I'm keeping her until the sheriff gets here. He has a room in his own house to keep women who break the law. I wouldn't want you to think we keep females in this here cell with real criminals. Got no one inside just now, though."

Jemmy spun in an abrupt about-face and all but ran out the door in confusion. *Why did the girl in buckskin hide from Jemmy?*

208

Who would be afraid of a respectable young female such as Jemima McBustle?

The woman puzzled Jemmy, but she could see no possible sense to it. Jemmy considered going back inside to ask, but what good would more questions do? She had little expectation either person would tell her the truth.

Thinking about Deputy Futcher's patronizing ways raised her ire once again. A piece of her mind was yearning to hop off the end of her tongue. If she went back inside, she would enjoy giving it to him. "How I wish I had the time to set him straight." She bristled under her breath, but didn't return.

In any event, more immediate problems pressed her. She had to find Hal and give him a piece of her mind. Jemmy never doubted she could spare sufficient pieces of her mind for both bossy males.

She sought about for someone to direct her to the city jail. The streets were all but deserted now. Jemmy saw only the backs of a distant horde following the baby elephant Pinto as if he were the Pied Piper.

She tried to open the door of the grand Romanesque sandstone castle that housed the Missouri Trust Company — locked. Apparently all Sedalia had taken half a day off to see Professor Gentry put his dogs and

209

ponies through their paces — all the respectable Sedalians, that is.

A half-dozen seedy characters were prying up boards from the boardwalk on Fourth Street. Deputy Sheriff Futcher was indeed derelict in his duty. Thieves were stealing the sidewalks not a block from his jail while he entertained himself with children's games and Indian maidens.

As Jemmy followed the crowd, she dreamed up a small crutch to prop up her spirits. *Maybe Hal has gone to Gentry's tent in hopes of finding the best place to take photographs. Yes, that's it. Probably. Maybe. Perhaps.* Even if she didn't really believe Hal would be at the dog and pony show, at least she had something to do — somewhere to go.

Jemmy's feet hurt good and plenty by the time she had walked another eight blocks on top of the twelve blocks she'd already walked in her quest to find that good-for-nothing Hal.

She paid no attention to the barkers outside the professor's tent. Hawkers carried trays of goodies hung round their necks. None tempted her in the slightest. She ignored the heavenly scent of buttered popcorn. Despite her thirst, she walked right past the lemonade stand. Roasted peanuts? No indeed. Saltwater taffy, spun sugar floss on a paper cone? None found a market in Jemmy.

She eschewed the line to the ticket wagon and marched straight up to the man taking tickets at the canvas flap. "May I have a look around inside? A friend of mine is missing and I think he may be here. I promise to return and buy a ticket if he is."

"You pulled a new one on me, miss. And I thought I'd heard every trick known to man or beast to get into the show free."

"I'm not trying to get in without paying. I simply want to see if my friend is there. I'm too tired to stand in line then find he's not inside. May I please have a quick peek?" Jemmy put on what she hoped was her most appealing smile.

"Indeed you may go inside, miss. As Jemmy started to thank him, he interrupted, "As soon as you hand me a ticket for the privilege."

Jemmy stomped off — which made her feet hurt even more. She considered slipping around the back to sneak in under the tent like a nasty little boy who had spent his ticket money on licorice whips. That procedure lacked a certain dignity.

With a sigh of dejection, she stood in line and dutifully paid her twenty-five cents. She took the ticket to the fellow manning the flap. He tore it in half and returned the stub to her. "There you are, miss. I hope you and your friend enjoy the show."

Inside the tent was at least twenty degrees hotter than the pleasant temperature outside. She pulled her fan from her reticule and set it in motion as she scoured the crowd for any sign of the tall redhead — nothing. She sat down to wait. Hal might come in. Even if he didn't, she was too tired to leave; and her feet felt like they'd been caught in a beaver trap. She longed to rub them, but soothing one's feet was not an action suitable for public display.

Besides, she'd paid twenty-five cents. If she expected to gain any value for her money, she'd better write a story for the *Illuminator*. On occasion, being a professional journalist was not the lark she had expected it to be. Sometimes it was no fun at all.

Any other time, she would have taken delight in the clever tricks of the dogs. One pair of poodles walked tight ropes, did back flips, and leapt through rings of fire onto the backs of galloping miniature horses.

A spotted terrier in a purple ruff brought uproarious laughter from the crowd. The little dog snatched the derby off a chimpanzee sitting in the audience as if he were a businessman come to see the show. The chimp loosened his tie as he clambered down the bleacher seats after the scrappy dog.

Tail straight up in the air, the dog raced to the center of the ring and dropped the derby in the sawdust. When the chimp came within inches of his hat, the dog grabbed the derby in his teeth and ran off a few feet.

The chimp would come a hair's breadth from catching his hat, then fall on his face — or on his backside — or somersault into a hilarious splat.

In the outrageous finale, the dog leaped upon the chimp's back and began tugging at his jacket. All of a sudden, the material separated with the dog still clinging to the collar. In an instant, the chimp's jacket tumbled to the ground with dog still attached. The inside of the jacket magically transformed itself into a mustard yellow skirt blotted all over with huge purple polka dots.

The dog kept a firm bite on the back of the skirt no matter how fast the chimp twirled in his efforts to catch the dog. Over and over again the chimp caught nothing but air amidst laughter growing ever more raucous.

Even so, worry kept jogging Jemmy's mind from the capering animals. *Where is Hal?*

Chapter Thirteen:

SEDALIA
THURSDAY EVENING,
SEPTEMBER 22, 1898

Henry Gentry was Indiana's answer to P. T. Barnum. The enterprising fellow billed himself as "Professor," but he had never seen the inside of a college classroom. In fact, he started in the humblest way imaginable. He rounded up a bunch of stray dogs in Bloomington, trained them, and began the most successful dog and pony show in the world.

The genius of H. G. was simple. He kept the operation small — one eighty-foot roundtop tent for the main ring and two outer tents for the animals. When he had more success than he could handle, he started a second troupe—then a third and a fourth — each managed by one of his brothers. The same troupe could play a single city for weeks by moving its tent to different neighborhoods.

Troupe number one played Sedalia that September. The band leader, Beach Parrott,

215

began the show by blaring out a fanfare. Children in the audience whooped with glee when the ringmaster, Wink Weaver, invited them to ride ponies free after the performance.

The show was a marvel, though Jemmy paid it less attention than she would a woolly worm on the sidewalk. A little pink pig dived from a platform into a teeny pool; goats climbed ladders and slid down slides. The baby elephant waved an American flag while dogs atop military ponies trotted in close formation around the ring to Sousa's "Stars and Stripes Forever."

Jemmy's head rolled up and down like a yoyo as she tried to see the show and find Hal at the same time. Starting at the top of the stands, she worked her way down section by section. She systematically scrutinized every face in the crowd. She made herself dizzy switching back and forth from the search to the sprightly antics of Professor Gentry's "150 ~ aristocratic ~ animals."

Jemmy scowled and stewed. Hal had deserted her, true; but now a big dose of pure concern softened her anger. No matter what photogenic sights had enticed him, he surely would have finished shooting them in less than six hours.

Guilt closed in from another quarter. *Is*

this any way for a professional journalist to behave? Not find Hal and not do my job either? I should be on my way to the train depot to send a finished "dog and pony" story to St. Louis by the next train. She was too dispirited to even begin the article.

As the show let out, she asked directions to Liberty Park and soon found herself back at the Koock home. She crossed her fingers as she knocked on the door. She never would have thought she'd yearn to see Hal's freckled mug. Her longing was so over-whelming she even wished for a repeat of Hal's disastrous debut as butler. She'd welcome Hal back even if he spilled a whole tureen of tomato soup on her best gabardine skirt.

Her spirits sank still lower when Dorothea opened the door. "Isn't the young man with the camera with you?"

Jemmy had to admit, "I haven't seen him since before noon. I hoped he might have returned here after we became separated in the crowd."

Dorothea sounded alarmed. "You've been out in public for hours with all manner of hooligans in town without an escort?"

"Please don't tell Aunt Tilly. She would never let me out of doors if she knew."

Dorothea patted her arm and spoke in a

conspiratorial tone. "Don't fret. Aunt Tilly wouldn't approve, but personally, I find the idea thrilling. I only wish I had half as much gumption."

"I need your help," said Jemmy. "I've been to all the places I think Hal would have wanted to photograph, at least the ones within walking distance. Where can he be? I'm too worried to concentrate on my articles for the paper. I must find out what's happened to him. Can you think of anything we might do?"

"We could go to the police."

"I've already been. The deputy said I would save myself grief if I stopped looking for brawlers."

"I see. He didn't take you seriously because you're female."

"Perhaps Lilburn might know something, or Jean Max. Perhaps one of them remembers a place Hal mentioned — someone or something he wanted to photograph."

Dorothea led Jemmy through the kitchen where Pélagie was peeling sweet potatoes. They stepped out the back door into the garden where Jean Max was turning over the compost heap.

"Jean Max, would you have any notion of where we might find Miss McBustle's photographer? He's gone missing."

Jean Max gave a Gallic shrug of his shoulders. Dorothea tried again. "Perhaps you heard him mention some scene he wanted to photograph — some place or some person."

Jean Max cocked his head, then nodded in the affirmative. "Beeg poster of Wild Beel. He try but light no good. Maybe light better now, eh?"

Jemmy brightened at the thought. Hal might be waiting for the right light to capture the immense barn roof sign on the road to Kansas City. A nagging bit of reality at the back of her mind told her not to hope. Still, it was something to try — something to occupy the next hour — something to free her brain from this maddening limbo.

Dorothea said, "Hitch up, Jean Max. We'll give him a ride home so he doesn't have to carry all that heavy glass."

Until dusk they scoured the city. They drove to barn roofs, hoardings, walls of vacant buildings plastered with posters. Hal was nowhere to be found.

Back at home, Aunt Tilly rebuked Jemmy and Dorothea for a host of improprieties: for being late to dinner, for failing to arrive at table in a proper state of dress and toilette, and — most of all — for failing to make cheerful conversation. Aunt Tilly didn't seem to miss Hal, though — perhaps because a newly hired and supremely efficient butler made the dinner flow seamlessly from butternut squash soup through apple cake without a single catastrophe.

Auntie did notice the undersupply of Koock gentlemen. She clucked her tongue over the absent young Mister Marmaduke and his father, Obadiah. Jemmy wondered when she would take those two males more firmly in hand.

After dinner Auntie whisked Fanny and Sissy off to the nursery. Dorothea looked at her stepson. "Lilburn, if you have any notion where Miss McBustle's photographer might be, please tell us."

Burnie said, "The only place I can think to go is the Maple Leaf Club. Hal was much taken with 'Perfessor' Joplin's music."

When the four arrived on East Main, Jean Max and Burnie left to seek Hal. Dorothea rolled down the blinds on her side of the carriage and pulled her shawl over her face. When Jemmy leaned forward, Dorothea tapped her with her fan. "Roll down your blinds. Don't let people see you in this neighborhood. You'll cause a scandal."

"I've already scandalized these people once. I don't think one more teensy disgrace can make much difference."

Jemmy turned her good ear toward the club. The ragged beat and tinkly descant made her a fan of Scott Joplin's ragtime from that moment on. She closed her eyes and stuck her head out of the carriage. In her heart of hearts she wished she would open those eyes to find a certain skinny robber asking her to listen to music with him.

A voice she recognized spoke, but not one she delighted in hearing. Her eyes opened to view the pimply forehead of Duke Koock.

"Damn me. You're almost as much of a nuisance as the old sow you came from St. Louis with. What are you doing here?"

"Hunting for you. When you didn't come home to dinner, Mrs. Koock was worried."

He snorted. "If my stepmother came chasing me every time I skipped a meal at home, my father would have to divorce her on grounds of desertion. Go back to the house or old Dotty and the old sow will both be hunting for you."

"How silly of me to try to spare your feelings by suggesting anyone would bother trying to find you. I have no interest whatsoever in your whereabouts. In point of fact, we're trying to locate my photographer Hal. Have you seen him?"

Duke bugged out his eyes and stroked his

chin. "Well, maybe." He motioned for Jemmy to lean forward, then cupped his hand to whisper in her ear. Instead of the expected whisper, he delivered a raucous sputtering that could only be described as a mighty good imitation of a fart. Ear itching from the raspberry and damp with spit, Jemmy shuddered and yanked her head inside the carriage. On the way she bumped her head on the window frame.

She winced as she dug in her reticule for her hanky. While Duke sauntered off laughing, she gave the mucky ear a vigorous cleaning.

Duke's "whoos" of laughter sounded like an amorous male peacock with the hiccups. His repellent sounds faded; but his presence lingered in her ear — her good ear, her ear drenched in Duke's obscene spittle.

Dorothea asked, "Did he call me Old Potty?"

" 'Old Dotty.' He called you 'Old Dotty.' "

"My stepson calls me a crazy woman? I must be a crazy woman to put up with him." Dorothea started to weep.

Jemmy patted her hand. "Better 'Old Dotty' than 'Old Potty.' "

"I don't see much difference. They both imply insanity."

"But the second one suggests you also

smell bad. You don't. You smell like violets in spring."

"Thank you, Jemmy. You always say the right things to cheer me. I'll surely miss you when you return to St. Louis."

Jemmy was still cleaning her ear and Dorothea was still sniveling when Burnie returned without news of Hal. "Did something happen while I was gone?"

"Duke favored us with a few moments of his precious time."

"I didn't see him."

"He went off that way." As she pointed in the direction Duke had gone, she saw three figures emerge from the shadows to meet him under the gaslight. She recognized the skinny robber and the pipe-smoking deputy from the sheriff's office. She couldn't identify a plump lady in a yellow plug hat. Jemmy drew the blinds in hopes they had not noticed her. *What are those four up to?*

Back at the Koock house, Jemmy's anxiety mounted with each chime of the clock. The slightest crack or rustle raised hope of Hal's return. Every time the noise turned out to be the creak of a house settling its bones. Disappointment wallowed in disappointment.

Jemmy slept little. One nightmare after another drubbed her brain. She dreamed she saw herself with pounding headache in place after ugly place — shackled in a dank cave — tied up in cobwebs in a musty cellar — drugged and suffocated by bedclothes that stank of formaldehyde. She struggled to free herself, but only managed to punch Aunt Tilly in the shoulder.

Aunt Tilly awoke in mid-snore. Jemmy pretended sleep. Soon Auntie's open mouth once again produced sounds reminiscent of grunts from hogs nosing each other aside to find the best place in the trough.

Jemmy gave up on sleep. She brooded until daylight under the burden of not knowing and the double burden of not do-ing. She fretted her lack of sleep would give her puffy eyes and a scattered brain. She stewed still more at her own lack of feeling. *How can I think of myself when Hal is still missing?*

Bleary-eyed and lacking any plan to find Hal, she rose early. This was Friday — the big day — the whole reason she had come to the Queen City. That very day the Wild West would return to Sedalia.

CHAPTER FOURTEEN:

THE COATES HOUSE HOTEL
KANSAS CITY
THURSDAY NIGHT, SEPTEMBER 22, 1898

As Louisa Cody climbed into the carriage, she set her lips in a thin hard line. After this short journey, she would have it out with Buffalo Bill. He might have missed Custer's last stand, but he'd be front and center for Louisa's.

I could go home. There's still time. Nobody recognized me at either performance. Do I have the nerve to go ahead with a plan so desperate?

The doorman tucked her valise beside her as he asked, "Where shall I tell the driver to take you, ma'am?"

Without looking at the doorman she said, "The Coates Hotel."

"I hope your moving to another hotel doesn't mean you're dissatisfied here at the Savoy."

"No, not dissatisfaction. My reasons are personal, entirely personal."

225

Frank Butler paused in front of the door to Buffalo Bill's suite of rooms at the Coates House Hotel. He steeled himself to face what he expected to find inside.

A voice boomed out, "What is it this time?" Cody yanked the door open. "Can't a man have . . . ?" His words trailed off as he stood aside for Frank to enter.

Frank picked imaginary lint from his hat. "I'm sorry to interrupt your midnight supper, but what I have to say won't wait."

Cody motioned him toward the chair at the dressing table, the only unclaimed seat in the room. Frank tried not to stare at Katherine, but his eyes couldn't resist a peek at the upsweep of her sun-blond hair. She wore a shimmering ball gown of sky blue satin. Loops of blue crystal beads danced down her pale arms and across her white bosom as they twinkled in the candlelight.

"Will, aren't you going to introduce me to the famous Frank Butler?" She stood and extended her hand.

Cody spoke in a monotone. "Katherine, I'd like you to meet Mr. Frank Butler, Miss Oakley's husband. Mr. Butler — Miss Katherine Clemmons — the famous actress."

Frank gave the white-satin-gloved hand a feeble shake born strictly of politeness. He didn't approve of Cody's lady friends — all the more because of his own guilt at deserting his wife and children for his lady love.

Like a proper hostess, Katherine offered refreshment to her guest. "Please, Mr. Butler, have this glass of champagne. I have not taken a single sip."

"No thank you, ma'am. I wouldn't deprive you of your wine."

"But I want this to be your wine." She dimpled in a winsome smile. "Let me tempt you." She waved the glass under his nose.

The sour smell of ferment offended his nostrils. He'd long since taught himself to abhor liquor fumes.

Katherine ignored his expression of disgust and held out the glass. "It's real champagne from France. I'll join you both as soon as I fetch my traveling cup from my portmanteau."

She moved toward her case, but Cody stopped her with a hand to her shoulder. "Mr. Butler doesn't drink, Katherine. Even a little trembling of hand or head could mean disaster in his line of work."

She dipped her head prettily in Frank's direction. "Since yours is not a social call, I imagine you gentlemen would like some privacy. I'll simply slip down to the lobby."

Frank and Cody spoke at the same time.

Frank said, "I don't want to put you out, but —"

Cody said, "Sit down, Katherine. This won't take long."

Katherine sat and took a sip from the glass Frank had refused.

"Well, Butler, what is it?"

"Colonel, are you sure Miss Clemmons should hear this?"

"Get on with it. What do you want?"

"You must hire more Pinkertons for the Sedalia trip."

Cody's eyes narrowed. "I take it you don't think Little Elk was shot by accident."

"I'm sure it was no accident."

"Your reason?"

"Someone is trying to kill Annie."

"Kill Annie? What makes you think so?"

"A shot grazed her horse on Tuesday."

"Tuesday — why didn't I hear about it until now?"

"I wanted to scout around and be sure."

"Who would want to kill Annie?"

"I can name a few people, including one who is working right here in Kansas City right now."

"Lillian Smith."

"Yes, Lillian Smith."

"Lillian Smith is a nice little girl. Maybe she is jealous of Annie, but I don't think she would ever —"

Frank's impatience trampled his tact. "Lillian Smith is not nice and never has been little. Will you hire the Pinkertons or not?"

"Nothing happened at tonight's show, did it?"

Frank shook his head. "No."

"Do you really think we need more Pinkertons? If you're convinced Lillian is shooting at Annie, just show the men who travel with us a picture of Lillian. Surely a pair of Pinkertons is enough to catch one little big girl — assuming she plans to be in Sedalia at all."

"So you won't hire any more men."

"Why don't you talk to the local police when we get to Sedalia? We give them enough free passes to get some consideration, don't you think?"

Frank turned on his heel and left the room before the hot blood in his arm planted a solid fist on his famous boss's famous face. He muttered to himself, "I should have known better than to talk to him when that actress was around."

He took the stairs instead of the elevator to work off his pent-up emotion. As his feet hit the lobby carpet, he saw something that curled his upper lip in a sardonic smile.

Boarding the elevator was none other than

Mrs. Buffalo Bill Cody herself. Lulu looked like a dark storm cloud come to blot out Katherine's blue horizon. She wore a gunmetal gray dress and gray hat trimmed with jet beads. Eyes glinting black as anthracite coal, she stared in Frank's direction. She tossed him a look fiery enough to light a cigar, but didn't seem to recognize him at all.

As he walked out of the hotel, he chuckled to himself. "Cody is going to wish he had hired more Pinkertons. They could protect my wife in public by day. They could protect him in private by night."

Chapter Fifteen:

THE COATES HOUSE HOTEL
KANSAS CITY
FRIDAY MORNING, SEPTEMBER 23, 1898

Before five o'clock in the morning, Frank Butler once again arrived at the Coates House Hotel. The train to Sedalia would pull out at six. He had but a few minutes to convince Buffalo Bill to hire more Pinkertons. The colonel had refused the night before, but things had changed.

He pinned his hopes on Mrs. Cody's surprise visit. *Maybe Lulu's appearance softened the old man up. Perhaps having Lulu pop in at a decidedly inopportune time would convince the colonel he needed added security to protect Annie in the arena — and to protect himself from the slings and arrows of an outraged Mrs. Cody.* He crossed his fingers in hopes Lulu had thrown a tantrum so spectacular Colonel Cody would be eager to hire more detectives.

Frank would not have been surprised to see the door to the colonel's room hanging lopsided on a single hinge, but nothing seemed amiss. He looked both ways down the corridor as he stepped off the elevator. The entire floor slumbered in heedless morning repose.

The colonel answered the knock on his door with a hearty, "Frank. I'm glad you're here. I want you to tell Johnny to take over for me. I'm not going to Sedalia. Tell the folks I'm sick."

"She got to you, then."

"Katherine is none of your business."

"I wasn't talking about Katherine."

"Who then?"

"Your wife — Mrs. Cody. You remember Lulu."

The colonel looked both ways down the hall before he pulled Frank inside. He shut the door and spoke in a low murmur. "What's this about Lulu?"

The question puzzled Frank. "Haven't you seen her? She was riding up in the elevator when I left late last night."

"You mean she's here in this hotel — right now?"

"I thought she would have pounded down your door along about midnight."

Colonel Cody heaved a sigh. "I don't know which one of those two females is more trouble. I had rather manage a million Indians than one soubrette like Katherine.

And they'd cost less. She told me she didn't think a lady could dress properly on less than forty thousand a year. I've been helping her prove it ever since."

The colonel closed one eye. "And Lulu. I understand my wife perfectly. She wants to find Katherine in my room in the morning after spending the night here. Heaven knows what this scandal will cost me if she succeeds."

"Perhaps she wants to divorce you."

Cody rubbed the middle of his forehead with two fingers. "I only wish she did. She flat refuses. Says good Catholics don't get divorces. Truth be told, she thinks to bring me to heel by turning me into a pauper. That would be her justice and her sweet revenge."

He stood up straight as a pin oak. "My wife refuses to learn this one simple fact: no woman will ever keep William Frederick Cody down on the ranch."

The colonel shook Frank's hand and patted his shoulder. "Thank you for giving me time to conjure up a way out of this mess."

He raised his voice and pitched it toward the door to the necessary. "Katherine. Get dressed, please, and don't take all day about it. Lulu's here." He pointed an index finger at the floor. "Right here. In this hotel."

Katherine appeared in the bathroom doorway holding a hairbrush. With her hair in loose curls and her uncorseted body in peach-colored silk, she shimmered — appetizing as orange ice on a hot day. In a contest with Lulu, whether beauty or charm, Katherine would win hands down. Frank admitted to himself the actress came close to competing with Annie — not that any other female, no matter how fetching, could claim his heart.

The colonel strode to the window and stuck his head outside. He bent over at the waist to scout left and right, then closed the window part way as he said, "No balcony. The ledge is about four inches wide though."

Katherine paled. "You're not getting me out on any ledge. I'm not some circus tightrope walker."

"Of course not. If she turns up, stay put in the bathroom. Lock the door and don't make a spitch of noise. Frank and I will manage."

Katherine hissed out a warning, though she sounded more frightened than angry, "See to it. One thing is certain. This time, I'm not letting her get close enough to yank out my hair. I had to cover my bald spot with a hairpiece for months."

"Then get moving. If you're gone from here before she makes her grand appearance, your golden tresses will remain on your scalp where they belong."

Katherine returned to the necessary.

Colonel Cody scowled at the clutter of jars and jewelry and perfume bottles on the dressing table. He placed one hand on his hip and sang out, "Katherine. Do you need any of these whatnots on the vanity?"

"Only if you want me to have a beautiful hairdo."

"We'd best make sure you have beautiful hair to do."

Katherine appeared in the doorway. "Not romantic, but sensible. Put them in my small portmanteau, the one that opens in two parts with special compartments. It's a fitted case, so you'll have to figure out what goes where."

He began cramming items in the case higgledy-piggledy. "Frank, round up all her bits and pieces and shove them in the trunk — the one in the closet there."

Frank smacked his kid gloves against his hand to get Cody's attention. "I came here for a purpose. Will you listen to me?"

"Here's what you do, Frank. If Lulu shows up, you tell her this is your room. It was just booked in my name to cover up your own little peccadillo."

"I can't believe you expect me to be party to your shenanigans. You want me to pretend Katherine and I . . . I won't do it."

"I can make it worth your while."

Frank tromped toward the door. "You've got to be crazy. You know I'd never do anything to jeopardize Annie's trust in me."

The colonel offered an apology, at least as much of an apology as he could manage. "Hold on, now. I was wrong to suggest it."

"You got yourself into this. You can jolly well get yourself out. I'm leaving." Frank yanked on a glove.

"Wait, don't go. I was way off the mark. We'll think of something else."

Frank hesitated with his hand on the knob. He turned back to face the colonel's pleading eyes.

Colonel Cody put his hands together in a gesture of prayer. "Lulu could be here any second. I promise to listen to every word you say the minute Katherine is safely gone. Now help me get her packed."

Even though Cody hadn't actually promised to hire more Pinkertons, Frank felt hopeful enough to stick around. He folded sundry articles and tucked them away in Katherine's trunk while the colonel tried to fit each silver-backed mirror, comb, jar, and vial into its own special place in her portmanteau.

Frank picked up one ice-blue silk stocking with bluebells embroidered at the heels. He was searching under the bed for the mate when a knock came at the door. Both stopped, looked at each other, and began a frantic rush to stash away all feminine furbelows.

Frank closed the trunk in the armoire. The colonel gave up finding a place for Katherine's gewgaws in her ladylike portmanteau. He slammed the two halves together with such force that her silver nameplate popped off and tinkled to the floor. Frank picked it up and stuck it in his pocket. He bit his lip to contain his laughter.

Cody shoved the portmanteau under the bed then dragged it out again. "That's the first place Lu would look." He finally thrust the case inside the bedclothes and piled pillows on top.

He feigned a smile and opened the door. The smile became a sigh of relief as he stepped back. With a gracious wave of his hand, he motioned a waiter in a white jacket to push a wheeled cart into the room.

On the cart, a single purple dahlia basked in a crystal vase between two silver food domes. The waiter hastened to clear the dishes from the day before and stow them on the bottom shelf of the breakfast cart. With easy efficiency, he replaced the table-cloth with fresh linen and set the table for two. In less than five minutes, he was gone.

As he dropped coins into the man's palm, the colonel heaved another sigh. "That was a close call. I was so busy with the vanity case I forgot the dirty dishes from last night's champagne dinner. I also forgot I ordered breakfast for five o'clock this morning."

Katherine appeared in the doorway, fully dressed and self-possessed until she scanned the room in search of her belongings. "Where is my hat? What have you done with my gloves and the handkerchief I laid out?"

The colonel's expression turned blank. Frank spoke up. "If you mean a yellow hat with a canary on it and long tails of stuff you could see through, I put it in your trunk. The gloves and the hanky, too."

Katherine rolled her eyes at Frank. "Have you never heard of a hat box?" As she marched to the armoire, she huffed under her breath. "Leave it to a man to flatten my new hat. I had it custom-made at Annette's Millinery in St. Louis." She retrieved the hat and set to poking it back into shape.

Before she could finish, another knock

came. Katherine snatched up hat and gloves and retreated to the necessary. The colonel assumed his feigned smile and opened the door. "Lulu, what a surprise."

The minute Lulu sauntered into the room, she spied the table with its silver domes and dahlia. "Breakfast for two? You always had a big appetite, but I thought old age might have forced you into more temperate habits. You're past fifty, you know. I'd say it's time to go on a diet."

"I don't plan to eat both. I have a breakfast companion. Frank Butler."

Lulu lost her composure when the colonel closed the door to reveal Butler standing behind it. It was Frank's turn to feign a smile. He nodded, "Pleased to see you, Mrs. Cody. You're looking well."

"I'm not looking well, Mr. Butler. I look like what I am — a harridan." She walked to the center of the room. "An old hag. Just ask my husband."

Frank had no reply.

The colonel said, "Frank and I must leave for Sedalia in a few minutes. I hope you'll forgive us for eating in your presence. Would you like me to send down for another breakfast? You can stay as long as you like."

Frank held his breath. Colonel Cody was taking a mighty risk. What if Lulu took him up on his offer? What if she decided to stay? He breathed easier when Lulu waved off the suggestion. She commenced circling the room like a turkey buzzard soaring overhead intent on spying something rotten.

As he took his place at the table, the colonel said, "Butler, eat. Don't stand on ceremony."

Frank removed the dome from a steaming bowl of oatmeal. He envied the colonel's platter of hotcakes with syrup and link sausages. He sought something sweet — jelly, sugar, honey — anything to make palatable the oatmeal — a dish he abhorred above all foods. He saw nothing but cream, salt, and pepper. "Where's the sugar for the coffee?"

"Sorry, I thought you took it plain. Well, dig in — though I don't know why you ordered oatmeal even if it is the latest word in health. Oats are proper food for horses. Can't imagine why people want to eat them."

Frank stuck in a spoon. It stood upright in the cereal. He gagged as he pulled it out and put it to his lips.

Lulu peeked in the armoire as she asked, "Mr. Butler, what brings you here so early on a travel day?"

"I came in hopes of persuading the colonel

to hire additional Pinkertons." Frank cast a meaningful glance in the colonel's direction. "In fact, he was about to agree to hire several more when you knocked on the door."

"Hire Pinkertons? Do you need more security?" She pulled at the lock on the trunk in the closet.

Frank was glad he had remembered to close the lock. "We do. I am certain of it."

"Indeed. Has something happened to make you think so?"

Despite the colonel's warning glare, Frank played his trump card. "Someone has been shooting at people in the show. One of the Indians, a man named Little Elk, was wounded day before yesterday. There have been other incidents, too."

Lulu sounded interested but detached, as if she were making small talk with a male acquaintance by asking about his mother's bunions. "Really? Do you suppose anyone could be trying to do away with Mr. Cody?"

"Possibly. Little Elk was shot while riding directly behind the colonel."

"Whom do you suspect of wishing evil on the Wild West?"

"Any number of people might want to bring the colonel down. He has competitors, you know. Pawnee Bill and Mae, the

Sells brothers. Gun people like Doc Carver, Captain Bogardus's son Ed, Ira Paine, and Ad Toepperwein are the main ones. That doesn't even count people outside of show business. There are a number of women like —"

The colonel cut him off. "Enough. You're frightening Lulu."

Frank saw more mistrust than fear on Lulu's face. She let her handkerchief flutter to the floor with an "Oh my. How clumsy of me."

She stooped down on the far side of the bed and pulled up the counterpane. She kept her head down and shuffled forward on her haunches. Frank could see her back bobbing as she inched toward the head of the bed. At length, she held up her handkerchief and waved it toward the men. "Dropped my hanky."

Lulu stared at the bed.

Frank held his breath.

The colonel stopped chewing. The sausage on his fork quivered in midair like a fat worm on a fishing hook.

Lulu peered at the jumble of bedclothes and pillows. She reached a hand toward it, then stopped. A sound of breaking glass from the necessary brought all heads to attention. Lulu's face twisted in a grimace of triumph as she made a beeline in that direction. The door opened before she could turn the knob.

Katherine sailed in like a majestic yacht floating over choppy seas. "Colonel, you must ring for housekeeping before you use the facilities. I'm afraid I broke your only drinking glass."

She turned smoothly toward Lulu. "Mrs. Cody, don't you look the picture of health. I was under the impression your ailments prevented you from leaving Nebraska. I am glad to see you looking strong as a horse."

Frank could barely stifle a grin.

Lulu rose to the challenge. "Bill, I'm ashamed of you and Mr. Butler. How could you two be so churlish as to eat in the presence of Miss Clemmons? I doubt you've offered her so much as a cup of coffee."

Katherine tossed the room a dazzling smile. "I abhor coffee, Mrs. Cody. Indeed, the thought of eating anything at this unholy hour is completely alien to my notion of how a lady should begin her day."

Lulu smiled in return. "Then, I wonder why you are here at this unholy hour. What could be so important as to deprive you of your beauty sleep?"

Without a playwright to supply dialogue, Katherine had no answer.

Frank leaped into the breach. "I brought Miss Clemmons along in hopes that her pleas added to mine would convince the colonel to hire more Pinkertons. Last night, I tried on my own with no success."

Katherine took the cue. "Yes, Mr. Butler convinced me the colonel was in peril. Naturally, I wanted to add my voice to his. I could never forgive myself if I had left undone anything that might save the colonel's life."

Lulu looked dubious. She spoke to her husband with mock concern. "And have they persuaded you to hire more Pinkertons, dearest? How we would all mourn if anything tragic should happen to you."

"Yes, dearest. As soon as we have finished breakfast, I am going down to the lobby to call Nate. He can take care of the details."

"Dearest, Nate Salisbury retired last year."

"Of course he did. Thanks for reminding me, dearest. I'm becoming more and more forgetful."

"You've always been forgetful, dearest — in some ways."

Frank choked down another speck of oatmeal. "Well, Miss Clemmons, we have succeeded in our errand. I think we'd best be on our way. I have much to do before the train leaves."

"Of course, Mr. Butler." She slipped a kid glove on one soft, white hand.

On the way out, Frank shook the colonel's hand to seal the deal. "I'm deeply grateful you've decided to hire a bigger protection group for the show. I'm confident you'll never regret my turning up this morning to persuade you."

The colonel shook Frank's hand and exchanged meaningful glances with Katherine as he closed the door behind them.

In the hall, Katherine and Frank grinned with relief over the close call.

"When you said this was too early in the day for breakfast, I thought the whole house of cards would fall."

Katherine giggled at Frank's words. "The minute I said it, I realized how absurd it sounded. If getting up early is against my constitution, why on earth would I be up and dressed and in the colonel's room? I owe you a debt for rescuing me."

"I'm sorry about your hat. Your fitted case didn't fare any better." He handed her the silver nameplate with its fancy scrollwork. "I'm still amazed Lulu didn't throw a conniption fit."

"The whole business may not be over yet. What will happen if she finds out the truth?"

He shrugged. "Murder, probably. She

might kill him. He might kill her."

"Don't joke about it, Mr. Butler. I don't find it humorous in the least."

"I was only partly joking, Miss Clemmons. The colonel said Lulu once tried to poison him. I think she might be behind the incidents at the Wild West."

Katherine put her hand to her throat. "Tell me you're still joking. If that woman could kill her own husband, the father of her children, what would she do to me?"

"Calm yourself. I shouldn't have said anything. The colonel swears all she really wants is to keep him home on the ranch. I feel certain that's the truth."

"My clothes are still in the room. Do you think she will find them?"

"I don't know. She may try, but the colonel keeps getting craftier as he gets older. We'll have to wait and see."

"Even if Louisa Cody hasn't marked me for murder, I have other reasons for wanting these events to be kept confidential."

Frank looked blank.

She pulled him into an alcove by the elevator and leaned toward him. Her French perfume wrapped his nose in a field of sweet lilies. The heady scent made him weak in the knees.

"You'll help me, won't you, Mr. Butler? I

couldn't bear to have any of this come out."

"Let's understand each other, Miss Clemmons. The only reason I went along with any subterfuge was my desire to have more Pinkertons working at the show. I believe Annie's life is in danger. I'd do anything to protect her. As for you —"

"Oh, but you must help me. I beg you."

"Save your begging."

"What if I promise not to see him again, not ever."

"I hesitate to call a lovely lady a liar, but I wouldn't believe you."

"Trust me, Mr. Butler. I never plan to see him again. This meeting was in the nature of a farewell."

"I believe you're telling me what you think I want to hear."

"I assure you I'm most sincere. The last thing I would want is for Harold to hear about last night."

"Harold?"

"Yes, Harold Gould, Jay Gould's son."

"The financier? The rich Jay Gould?"

"Yes, the very same Jay Gould. The man who caused the panic of sixty-nine. The man who singlehandedly caused the Black Friday stock market crash."

Frank blinked his eyes in astonishment.

A smile played around Katherine's lips.

"My prospective father-in-law made millions in his attempt to corner the market on gold. I find that audacity to be an extremely attractive family trait. That along with the vast family fortune make the Gould heir well nigh impossible to resist."

Katherine arched her hands together to push her gloves between her fingers. Frank had no doubt she relished her intended's potential millions and didn't mind in the least how the infamous robber baron father had grabbed them up.

When Frank shook his head in disgust, she dimpled and leaned toward him. "Yes. I'm marrying his son in two weeks. On October twelfth, eighteen ninety-eight, Katherine Clemmons will become Mrs. Harold Gould."

Chapter Sixteen:

SEDALIA
FRIDAY MORNING, SEPTEMBER 23, 1898

Jemmy could not abide lying in bed. She rose and rubbed her swollen eyes as she stumbled into the hall. She tapped lightly on Dorothea's bedroom door. It swung open so fast Jemmy realized her hostess must have been waiting for the knock.

Dorothea tucked her brows down to meet her droopy nose. Jemmy silently compared the picture to a brown butterfly landing on a carrot. She pulled her lips together to smother a giggle.

Mrs. Koock pulled Jemmy inside and straight to the washbasin. She poured water from the ewer and pointed to the bed. After her guest stretched out — obedient but antsy — Dorothea placed a damp linen towel over Jemmy's swollen eyes.

Dorothea's soothing hand brushed hair back from Jemmy's forehead. "I know how upset you are over Hal. Have you thought of anything else we might try?"

The cloth fell as Jemmy sat upright. She nodded toward the door to Mr. Koock's bedroom and murmured, "Is Mr. Koock in there?"

Dorothea reassured her. "You may speak in a normal voice. I heard Obadiah leave a half hour ago."

"I can't think of anything worthwhile. It all seems impossible — impossible Hal has gone and impossible to find him." Her restless fingers twisted the compress in a knot. "Do you suppose Burnie or Jean Max has remembered . . . ?"

Dorothea dipped another towel in the water.

Jemmy tried to convey a hopefulness she did not feel. "We could bring them with us to the police. They're male. Maybe the police don't listen to us because we're female."

Dorothea exchanged the cloth for a fresh one. "Police don't take boys any more seriously than they do ladies, or servants, either. I think we shall need Mr. Koock's aid. Yes, we must ask Obadiah."

Even though Jemmy hated to admit she needed help from her intimidating host, she had to set aside her feelings. Her bad ear hissed in her brain to do everything in her power to find Hal.

"While you dress, I'll have Jean Max hitch up. We'll have a bite of breakfast before we leave."

"With my stomach churning as it is, the thought of food makes me queasy. Please, you have something to eat. We can be off as soon as I make myself presentable. Thank heavens Aunt Tilly is a sound sleeper. I'd hate to wake her." Not until that moment did Jemmy notice Dorothea was already fully dressed.

Less than a half hour later, the ladies were in the carriage. They said little on the way to the MKT repair shops. Jemmy wondered how the stern Mr. Koock would react. *For once I'm glad to be a girl. If I were a boy, he would probably take me out to the woodshed and whip me for being so careless as to lose my bodyguard.*

The repair station grounds of the Missouri Kansas Texas Railroad (known as "Katy" for short) bustled with action. Steam engines pushed red boxcars, their sides painted with union-shaped shields blazoned across with MKT in bold white letters. Men moved cabooses, coal tenders, and flatcars from track spurs into vast sheds. The smell of coal fumes clouded thick as ash from Vulcan's bellows. The bang of hammer on metal rang in Jemmy's bad ear to clang

251

against her jangled nerves.

Dorothea picked her path deftly across rails and over cinders. She pointed the way up a wooden stair leading to a tin-roofed tower.

As she walked into the superintendent's office, a surprised secretary popped up from his chair and pulled on his jacket. Eyes wide in surprise, he blurted, "Mrs. Koock, I hope no serious problem causes you to come here during business hours."

"Would you be so kind as to announce Miss McBustle and me?"

With something akin to terror on his face, the secretary rapped on the inner-office door, then entered. In seconds, Mr. Koock appeared, derby in hand. "Dorothea, has something happened at home? The girls . . . ?"

She patted his hand. "The girls are fine — so are the boys, and so is the house. The problem belongs to Miss McBustle."

"Indeed." Mr. Koock looked relieved. "What is the trouble, Miss McBustle?"

"The young man who came with me from St. Louis — my photographer, Harold Dwyer — has gone missing."

"Missing?"

"We went to the courthouse yesterday morning. While I was interviewing a medicine show man, Hal disappeared."

"Perhaps he saw something he wished to capture with his camera."

"What could possibly take him all day and all night to photograph?" Jemmy searched Mr. Koock's face for signs of disbelief. To her amazement, she saw none. She added, "Besides, he's supposed to be my escort, my bodyguard."

"Has he been lax in these offices before?"

"Never." Jemmy conveniently forgot Hal's absence at the crucial moment in the train robbery three days earlier.

"Have you any idea where he might have gone?"

Jemmy shook her head. "I waited for him at the courthouse. I searched for him at the parade and at Professor Gentry's show."

"The police — did you see them?"

"I tried the sheriff's office. The deputy was less than helpful. He wouldn't even tell me where the city police building is located."

"I shall have to speak to him about his lack of manners. Let us return to the sheriff's office. Perhaps I can set him straight."

Putting on his hat, Mr. Koock opened the door for the ladies, then followed them down the stairs. His secretary jotted notes while Mr. Koock issued orders.

"Go round personally to all the foremen.

Make sure their crews know we expect everyone to be at work tomorrow. Having the Wild West come to town does not mean anyone can take a Saturday holiday to sleep off Friday revels. The Katy owners don't allow goldbricking and neither do I. You may tell them failing to work a full shift tomorrow will cost them not only tomorrow's pay, but today's as well — and might result in dismissal."

"Yes, Mr. Koock. I'll see to it." Still scribbling, the clerk hurried back upstairs. The party of three rode in stark silence to the Pettis County Sheriff's Office. Mr. Koock stared out the window with his derby on his lap and his fingers interlaced around the brim. His thumbs met with every bump in the road.

Dorothea darted sidelong glances at him. She seemed to want to talk. Jemmy understood. She herself often said nothing when she wanted desperately to speak.

She remembered Auntie Dee's caution. "Wise women know to keep their tongues to themselves, especially when menfolk are trying to think. Cogitation requires great effort on their part — all the greater because they so seldom exert themselves in cranial calisthenics of any kind."

Mr. Koock followed Dorothea and Jemmy

into the sheriff's office. The angular deputy rose to his feet so fast he dropped tobacco embers on the sheriff's desk. "Mr. Koock, sir, what brings you here?"

"I see you know who I am, but I don't believe we've met, Deputy . . . ?"

"Futcher, Budoc Futcher. I was named after the Irish Saint Budoc who was born at sea in a barrel."

"Were you born at sea in a barrel?"

"Not exactly. Not exactly in a barrel. Not exactly at sea. I was born upside a poker table on a riverboat going down to Cay-ro Illi-noyze."

Obadiah didn't introduce the ladies or even shake Deputy Futcher's extended hand. He nodded toward Jemmy. "My houseguest, Miss McBustle, informs me you treated her in a surly manner yesterday."

The deputy stammered out, "Beg pardon, Mr. Koock. I had no idea the young lady was an acquaintance of yours."

"It shouldn't matter, Deputy. The citizens of Pettis County expect you to be polite to all ladies, regardless of their friends or their station in life. Am I making myself clear?"

"Yes, sir. I'm right sorry I offended the young miss."

Obadiah nodded in Jemmy's direction. "To her, Deputy. Apologize to her."

255

The deputy pushed a hank of greasy hair behind his ear and bobbed his head at Jemmy. "Beg pardon, miss. I was out of order and I hope you'll forgive me."

He didn't wait for Jemmy to forgive him, but cast a hangdog glance at Mr. Koock.

Jemmy relished having the upper hand. "I'll forgive you, Deputy Futcher, on condition you find my photographer. Hal has been missing for nearly a whole day."

Dorothea chimed in. "We searched every place we could think of — all the sights he wished to photograph. We even went to the Maple Leaf Club last night because he enjoys Mr. Joplin's music."

Mr. Koock's head shot up as his bottom jaw dropped. "Mrs. Koock! The Maple Leaf Club? North of Second Street after sundown?"

Dorothea pulled her shoulders back and stuck out her chin. "Yes, Mr. Koock. The Maple Leaf Club."

The deputy said, "Well, seeing as how we know the kind of places your Mr. Dwyer likes to go —"

Obadiah put up a hand to stop the deputy from saying anything further. "Mrs. Koock, you and Miss McBustle will stay here while the deputy and I seek Mr. Dwyer on the other side of the tracks. We'll take the car-riage."

As he followed Mr. Koock out the door, the deputy said, "Make yourselves at home, ladies. This might take a considerable while."

Jemmy plopped down on a bench. Doro-thea's rumbling stomach broke the silence like a three-story building collapsing on a brick street. They exchanged glances and tittered behind pursed lips before they broke out laughing.

Jemmy said, "I thought you ate breakfast."

"I tried to eat while you were dressing, but all I could get down was half a cup of lukewarm coffee. Let's have breakfast now. We accomplish nothing by staying here. I'll leave a note in case they should return before we do."

She took Jemmy's hand and pulled her up from the bench. "I know a restaurant that serves lovely corn muffins with peach but-ter. We need to keep up our strength."

Without much enthusiasm, Jemmy nod-ded. She understood what Dorothea meant. If the news about Hal should be more troublesome than a little too much whis-key . . .

She couldn't bring herself to think about the worst that could happen.

They walked out Fourth Street to Osage and down to the Coffee Cup, a cheerful eatery with red-checked tablecloths. Lively chitchat floated atop the savory aroma of fried eggs and ham. The place exuded vitality with every tink of silverware on ironstone china. When the cook called, "Order up, table five," Jemmy felt as much at home as she did in her mother's boardinghouse.

The pair sat at a cozy table by the window and ordered poached eggs with bacon to go with the corn muffins. Before the warmth of the place and a big cup of coffee with heavy cream could thaw out the ladies' frozen tongues, Jemmy inexplicably leaped up and dashed out the door.

Jemmy left Dorothea three words of explanation — three words that lost themselves in the din of the restaurant. What Jemmy said was "There he is." It's probably just as well Dorothea couldn't possibly have heard those words. The "he" Jemmy saw was not Hal, but the skinny train robber.

When Jemmy reached the street, she could spot no sign of the boy she had seen through the ruffled curtains. She lit out in the direction he had been walking when she first spied him. Skirts lifted to a most unladylike mid-shin level, she ran down Osage. She raced toward Main Street as fast as high-heeled boots and corset stays would allow.

She should have paid more attention to the alleyways. As she passed one, a figure grabbed her from behind and spun her into the alley. The skinny fellow pinned her hands against the rough surface of a limestone building and demanded, "Why are you chasing me?"

"I already told you once. I am a journalist. You have a story. Tell me what I want to know and I'll trouble you no more."

"And get me killed into the bargain. Doesn't sound like a good deal to me."

"What if I can arrange it so the others get caught, but you don't? Would you consider that a good deal?"

"If even a single one of them goes free, I am as good as dead."

"I can do it. See to it not a single crook goes free — except you, of course."

A wry smile played on his lips. "Maybe I like being a crook."

"I hate to spoil your illusions, but I don't think you are meant to be a thief. Being a successful criminal takes luck. If I may say so, I think finding a four-leaf clover would only bring your luck from bad to none at all — especially where I'm concerned."

He took on an injured air. "I don't know what you're talking about."

"Who stopped you from robbing the train passengers?"

"Not you."

"Yes, I know. It was Aunt Tilly and her umbrella. But don't you see. She would never have been on the train but for me. She's my chaperone. Without an older lady as traveling companion, the family would never have let me come to Sedalia."

"What does your chaperone have to do with my luck?"

"Are you blind? Aunt Tilly and I together stopped the robbery."

"Let me see." He cocked his head to the side and screwed up his eyes in mock meditation. "The robbery went sour because you and Aunt Tilly took stupid risks. Nothing to do with my luck — good or bad."

Jemmy stared at his hand, still jamming her arm painfully against the wall. He let go. She rubbed her wrists and posed more questions. "All right. Let's say the train affair was no more than coincidence. What about the other times? Were they coincidences, too?"

"Other times?"

"At the Maple Leaf Club. I recognized you. If it hadn't been for Duke's drunken brawling, I would have found out all about you. You'd be in jail this very minute."

He looked puzzled. "So where's the bad luck? I did not go to jail. Sounds like good luck to me."

"And what about right now? Sedalia has lots of streets. I was looking out the window at the very instant you chose to walk down this one. What do you say to that?"

Jemmy shook off the possibility he might have come down Osage on purpose because he had been following her. *I suppose it's also possible all my arguments might be easy to refute.*

He crossed his arms but said nothing.

Jemmy pressed her case. "Could it all be mere happenstance? Or could it be I'm your nemesis?"

"My what?"

"Your bad luck, your downfall. I've found you twice before and I can find you again."

"So maybe I'm not lucky. What of it?"

"The sheriff will catch your gang. Tomorrow. I guarantee it."

The skinny robber's eyes snapped wide open. He grabbed Jemmy's wrist and squeezed it until she cringed. "What do you know?"

Jemmy knew no facts, but she knew how to bluff. She had studied Aristotelian logic at St. Louis Branch High School No. 3. She learned how to find logical connections.

"Seems to me the gate receipts at Buffalo Bill's show would make a tempting target for crooks — any crooks — all crooks."

She had hit a nerve. She milked the moment for all it was worth. "Better be quick, lest some other outlaw gang should beat yours to Buffalo Bill's ticket wagons. Of course, you might prefer that outcome. Other robbers would end up in prison instead of your mob."

The skinny robber dropped her hand but leaned closer to her face. "What do you expect me to do?" His warm breath smelled faintly of apples. Jemmy found the sensation more pleasant than she wanted to admit.

"Well, you could warn your gang not to steal the ticket money."

He shook his head. "It's not my gang. They don't listen to me."

"Or, you could work with the sheriff to put the rest of your gang behind bars."

"And me along with them."

"Not if I tell the sheriff you came to enlist my aid in catching the gang — came of your own free will."

"Would you?"

Jemmy kissed the tips of her middle and index fingers. She offered to touch the kissed fingers to his lips. "I'll seal the

262

bargain with a kiss."

He ignored the gesture. "Why help me? What would you get out of it?"

"I told you. I'd get your story."

"Well . . ."

"Come with me now. We'll find a quiet place and you can tell me all about how you fell in with bad company."

"Oh, no. If one of them saw me, I'd be a dead man. I'll tell you nothing."

"Tell me after they're caught. You'd have nothing to fear then."

"I'll give you my story, but only after every single one of them is behind bars."

She stuck out her hand to shake.

He raised his arms as he backed away. "Not so fast. You're not to mention my name to anyone — ever. You promise?"

"I promise."

"Ticket wagon at nine tonight. They'll come dressed like an act in the show. Perhaps like soldiers or Cheyenne Indians."

He spat on his palm and held it out for her to shake. "Deal?"

No one had ever asked Jemmy to spit shake. It seemed almost as disgusting as eating a caterpillar. *Just one more thing I have to stomach. It isn't easy being a woman in a man's world.* She spat into her palm and stuck out her hand. "Deal."

He crushed her fingers in a grip so excruciating she had to fight back tears. "Deal." He bored her eyes with one last penetrating stare before he pulled up his coat collar and trudged off down the alley.

Jemmy plucked her hanky from her sleeve and wiped her palm with some vigor as she walked back to the Coffee Cup Restaurant. Dorothea jumped up and greeted her with a question. "Where did you go? By the time I reached the door, I couldn't see you in either direction."

"I thought I spotted someone who — but I was wrong." Jemmy hoped her I-know-something-you-don't smirk didn't arouse Dorothea's suspicions.

With a "Here's your breakfast, dearie," a red-faced waitress plunked down steaming oval platters.

Dorothea said, "No need to hurry. The newspaper ad said the Wild West parade would start at nine-thirty, rain or shine."

Jemmy dug into her eggs with gusto until she remembered Hal might not be enjoying a hot breakfast, or any breakfast at all. She put down her fork and tucked her hands in her lap. *What's wrong with me? What kind of monster am I? I was so bent on getting a story, I didn't even remember to ask the robber about Hal.*

CHAPTER SEVENTEEN:

Dorothea and Jemmy returned to the sheriff's office. They found nothing better to do than stare at cheerless walls — wait, wait, and wait some more. Jemmy tried to write an article about the Queen City, but every attempt faded after the lead sentence. Stewing over Hal's disappearance banished all attempts at concentration.

The clock ticked its way to eleven o'clock as Dorothea took up work on her petit-point bell pull. Jemmy stared at her tablet. *What's the matter with me? I can't seem to do anything at all — not search for Hal — not even write a story.*

What kind of a reporter am I? A worthless kind, that's what kind.

Lost in self-doubt, Jemmy didn't hear the distant sound of a marching band.

Dorothea rose to her feet. "It's about time. The parade was scheduled for nine thirty. I wonder whether the Wild West encountered obstacles in getting here. Weather could hardly be counted a difficulty. The day is most agreeable."

"I suppose problems are apt to crop up. Moving hundreds of horses and tents can't be easy."

Dorothea pulled Jemmy up from the bench. "I propose we view the parade on its way to the fairgrounds. We'll stay close by the sheriff's office. That way we can keep watch for Mr. Koock and the deputy."

Jemmy relished leaving the stifling office as they moved toward the courthouse steps. She stood up straight and reminded herself that covering the parade was her job. *I am a reporter. Reporting the news is my job — with or without Hal. Who knows? Maybe I'll even find my missing photographer.*

The holiday excitement outside should have been enough to raise anyone's spirits. Little boys shinnied up lampposts on the courthouse lawn. Jemmy envied them. She and Dorothea had to crane their necks even though they managed to find standing room on the highest steps of the portico along with other sensible ladies of breeding.

In size, hoopla, and noise, Colonel Cody's parade easily eclipsed Professor Gentry's. First came spotted ponies bearing Native Americans. Both men and horses wore fearsome slashes of red, white, and ochre paint.

Next came Cha Sha Sha Opogeo, the bushy-bearded husband of Red Cloud's daughter. His real name was John Nelson, but his honorary Sioux title had more show-biz appeal.

A color guard of veterans from the Cuban campaign of 1898 carried a banner with the words ROUGH RIDERS. To inspire his sol-diers of the First Regiment of U.S. Cavalry in the Spanish-American War, Teddy Roo-sevelt appropriated the term from Buffalo Bill. With a fine sense of fair play, Cody had stolen back the pilfered label.

Buck Taylor, the first "King of the Cow-boys," led a band of genuine rough riders: bronco busters. Vicente Oropeza's vaqueros twirled ropes. Frontier girls waved, and South American gauchos tossed bolas around the horns of Texas cattle.

Even though the animals were a hundred feet away, Dorothea put her perfumed hanky over her nose to cover the reek of bovine flatulence. Jemmy stuck her nose in the air and inhaled a deep whiff on purpose. How else would she be able to describe the smell?

Conestoga wagons rolled up Ohio Street advertising the show. The first boasted oversized portraits of the stars. Framed by filigree and curlicues in gaudy paint was an oval portrait of the international celebrity, Col. W. F. Cody. Smaller ovals of Annie Oakley and Johnny Baker graced either side of the most famous showman in the world. All three names were emblazoned on gold-painted streamers under their pictures.

Wagon canvas depicted Rough Riders charging up San Juan Hill and a Puzta horseman from Hungary in a long purple coat standing atop five galloping horses.

One featured Native Americans engaged in occupations as varied as killing a bear or playing tennis. Another depicted the Sixth Cavalry riding behind a billowing U.S. flag with forty-five stars in its blue canton.

Tallyho, Cody's own coach, was missing. Folks would have to be satisfied with his picture as a young cross-country rider. Dorothea read Pony Express owner Bill Major's words aloud. "I gave him a man's pay when he was fourteen because he could ride a pony as well as a man."

Canvas roll-downs at the windows of the Deadwood stagecoach advertised RESERVED SEATS $1, REGULAR ADMISSION 50¢, and CHILDREN UNDER TEN HALF-PRICE.

The grand star Annie Oakley marched with thirty or forty orphans who were to be her guests for a meal in the Wild West cook tent. She was famous for her kindness to needy children, especially for "Annie Oakleys" — free show tickets. The crowd approved with much foot-stomping and applause.

As Annie and the orphans passed by, a shock of monstrous proportions chased any thought of the parade from Jemmy's head. She clapped eyes once more on the skinny robber as he ambled past.

She bounded off the portico with her mind made up to atone for her failure to ask about Hal. Without a word to Dorothea, she once again bolted in most unladylike pursuit. She weaved and elbowed her way through the crowd until she could reach out to pull at his sleeve.

He stopped and turned back with a smile as if he expected to greet a friend. He beamed even wider to see a pretty girl had latched onto his arm.

His expression turned from pleasure to dismay. When his eyebrows shot up, Jemmy knew he recognized her. He jerked his arm free and ducked into the crowd at a speed she could not hope to follow in long skirts and high-heeled boots.

In seconds she could see nothing of him, but she remembered all too well how he looked. Five-feet-five inches tall; a hundred and fifteen pounds. He even wore the same blue shirt and dark blue neckerchief. He fit every note in her notebook except "Smoked sausage bits on shirt."

She had only a brief glimpse of that particular thin fellow with light brown hair parted in the middle, but she knew beyond a doubt this was the skinny train robber. His face told the whole story. A blue-black knob of a bruise perched on his cheekbone like a lump of melting coal. A red scab line beaded across his jaw and down his chin. A yellow-purple half-moon under one swollen eye testified to the beating he had suffered on the train.

Jemmy fumed over her own stupidity. *How could I be so dim-witted? Heavens in a handbag, I even told myself his bruises would help me identify him if I managed to see him before they healed.*

But what did I do? I went right out and decided the skinny boy I saw at the Maple Leaf Club was the skinny robber from the train.

Did I notice anything at all about him? Did I notice he had only one single bruise on his jaw? Heavens in a handbag, how could anybody not be battered after being beaten and thrown off a train!

Did I notice he had light brown hair parted in the middle, not dark brown hair parted on the side? She stopped short and peered into the crowd for a minute or more. *When, oh when, will I start to think like a newspaper-woman?*

Jemmy dragged her feet back to Dorothea. Her hostess wore an expression of worry or agitated stomach. "Why are you so down-cast?" She burped behind her hanky.

"I thought I saw someone I knew. I was mistaken."

"Jemmy, my dear, I beg you to stop rushing off without a word of explanation. I can understand your need to find Mr. Dwyer, but your actions set my teeth on edge. You've dashed off twice already this morning."

Dorothea gave another genteel burp behind her white gloved hand. "Each time you take flight, my innards rumble. If you flee again, I fear my stomach will cast up more than wind."

"Forgive me, Dorothea. I am at fault for upsetting your digestion. Mother says tranquility in one's digestive system is the key to good health, and good health is the key to a happy life. I promise not to run off again without the most compelling reason."

Dorothea looked less than reassured by Jemmy's answer. And neither of them could have been reassured by the downcast looks on the faces of Mr. Koock and Deputy Futcher when the men returned. The two had had no success in locating Hal at any of the less-than-respectable places they visited on the wrong side of the tracks.

They had accomplished only one thing. They stopped by the Sedalia police station — which the deputy now remembered was located on Second Street. Mr. Koock had described Hal and asked the local police to help find him.

Deputy Futcher fawned on Jemmy. "Perhaps we could discuss this over lunch if Mr. Koock's business would permit. It'd be my pleasure to treat. I'd like to make up for my lack of manners yesterday. They got ham and beans at the Presbyterian and beef stew at the First Methodist. Church ladies do a fine meal and make a little money for missionaryin' when the big shows come to town. Wouldn't be enough restaurants in the whole county to feed the crowds without 'em."

Jemmy welcomed his attentions about as much as she would a pimple the size of a grapefruit. "I'm sure we all appreciate your kind offer, Deputy, but Mrs. Koock and I must leave to interview members of the Wild West."

Once he knew how important Jemmy was

to the Koocks, Deputy Futcher's zeal to help her assumed heroic proportions. He leaned close enough to Jemmy to bathe her in his tobacco-breath. "I'll hunt for him on my own time soon as the afternoon deputy comes. I know a couple of places outside of town where he might have gone for a little —"

Mr. Koock interrupted. "Yes, Deputy Futcher, we'd be most grateful for any assistance."

Obadiah ushered the ladies out the door and into the carriage. He told Jean Max to drive to the place where Buffalo Bill's roustabouts were setting up. The campgrounds lay past the Katy shops southwest of Sedalia.

On the way, Jemmy replayed her conversation with the other skinny man — not the real skinny robber — the skinny man in the alley by the Coffee Cup Restaurant. She remembered his startled reaction when she implied she knew the Wild West would be robbed. In a flash, she realized she had stumbled on a truth. The skinny man was actually planning to rob the Wild West.

She had to tell somebody right away. She started to ask Mr. Koock to turn back to the sheriff's office, but changed her mind. Surely the sheriff had experienced big shows coming to town. No doubt he was prepared for trouble.

Hal's absence tortured Jemmy. What if her warning caused the deputy to stop searching for him? If anybody knew the scum of Sedalia, Futcher would be the man.

What's more, she had a job to do, a reporter's job. She had devoted precious little time to duty of late. She could ill afford to waste any more.

No, she had to be subtle. She would tell her host. She took a deep breath and blurted out the words as if she just had a revelation.

"Mr. Koock, in my distress over Hal, I quite forgot to mention something of grave importance. Perhaps we should go back so I may impress upon Deputy Futcher the need for extra vigilance at the show tonight."

"What is it, Miss McBustle?"

"I have good reason to believe the thieves from the train plan to rob the show this evening."

"Why do you think so?"

If Jemmy told him the truth, she would have to explain her lies. She would have to tell why she had run off from her companion and chased a crook into an alley.

Fortunately, she was gaining a real knack for making up little white lies. "The fellow I took the gun from on the train threatened the show. He said, 'Just wait until the Buffalo Bill show Friday. We'll buffalo everybody.' Those were his exact words, near as I can remember."

"You've told this to no one — not in three days?"

"At first I didn't know whom to tell. Then it slipped my mind, and now I'm so upset over Hal's disappearance . . ." She pulled her hanky from her sleeve and dabbed at her nose in hopes she had satisfied his doubts. Even if the words sounded odd, she really did believe the robbers would be after the ticket money. Tears would sway him — at least they would if Mr. Koock happened to be a typical male of species *Homo sapiens.*

"I'll telephone Sheriff Williams and Police Chief Prentice from my office. I'm sure they have everything well in hand, but one can't be too cautious. Forewarned is forearmed."

"Thank you, Mr. Koock. I apologize for giving you nothing but problems. I'm beside myself trying to think where Hal might be."

By then, the carriage had reached the Wild West campgrounds. Mr. Koock preceded Dorothea and Jemmy out of the carriage so he could steady them as they climbed out. As he handed down the ladies, he said, "Try not to fret, Miss McBustle. I daresay I shouldn't impugn your photographer's character; but after all, he is Irish. I feel certain your Mr. Dwyer will turn up with nothing worse than a bad hangover."

The temperature of Jemmy's own Irish blood rose a few degrees. She muttered under her breath the rest of the line — the words Mr. Koock would have added in male company. "Bad hangover or a dose of the clap."

She forced a smile. "I'm sure you're right, Mr. Koock. Thank you for all you've done for me. I fear I've repaid your kind hospitality with nothing but troubles."

"Mrs. Koock and I are happy to do whatever we can."

Dorothea looked hopeful as she asked him, "Will you be escorting us to the Wild West this evening?"

"I only wish I could, but I fear Lilburn will have to serve in my stead. I must stay at the shops. With out-of-town rowdies about, I always post sentries as a precaution. The Katy shops are too close to the Wild West to take chances."

"But must you stay, too?"

"I would never ask my men to do anything I'm not willing to do myself, or to deprive them of any pleasures unless I forego those pleasures myself."

It was Dorothea's turn to force a smile.

"Of course, Mr. Koock. I quite understand."

With a finger pointed toward the ground and the parting words, "I'll send Jean Max back to wait for you in this same spot," he climbed back in the coach, knocked twice to signal the driver, and waved out the window as he rode off.

Dorothea fluttered her hanky at the departing coach. She was still smiling, a genuine smile. She motioned toward the canvas going up. "Shall we go?"

Jemmy wondered why Dorothea was smiling when Mr. Koock had refused to escort his wife to the show.

Dorothea must have felt the need to explain her apparent lack of disappointment. "For the first time in years, he looked at me when he waved goodbye."

Wrapped in their own thoughts, the pair walked in the direction of a swarm of workmen setting tall fence posts around a rectangular field. Other workers attached canvas to the posts.

Jemmy took notebook and pencil from her satchel as she headed toward the person giving orders. The scent of fresh-cut grass lingered in the air.

"Excuse me. I work for the St. Louis *Illuminator*. Perhaps you've heard of me, Ann O'Nimity." Her ridiculous pen name gener-

ally elicited a snort or at least a grin. Not with this foreman. He kept right on issuing orders.

"Pardon me, sir. Might I prevail upon you to answer a few questions?"

"Can't take time off. Happy to answer if you can keep up." He raced off at a pace that forced the ladies to trot.

When he reached a pair of diggers driving a post, he said, "Hole got to be deeper. See the red line on the post? There for a reason. Got to go down that far in the earth. Else a big wind come along and blow down the whole shebang." The men pulled up the post, tossed it aside, and began hacking at the hard clay with spade and pickax.

The foreman walked as he cast back over his shoulder, "Hire local boys to help out. Work hard. Not bright, though."

Jemmy wasn't sure if he was talking to Dorothea and herself, talking to the workers, or talking to himself. He strode off toward the grandstand. From his tongue rolled a spool of statistics born of practice in giving facts to reporters and getting rid of such nosy pests without being crude.

On the way he pointed to yards of canvas being hammered into place around the vast rectangle. "Fifty-two train cars — fourteen more than Ringling. Seventy thousand yards of canvas. Eleven hundred and four stakes. Twenty miles of rope. Fence off eleven acres of ground. Grandstand tent four and a half acres of canvas for the roof. Don't want paying customers wet."

He pointed toward a platform near the top of the grandstand. "Electric plant cost fifteen thousand dollars."

He changed direction so often, Jemmy could in no wise keep her good ear trained on him.

"Two gas-powered plants other side of grandstand. Three searchlights. Electric carbon-arc floodlights. Hundred and fifty thousand candle power. Hope I helped." He tipped his hat, turned, and fairly galloped across the arena.

Jemmy raised her voice, "Please, sir, where would I find Buffalo Bill?"

"Not here."

"Annie Oakley?"

"Cook tent or her own."

He was almost out of earshot when she hollered after him, "What is your name?" She raised her voice louder still. "I want to spell it correctly in my article."

He kept walking but tossed back, "Best go to Johnny Baker's tent. You're already late for reporter powwow."

She turned to Dorothea. "He didn't even

let me thank him."

"He's a busy man."

"I couldn't keep up. I don't think I wrote down half of what he said. My bad ear . . ." Jemmy pursed her lips in vexation.

"Let me help. I have two good ears and a good memory." With Dorothea's aid, Jemmy filled in the blanks in her notes.

Their attempts to find the press conference met with shrugged shoulders until they came across one of Annie's orphans. A little boy in oversized pants held up by a rope belt took off at a trot. When he ran too far ahead, he loped back to encourage the ladies to move faster. Eventually, they arrived at a tent with the front flaps open and the sides rolled up a few feet to let in breezes.

Inside Jemmy could see a man holding forth to reporters, a man who was clearly not Buffalo Bill. The "Cowboy Kid" wore black from his boots to the sombrero he flourished to punctuate his quotable words. White fringe dangled from his embroidered shirt. Silver conchos down his trouser legs made him stand out from a ring of press men taking notes.

"I am proud to call myself the colonel's son." Johnny Baker motioned toward the note-takers with his sombrero. "You can write that down. 'Colonel' is what he likes to be called."

Johnny curled the hat brim with the heel of his hand. "The colonel adopted this orphan boy when I was just seven years old. Taught me everything I know about shooting and show business. Yes, Pahaska — spelled P-A-H-A-S-K-A, that's the colonel's Indian name — saved my life and made me famous. I owe him everything and I'm proud to say so. In fact, I make it my life's work to say so whenever I get the chance. I'll take questions now."

A deep voice demanded, "Where is Buffalo Bill?"

"He is indisposed and was unable to make the trip."

"So he won't be at the show tonight?"

"Unfortunately, no. But I promise you a Wild West worth five dollars of anybody's money. And you get it all for the amazing bargain of a mere fifty cents."

Johnny smacked his sombrero against his knee as if he suddenly remembered something. "Of course, you don't have to pay. Every reporter comes in free on a press pass. Buffalo Bill has vowed to do all he can for the greatest democratic institution the world has ever known — the free press of the United States of America."

A sarcastic voice came from across the tent, "Aren't you a little old to be playing the Cowboy Kid?"

"I only bring out the Kid costume when I'm taking over for the colonel. He says a sombrero has more razzmatazz than a ranger hat."

A baritone voice in front of Jemmy set a friendlier tone. "Do you still hit targets standing on your head?"

"Indeed I do, though folks say the years will one day keep my feet on the ground. Not soon, I hope. I like the look of the world when it's upside down. Makes more sense that way."

The sarcastic voice chimed in, "Most fellers prefer their headquarters over their hind-quarters."

The quip earned guffaws until Johnny rebuked the "for men's ears only" remark. "Gentlemen, we have ladies in our midst." He bowed to Jemmy and Dorothea. "Do either of you have a question?"

Instead of asking about Annie Oakley's costume as the group probably expected, Jemmy surprised the crowd with "How often has the show been robbed?"

Laughter of the nervous tittering variety followed. Ladies were not supposed to concern themselves with anything so down-

and-dirty as thievery.

Johnny answered by not answering. "No one would rob the Wild West, miss. Colonel Cody is too well-loved."

A friendly voice brought Johnny back to more genial territory. "What's the best you ever shot?"

Jemmy supposed the voice probably came from one of Cody's own publicity men.

"I guess you mean in Hamburg, Germany. I fired one thousand and sixteen times and hit a thousand flying objects. My record still stands — less'n somebody broke it in the last week."

The deep voice boomed, "What does it feel like to shoot a thousand rounds?"

"My shoulder felt like someone took a ball-peen hammer to it; I would have sworn devils propped my eyes open during a Kansas twister; and the colonel had to pry my fingers off the trigger. Considering everything . . ." He paused for a full twenty seconds, then hit them with a zinger. "I felt like the emperor of the rifle and the sheik of the shotgun."

From the corner of her eye, Jemmy caught a shape slipping under the canvas on the far side of the tent. She could scarcely believe it. The skinny robber, or the one pretending to be the skinny robber, was about to elude her for the third time in the same day.

She dashed out front and raced around the tent so fast she tripped over a tent peg and fell with a most unladylike "Eeech." Her knees, elbow, and chin met the ground all at the same time.

Before she recovered enough to push her hat back from blinding her eyes, a firm hand pulled her to her feet. As her gaze rose from boots to shirt to face, she planned what to say to the skinny robber.

But when she stared into a middle-aged man's bearded face, she realized her powers of observation had played her for a fool yet again. His backside may have resembled the skinny robber's. But his bushy bearded face belonged on a package of Smith Brothers cough drops.

"Are you hurt, miss?"

Jemmy rubbed her elbow and felt something damp run down her chin. "Is my lip bleeding?"

"No. A little drool is all."

"Thank you for coming to my assistance."

"My pleasure, miss. Can you walk? I'd be happy to escort you." He offered his arm.

"I appreciate your courtesy, but it's not necessary. I can walk. I do thank you for your help."

He tipped his hat and went on his way.

Head down, Jemmy picked her way over the ropes and tent stakes, then stopped short. *Wrong again. I must stop leaping to conclusions and over tent stakes. His eyes trouble me. The set of his chin seems off kilter. Maybe I'm trying to make something of it because I don't want to admit I made a dunce of myself for the third time in one day.*

Confusion banged in her head like mallets on a bass drum. *How many skinny men are in Sedalia, and why can't I tell them apart?*

Where is the one I want to talk to — the one with the beat-up face — the robber from the train?

Her confusion swelled to the clatter of a thousand snare drums in her bad ear. *Who is the other one? Who is the fellow with the bruised jaw? Why would he pretend to be the robber from the train?*

And where on earth is Hal?

Chapter Eighteen:
THE WILD WEST FAIRGROUNDS
SEDALIA
FRIDAY AFTERNOON,
SEPTEMBER 23, 1898

The powwow broke up as reporters drifted off to write their stories. A man in a straw boater hat with a plaid hatband winked at Jemmy. He joked, "I'll bet a silver dollar, Wild Bill is on the bandwagon — that would be on the wagon with the Jack Daniels Silver Cornet Band." When Dorothea sent a scathing glare in his direction, the tops of his ears turned red and he ceased laughing. He tipped his hat as he made a wide berth around the ladies.

Jemmy wondered whether the jokester would have received a dagger-look if Dorothea had been bold enough to aim it at Jemmy. She picked at a grass stain on her skirt as she apologized to her companion. "I cannot tell you how sorry I am to upset you with my careless actions. I thought I saw the robber from the train. I ran after him to ask about Hal. Once again I was wrong."

Dorothea answered with a sad small burp.

"I suppose my digestion will have to become accustomed to your proclivities."

Jemmy's own stomach sank as she realized she had joined the rest of the uncaring mob who populated Dorothea's world. The poor woman had to accustom herself to the proclivities and peculiarities of four unruly children and one uninterested husband. Would Dorothea ever be daring enough to claim an eccentricity or two of her own?

Shame reddened Jemmy's cheeks. "What can I say, except to apologize again? I have no right to disorder your digestion. Auntie Dee says the only thing better for a person's health than goodly digestion is a goodly sum in Boatmen's Bank."

Dorothea offered a half-smile at the feeble jest, then changed the subject. "I inquired of Mr. Baker where we might find Miss Oakley. He said Mrs. Butler might be in the cook tent."

"You embarrass me with your sweetness." Jemmy brushed away a rueful tear. "You return my bad behavior with new favors."

Dorothea patted her shoulder. "Don't give it a thought. Friends are happy to do what they can for one another."

Jemmy sniffed, then blew her nose. "I don't deserve a friend like you." The pair walked arm in arm to the huge cook tent.

The bedlam inside as the staff pulled red tablecloths off blue tables took Jemmy by surprise. Mother hen and woman-in-chief Marm Whittaker bustled about serving up advice to new workers and sharp words to laggards as she urged all to greater speed and efficiency.

Jemmy chuckled when her attention fell on the fat rump of a fellow scouring one of four gigantic kettles. His torso completely disappeared as his tan-trousered behind gyrated and jiggled like the backside of dock-tailed English bulldog dancing a polka.

Dorothea waved a hand toward the kitchen end of the tent. "Would you look at the size of the gas stove. A half-dozen horse troughs would take less space. I've never seen anything remotely like it. Sixty men work in this tent alone. You can write that down. Mr. Baker gave the number when you were gone."

She ticked off other gems about Cody's vast organization. "The Wild West has its own barber, laundry, costume tent, blacksmiths, ticket sellers, ten publicity men — even glassblowers to make target balls for the sharpshooters."

The pair arrived too late to see Annie Oakley presiding over lunch with orphans. An Asian scullery boy throwing out dishwater pointed them toward a row of smaller tents. "Easy find Missy Butter. Have frowers in front."

At Annie's tent, Jemmy admired a gleaming bicycle and yellow primroses in a terra cotta pot. The brass plate on the front center pole announced to all this was the star's personal tent. The flaps had been pulled back to reveal the comforts of home — Axminster carpets, trunks and pictures everywhere, cougar skin rug, couch with satin pillows, and too many guns to count.

Annie Oakley sat in a rocking chair threading a big needle with black yarn.

Jemmy knocked on the center post. "Miss Oakley, I hate to bother you. I'm Jemima McBustle, a reporter for the St. Louis *Illuminator.*"

She waved an arm in Dorothea's direction. "This is my friend, Mrs. Obadiah Koock, from Sedalia. I'm hoping you can spare a few minutes for an interview."

Annie laid her darning apple in her lap. "Please, do come in. Bring your sewing if you have it with you. I've never found anything to compare with needlework for giving me peace of mind."

She motioned toward the couch for the pair to seat themselves. "I'm always glad for a bit of female companionship. Ladies are much outnumbered in the Wild West."

Jemmy opened her notebook. "It's most kind of you to speak with me."

"I'm glad to do what I can for the ladies of the press, few as they are. I will tell you though, you really should make an appointment beforehand. Arrange a time with the show's publicity man. Didn't your editor explain proper protocol?"

Jemmy ducked her head in embarrassment. "My editor wouldn't tell me if my hat was on fire."

Annie shook her head. "How sad so few men appreciate the abilities of the ladies in their employ. I am fortunate to work for a man who not only knows my worth, but rewards all ladies of the Wild West in proportion to their value to the show. The colonel believes in giving women equal pay for equal work."

Annie put down her thimble and rose from her rocking chair. She removed the napkin covering a pitcher of lemonade on an ornate table inlaid with ivory. She poured three tumblers and handed two of them to her guests. "The colonel is generous in many ways. He keeps lemonade on hand around the clock. Free to all who work here. In the heat of summer, I live on practically nothing else."

She took a sip. "Now then, miss . . ."

"Jemima McBustle. My friends call me Jemmy." Jemmy's intuition to drop her "Ann O'Nimity" moniker turned out wiser than she could have imagined.

Annie beamed. "Jimmy? How delightful. I often call my husband 'Jimmy.' Of course, his name is Frank. But once when I was sick, he performed the silliest antics to make me forget my ailments. Since then, I've called him 'Jimmy the squirrel' when he's clever."

Her face clouded with sudden alarm. "You're not going to print that, are you? It might be taken as undignified."

"I won't print it if you wish me not to."

"Well, then, my second Jimmy, ask your questions."

"How did you come to join the Wild West?"

"My husband and I had been on shooting challenge tours and worked for a time at Four-Paw and Sells Brothers Circus — which we quit because they took little notice of safety.

"This show's manager, Nate Salisbury, saw us in Louisville and hired us on the spot. The show needed a replacement for Captain Bogardus in — let me think — eighteen eighty-five. We've been with the

Wild West ever since, except for a brief period while the colonel took leave of his senses. When he regained them and proved he preferred me above Lillian Smith and all others who wished to take my place, we returned."

Jemmy tapped her pencil on her tablet. "I'm hoping for something a bit different from the usual. I know about your struggle to help your family after your father died. You paid the mortgage on your mother's house with money you made shooting game for restaurants. How old were you then?"

"Fifteen."

"Fifteen. So young for so much hardship and tragedy. Two of your sisters died from tuberculosis. How sad."

Annie opened her locket and leaned forward so Jemmy could see tiny braids of dark hair. "I wear this to remember them." She turned the locket in Dorothea's direction. "And, yes, I donate to sanatoriums in hopes one day we'll find a cure for consumption."

"I hear you even melt down your shooting medals for charity."

"A fine use for the medals. I hope you don't think me immodest when I tell you I have so many I can't imagine where to put them all. I can't abide to see anything or anyone lying idle which may be put to better use."

Annie gave Jemmy a nod of approval. "I see you're not idle. Clearly, you've done your homework."

Jemmy grinned at the compliment. It gave her courage to press Annie to reveal her inner thoughts. "You're well known for your generosity. And your belief shepherding one's possessions is essential to living a good life."

Annie sat straight and edged forward in her chair. "I trust you do not mean to call me a cheapskate, Miss McBustle."

Jemmy's head bounced back in surprise. She had not expected to upset Annie. She rushed to explain. "No, no indeed. I can scarcely express how much I admire your integrity as well as your talent. Please believe I have nothing but the deepest respect for both."

Annie sat back in her chair, apparently satisfied with the answer.

Jemmy tried to pick up where she had left off. "I know the famous stories — shooting a cigarette out of Kaiser Wilhelm's mouth. I hoped for something uncommon."

Annie pursed her lips in thought. "Perhaps this is the kind of story you want. A bank clerk refused to cash a money order for me.

He bragged about how often he had seen Annie Oakley shoot. Hot air — nothing but hot air."

She rocked her shoulders in imitation of the clerk's swagger. " 'Annie Oakley, Little Miss Sure Shot, is much smaller than you. Why, you're a great ox in comparison.' I told him I could prove I'm Annie Oakley. I fetched a pistol from my carpetbag and said, 'Hold the envelope up and I'll put a bullet through the stamp.' He cashed the order without troubling himself to find out whether I could really shoot a hole through the stamp."

Dorothea tittered behind her hanky. "A delightful story."

Annie rewarded both guests with a dazzling smile.

Jemmy took a deep breath. Now the ice had been broken, she felt bold enough to ask for more. "Mrs. Butler, I wonder whether you have suggestions for other ladies who would like to follow in your footsteps to become markswomen. Or indeed, have you advice for any and all women who aspire to succeed in a man's world?"

"I'm not political, Miss McBustle. I do not campaign for woman suffrage. I fear for this country should bad women and bloomer-wearers be given the vote, but I applaud any woman who is a true professional.

"I also believe all people — including women — should be proficient in firearms. Every school should have a shooting range and should teach safe use.

"I know many condemn shooting as unladylike. I defy anyone to find my actions less than ladylike at any time. Why, when I shoot standing on my head, I tie my skirts to my legs so as not to be immodest."

Silence fell as Jemmy bent over her notes. Annie sipped her lemonade, then stood and made a surprising offer. "I give shooting lessons to ladies whenever the opportunity arises. I am working on a booklet. I hope to publish it next year. I mean to give it out free, though I think I shall need to charge for postage. I'd be happy to give the pair of you a few pointers, if you would like."

"Would you, Mrs. Butler? We'd be most grateful. You know, Dorothea, Mrs. Koock is quite a good shot already. I'm afraid I am less than a novice."

"Well, Miss Jimmy, novice at firearms, come with me." Annie picked up a box of cartridges and three small-bore rifles as the trio walked to the front of the tent.

Dorothea's voice was hushed. "I've never

seen so many shooting pieces. They must have cost a fortune."

Annie crinkled her nose. "People, even strangers, give them to me. I refuse a great many, but still . . ." She waved at the display in the tent. "These are only a few. You should see my arsenal at home."

Dorothea's eyes sparkled with admiration.

Annie demonstrated the safe way to load and carry a rifle, then told her students what not to do.

"Here are the rules I plan to list in the book. Perhaps you'd be kind enough to tell me if you find them easy to understand and to the point.

"The first rule is 'Do not shoot until you know your target beyond any possibility of doubt.' You must wait until your mind clears. Confusion always comes in the seconds right after you sight a moving object. You must master your breathing and calm your heartbeat." She raised her brows as if to ask whether the pair understood. Both nodded to show they did.

"My second rule is, 'Don't shoot at a noise.' The third is 'Don't shoot at a moving bush.' The last is 'Don't — under any circumstances — allow your gun muzzle to point for one moment at any living thing you do not mean to kill.' "

She waited for the rules to register. "I know all four are no more than different words for saying the same thing. A person holding a gun must be absolutely sure not to mistake a horse or, heaven forbid, a child . . ." Her words trailed off, but the meaning was clear.

Jemmy agreed wholeheartedly. "I believe you're entirely correct in repeating an important message until it sinks into the hardest head."

"I am considering adding one more rule, 'Don't shoot at small game such as rabbits, grouse, or squirrel with big ammunition.' I've seen so-called hunters blast little creatures into pieces only buzzards could find. What a waste."

Dorothea added, "Yes, do include it. Even small shot can make game hazardous to eat. More than once biting down on bits of lead has caused Mr. Koock great pain in his molars."

Not until then did Annie tell them what to do. She taught them how to stand and how to seek inner calm. She demonstrated a wide stance with her right foot in front and leaned forward. "Mind, nerve, and will must all be in harmony. Don't look at your gun. Think of it as the point of your finger." She raised Jemmy's arm so she could sight down her knuckles.

"The secret of the true marksman or markswoman is to see with the rifle, not just through the sights — to see with the rifle itself. With both eyes open, I look straight at the object. The moment the butt of the gun touches my shoulder, I fire. If I hesitate for an instant, I miss. I've learned I must take it for granted I am going to hit. I fire away before I have time to doubt, to think I might fail."

Annie pointed to an elm tree twenty yards away. She put the .22 to her shoulder and squeezed the trigger. A twig fluttered down with a few leaves attached.

Dorothea hugged her .22 between head and chest so she could applaud.

Jemmy's mouth fell open in awe. "Is that how you prune trees at your house?"

When both Dorothea and Annie laughed, Jemmy's thoughts bubbled out in a disconnected rush. "You make it look so easy. It isn't. I know it isn't. How do you do it? When I was aiming at crows, I nearly hit the dog."

Annie grew serious. "While shooting I scarce realize I have a gun in my hands. But getting to the place where a marksperson becomes one with a firearm takes practice. No one should expect to succeed at shooting or anything else without being willing to devote the long hours it takes to achieve perfection."

She faced her pupils. "Of course, I am used to hard work. I lift a thousand pounds every day. I put a seven-pound shotgun to my shoulder a hundred and fifty times daily. You can see why I never have trouble falling asleep at night."

She pulled back Jemmy's shoulders and widened her stance. "Your turn to prune the elm tree. On the right side — as near to mine as you can."

Jemmy tried to remember all the steps. Stance, posture, inner calm, both eyes open, fire the minute the gun butt hits the shoulder. The crack split the air but nothing else. "What happened?"

Dorothea giggled. "You came close to shooting the tail off a squirrel on the ground."

Annie pushed the gun butt into Jemmy's shoulder and held it. "Keep the gun tip level with your eye."

Jemmy tried again. No leaves tumbled to the ground.

"I fear you lack strength, Jimmy. You must practice lifting and holding the piece steady. I hope you won't think me overproud if I tell you this. At Dresden, German officers tried to play a trick on me. They asked me to test the sights on a gun made from solid iron. It was heavy, but I raised it to firing position. The officers stomped and clapped, then told me the gun weighed thirty-five pounds. When you can lift a third of your body weight to your shoulder, Jimmy, you will find shooting much easier."

Jemmy tried a few more shots without showing a single whit of improvement. As her feeble muscles stiffened, she gladly exchanged places with Dorothea and traded the .22 for her notebook.

With every shot Dorothea clipped twigs from the elm. Annie nodded in approval as she pointed to a pin oak ten yards past the elm. Dorothea clipped off more twigs. Annie smiled as she pointed to a willow tree still farther away. Jemmy couldn't see anything fall, but something must have.

Annie placed a hand on Dorothea's shoulder. "If you're as good with moving targets as you are with stationary ones, I may have a new rival."

Jemmy jumped in, "Can she hit moving targets? You should see her whack crows."

Dorothea lowered her head in modesty. "Good eyesight has given me whatever ability I have in shooting. But I would never have the confidence to enter a competition or face an audience."

Dorothea raised her eyes to meet Annie's. Something beyond Jemmy's understanding passed between the two women.

Annie turned to her less-apt pupil. "Jimmy, aim at a high mark and you'll hit it. Not the first time, nor the second time — maybe not the third. But keep on aiming and keep on shooting. Only practice will make you perfect. Finally, you'll hit the bull's eye."

"What a splendid quotation, Mrs. Butler." Jemmy wrote so fast her pencil lead broke. Dorothea was quick to lend her own gilded silver mechanical pencil. "I'm sure my readers want to know which firearms and ammunition you use."

"Nitro powders for ammunition — perfectly safe if properly used. As for firearms — none but the best — made by the J. B. Stevens Arms and Tool Company of Chicopee Falls, Massachusetts, my sponsor."

She leaned forward to murmur an aside. "I am expected to mention them whenever I speak to the press."

In a louder voice, she proclaimed, "I not only endorse them fully, I believe nobody with sense would risk life and limb standing behind a cheap gun. Never trust a gun costing less than a hundred dollars."

Annie peered over Jemmy's shoulder. " 'Chicopee' is spelled with a 'c,' not a 'k.' "

At that instant, a rifle crack split the air. A sharp ping from the brass plate on the center post sent Annie and Dorothea ducking down as they scurried inside the tent. Jemmy had no idea what was going on until Annie hollered. "Fall to the earth. Jemmy, you're making yourself a big target. Fall to the earth."

The enormity of what happened hit Jemmy. *That must have been a shot — a shot fired at us.* Nothing else would send Annie and Dorothea diving for cover. Stark terror froze her limbs as she lay prone on the ground. She needed all her will to keep from whimpering while she shivered in front of the tent.

Annie and Dorothea crawled onto the rug behind the center post. They lay flat to peer out the front. In seconds Jemmy's body shifted from shivers to sweat. Fear-heated blood charged through her muscles and let her move again. She managed to crawl inside the tent. Hidden behind canvas, she stopped to think.

From her jangled emotions, she seized on one — loneliness. She cowered alone against one side of the tent. Fifteen feet of spongy grass separated her from Annie and Dorothea. A frenzy of self-pity drove her forward. She hit on the idea of hiding behind the tent flap and pulling it along with her. Canvas in hand, she began snailing on knees and elbows toward the pair behind the center pole.

All of a sudden, both Annie and Dorothea rose up on their knees as if they believed the danger had passed. Annie pulled a pair of field glasses from a nail on the center post. She used the binoculars to scan the trees leading off toward a watering pond.

Presently she stood and turned around to answer unspoken questions. "Someone ran off toward the tracks. I couldn't see anything but the backside of someone wearing trousers."

Dorothea pulled Annie down to a kneeling position. "Do you think more than one might be out there?"

Annie scanned the area then handed the field glasses to Dorothea.

Annie took the brass nameplate from its nail then searched the ground in front of the tent until she found the spent bullet. She studied the name plate and handed it to Jemmy. Above the "i" in "Annie Oakley" was a neat round indentation — a second dotting of the "i." Jemmy felt the dent with her thumb.

Dorothea stayed behind the center pole while she asked Annie, "What does the dent mean?"

"The person who fired was either a very good shot or a very bad one. Very good if he meant to dot the 'i' — very bad if he meant to hit me."

Jemmy was dumbfounded. "I can't believe anyone would try to shoot you, Mrs. Butler."

Annie said gently, "You're a novice in more ways than one."

A breathless Frank Butler ran up to the trio. He pulled shut the open flap as he breezed into the tent and took off his hat. "Excuse me, ladies. I hate to be rude, but I must speak to my wife now. I'm sure you understand. If you'd be so kind?" He held the flap open to let them leave.

Dorothea brushed a blade of grass from her skirt as she hustled Jemmy from the tent. "Of course, Mr. Butler. We quite comprehend."

Jemmy stood near the opening, just far enough away from the gap to avoid being seen. Dorothea hissed. "Jemmy, what are you doing? You mustn't eavesdrop."

Jemmy motioned Dorothea to be quiet as she trained her good ear on the conversation. Dorothea tried again. "Jemmy, I can't believe you're doing something so rude.

Come away from there."

Dorothea tried pulling Jemmy away. "What would Aunt Tilly say?"

Jemmy pried her friend's fingers off her wrist. "And what if the shooter comes back? Why don't you keep a lookout?"

When Dorothea reached forth once more to grab the same wrist, Jemmy batted the hand back. Defeated, Dorothea walked off a dozen yards. Standing with arms akimbo, she tapped her foot.

Jemmy listened harder to the male voice inside. It rose and fell in volume as if he were pacing the tent. ". . . to shoot at you just now? And with those two women here."

Annie murmured in a voice so low Jemmy could barely hear. "I don't know what to make of it. Little Elk near death. Tiffin wounded, and now a shot fired at my own tent."

"There's more. After all I went through to get the colonel to hire extra Pinkertons — after he promised me — he didn't hire anyone. Not a single one."

"How did you find out?"

"Not by his telling me, that's for sure. He wouldn't answer my telegram. I finally wired Pinkertons in Kansas City direct. None extra hired. Blast it all!" His voice dropped from angry and ranting to sad and solicitous. "But I'm running off at the mouth when I should be seeing if you're all right."

"I was never in danger because he didn't mean to hit me. He or she — it could have been a woman in men's clothes."

"So you still suspect Lillian Smith?"

"I do. Even a mediocre shot would be able to hit something as large as a person. I make a much easier target than this piece of brass. It would take someone like Lillian to put a second dot over the 'i' on my nameplate."

"And maybe he or she was aiming at you and is a bad shot." He adopted a commanding tone. "Either way, I won't chance it. You're not going on tonight."

"Mr. Butler, you can't be suggesting we cut the main attractions from the show. The colonel isn't here. If I don't perform, people will demand their money back."

"I can't help it. I will not have you risking your life to put money in the colonel's pocket."

"The show puts money in our pockets, too. And the pockets of a thousand other people as well. If I don't perform and the show's reputation is damaged — if people stop coming because we're unreliable — how could we ever look our friends in the eye?"

Frank sputtered, "What do I have to do to

keep you here? Tie you up?"

"I'm going on. How many days have I ever failed to perform?"

Petulance gave the lie to Frank's "I don't remember."

"Of course you remember Staten Island. How many shows did I miss?"

"Five."

"Five shows in twelve years. Four of them on Staten Island. Now tell me why I missed those four shows."

"I don't remember." Frank said this louder, but the words sounded more defensive than true.

"You do remember. Why did I fail to perform?"

"Blood poisoning."

"Right. Infection from a bug in my ear. I had such fever I could barely sit a horse, but even then I rode in the parade."

"You are a stubborn female, but this time I won't give in to you."

Annie's voice had an air of finality. "I am fit. I am unafraid, and I am going to perform."

"I was only joshing about tying you up, but if you don't promise not to go on tonight, I may have to do it."

Jemmy pulled back the tent flap and walked inside. The Butlers stopped arguing as they stared at this interloper.

"Please forgive me for interrupting." With heart beating like hooves in a buffalo stampede, Jemmy took a deep breath. Hands shaking and voice trembling, she held up her head. Into the unnatural hush she said softly and firmly, "I believe I know how to solve your problem."

CHAPTER NINETEEN:

SEDALIA
FRIDAY EVENING, SEPTEMBER 23, 1898

Frank Butler took comfort from the pistols he carried in each pocket of his suit jacket. He scanned faces in the stream of showgoers moving toward the three lines forming at each of the ticket wagons. Tanned farmers in straw hats, doddering Civil War widows in solemn black, little girls in dresses made from flower-printed feed sacks, farm boys in blue overalls, society belles in enormous hats covered with artificial roses — none was a face he sought. He saw no sign of Lillian Smith or any other show rivals.

One face came as a shock: Mrs. Colonel Cody. Louisa was in Sedalia. *Why would Louisa Cody leave Kansas City to attend a show in the middle of Missouri? Still more puzzling, why would she come when her husband wasn't even in town?*

Frank had little time to ponder what might have happened at the Coates Hotel after he and Katherine left. He needed to focus all his attention on his impossible task — finding a would-be killer in a crowd of ten thousand people before the spotlight fell on his own Annie.

He wanted to throw up his arms and quit this whole insane scheme hatched by that impossible female from the St. Louis *Illuminator.*

Why did I think she was a reporter? What newspaper owner in his right mind would hire a woman — not even a woman — a slip of a girl — to do actual reporting? If she were harmed while doing dangerous work for him, the rest of the press would crucify the dimwit. Of course Joe Pulitzer hired Nelly Bly, but Joseph P. is in a class of his own when it comes to lunatic tricks.

Why did I agree to this idiotic plan?

He knew full well why: Annie had endorsed it. She would never refuse to perform out of fear. He had married a lady with true courage, too much courage for her own good.

Short of tying her up as he had threatened to do, he knew of no way to keep her out of the arena. Tie his wife up? Pure bluff — he would never do that. Frank's dread of losing her love rose up to collide with his fear of losing her to a bullet. Together the two polar opposites made his mind carom between anger and helplessness.

He moaned inwardly. *Annie, why can't you be sensible? Why won't you let me protect you? What does it take to scare you, woman? Isn't being shot at today along with the shooting of Tiffin and Little Elk enough?*

He realized Annie would never admit being frightened. What else was there to do but turn his anger on the nameless, faceless threat that could be lurking around any corner or sitting in the stands that selfsame minute?

Why won't you show yourself, you monster? Let me get my hands on you. You'll wish you'd been lucky enough to die with Custer at the Little Big Horn.

The day was racing ahead of him even though his love had given him extra time. Annie stunned him when she agreed to delay her act until next-to-last on the bill — right before the grand finale. *Did the fact that she had compromised prove she was afraid?* Too much had happened for him to take it all in. He found comfort in only one thing. That McBustle girl's crazy plan gave him a little breathing room — time to rally the company.

Show folks had put on full dress and makeup early, two hours before the opening parade. By the hundreds, they pitched in to roam the grounds. They shook hands as they pretended to greet customers while working on their real mission, scouting out potential assassins.

Strain began to show in the higher-than-usual pitch of Frank's voice. The pain in his throat made him realize he had been clamping the hands of the revelers instead of clasping them in a friendly handshake. A hard-palmed farm boy took Butler's punishing grip as an invitation to arm wrestle. Frank could not extricate himself until he dropped to his knees and gave the boy a silver dollar in "prize money." The boy strutted off holding the coin aloft as he proclaimed his victory to admiring girls.

From that moment on, Frank eased his tension by clenching the hard wood handles of the revolvers in his pockets. The carved walnut gave him small comfort. He fought to keep a smile on his face as he reached for another hand to shake, "I'm Frank Butler. Welcome to the Wild West. Lovely evening, isn't it? I know you'll enjoy the show."

Then everything changed.

In a single instant the agony of his double life fell away when he spotted a plug hat with a plump woman under it — Lillian Smith.

She was walking arm in arm with a tall, lean man in an old-fashioned frock coat. Graying hair curled down over his collar from under a top hat. He wore attire suitable for an opera — or a funeral.

Frank gave the "attack" signal and nodded in her direction. A half-dozen Cossack Rough Riders in fur hats and high black boots separated the pair and whisked the aging dandy off in the direction of the cook tent. The man didn't resist or even call out — a sure sign of guilt — or innocence.

Frank smoothly took the dandy's place at Lillian's side and wrapped her arm around his. He held it there with a grip on her wrist strong enough to cut off circulation. "Say nothing. This won't take long provided you don't become foolish. Don't even think of screaming. Your dandy in the top hat is in no position to rescue you."

He steered her to the back of a ticket wagon and knocked on the door. When it opened, he shoved her up the stairs. She tripped into a space shielded from the ticket takers by a heavy black curtain. Without warning, he tore off her hat then began a most unceremonious pawing of her person.

Lillian seemed to understand why she had been kidnapped. She clenched her jaw and submitted. The fact that she refused to fight vexed him. "Why don't you say something?"

"I've learned Frank Butler finishes what he starts."

He found no firearms of any kind. "Say something."

"Not until you're ready to listen."

Lillian's calm answers and stoic dignity goaded him to search with even greater frenzy. He turned up his nose at the smell of her greasepaint and powder.

He found nothing more interesting than a return ticket to Kansas City and a flyer. It advertised "Cheapest Rate Excursions" on the Missouri Pacific Line round trip to Sedalia for $1.60, including show admission. In disbelief, he pawed her all over once again. He even pulled out her hair rat. He found nothing more lethal than a hand full of hairpins.

Lillian dropped the brown-dyed cotton hair rat in her reticule and calmly began re-pinning her hair.

He grabbed her by the waist and plopped her on top of the safe. "The dandy in the top hat. He has the rifles, right? He wore a frock coat to hide them. A suit jacket wouldn't be long enough."

She crossed her arms in surly defiance. "What? No club to conk me over the head? However will you prove what a caveman you are? Still protecting feeble little Phoebe from big bad Lillian?"

"Cut the sarcasm and tell me what I want to know."

"I'll tell you what you don't want to know. I'll have you up on charges for molesting me."

"There's not a bruise on you. Who will take your word over mine?" His sarcasm could match hers any day. "You — an actress on the stage."

Lillian whacked her forearm against the edge of the safe, then tore the lavender dimity sleeve to expose white flesh that would soon turn blue. "No bruises you say? What could be easier?"

As she raised her other arm, Frank pinned her legs against the safe with his thighs and grabbed both arms. "You think I wouldn't go to jail to save Annie's life? You think I wouldn't kill you to save her?"

There. He said it. For the first time he put words to his raw need for Annie. It feels like standing naked in church so all the congregation could see how pitiful and useless I am.

Lillian dropped her bravado. "I see you're serious. What I don't see is proof I have ever done one single thing to make you think I want to kill Annie."

Frank's words came softer but still bitter

and accusing. "For starters, she can make a thousand dollars a week. What do you make at that sleaze parlor you call a theater in Kansas City?"

"None of your business, but I do all right. I own a townhouse and a farm with a few acres. Do I look like I'm starving?"

"You'd do better if you had Annie's job, wouldn't you?"

"You probably won't believe this, but I don't like being on the road. I like sleeping in my own bed and watching corn grow in my own fields when I have a day off."

"So, you came to Sedalia on your day off to watch corn grow. And what a lucrative business you must be in. No successful show I've ever heard of would be closed on a Friday."

"Not that it's any of your business, but the theater is dark tonight on account of a fire in my dressing room. If you want proof, read the Kansas City *Star*."

"Clever. Set a fire in your dressing room so you can be free to come to Sedalia to kill Annie Oakley."

"I didn't set the fire. The magician, the 'top hat dandy' you had strong-armed, was practicing a trick using fire in my dressing room. Mine is the biggest one, the star's dressing room. His trick misfired. I hope you'll pardon the pun."

Frank's eyes narrowed. "If all you wanted to do was see this show, why didn't you see it in Kansas City? Why travel a hundred miles?"

"Would you loosen your grip? My fingers are turning blue."

Frank obliged, but didn't let go.

"Who could resist the cheap excursion rates trains offer? Under two dollars for ride and show ticket, too. I came here cheaper than I could hire a carriage to ride across Kansas City."

He tightened his grip again and shook her. "No more sass. I'll have real answers from you, and I'll have them now."

"Ease up and show a little common sense. You already know the reason I couldn't see the show in Kansas City. I was working in a show of my own. The fire closed my show temporarily. That is the only reason I can be here now."

"And you have no idea who shot at Annie this afternoon."

Lillian squinted. "Somebody shot at Annie?"

"Not only today. During Tuesday's show someone shot her horse. On Wednesday someone put a bullet in Little Elk. It was you, wasn't it? You didn't mean to wound

317

Little Elk. You were aiming at Annie."

"When you pushed me in here and mauled me — even when you accused me of trying to kill Annie, I put up with it. I thought you were just being the overprotective Frank Butler I knew of old. But now I think you've gone completely round the bend. I am one great shot. If I had aimed at Annie, I wouldn't plug some poor Indian by mistake. If I aimed at your scrawny twig of a woman, she'd be dead. What's more, you know I'm telling the truth."

Frank had run out of questions. Lillian's answers made sense, but what about the top hat dandy? "Pull yourself together. We're going for a walk."

On the way to the cook tent, Frank wrapped Lillian's arm around his and held it there to prevent her running away. To his disappointment, she didn't try.

Entering the cook tent gave him an even bigger let-down. The top hat dandy had transformed his abductors into an applauding audience. On a table lay a heap of colored scarves, a half-dozen identical bottles, a dozen or more interlocking rings, and three bouquets of artificial flowers. The magician was at that moment using playing cards to delight his captors with sleight of hand.

Frank let loose of Lillian's arm and stomped to the magician's side. To the Cossacks who held the man prisoner, he spat out a few words — words he knew the Russians would understand. "Guns. You take guns? Guns from coat?" He pointed to the magician.

"Guns, no. Toys. He have toys. Isss all toys."

Frank's anger rose. He stripped off the man's frock coat and felt it for weapons. He found only some balls of red-painted sponge. He threw down the coat and began putting his hands all over the dandy. He searched in forbidden places — places that would have demanded satisfaction under the code duello until recent years.

The magician suffered the groping in good humor, all things considered. As he put his coat back on, he tipped his top hat and offered Frank his card. "Mr. Butler, do call on me when you're in Kansas City. Should you tire of fondling me, I think I can find others who would esteem a fellow with your manual skill."

Frank turned the color of a Cossack's coat. He scanned the faces of the Russians to see whether they grasped the meaning of the dandy's words. They didn't.

Lillian understood, though, and uttered a

combination snort and whinny. Her high-pitched horse laugh made him want to give her some bruises to match the one she'd given herself. "Get out of here — both of you. But don't think I won't be watching you. Go!"

The magician began nesting the hollow-bottomed bottles together until they fitted into a single unit. Lillian smoothed his hair with a comb from her reticule. It was some time before the magician finished tucking away his treasures. With great ceremony, the pair bowed to the Russians and then to Frank and then to each other. Lillian giggled as the pair started to leave.

Johnny Baker and Annie appeared at the tent opening. Frank strode toward them as he motioned toward Lillian and the dandy. "They have no weapons, not even a pocket knife." He took Annie's arm to clear the path for the twosome to leave.

Lillian stopped giggling. "Mrs. Butler, I have no wish to hurt you. If I can be of help with whatever is going on here, you have but to ask."

Annie raised her head higher, but said nothing. Frank offered, "Most generous, especially considering my offenses against you."

"I'm sincere, Mr. Butler. If given the opportunity, I'll prove it."

"Well, then. If you should recognize a rival marksman, you might point him out to any people in costume. They can get a message to me or to a Pinkerton."

"I will."

Johnny Baker wrote something on two pairs of passes. "Miss Smith, please take these with our deepest apologies. Let us treat you to the best seats in the arena, the governor's box."

The dandy took his pair of tickets and touched them to his hat brim in a farewell salute. The pair swept out arm in arm.

Annie turned to Frank. "Now what?"

Frank shrugged his shoulders in defeat.

Johnny Baker called out, "Saddle up, folks. It's show time."

CHAPTER TWENTY:

THE WILD WEST FAIRGROUNDS
SEDALIA
FRIDAY EVENING, SEPTEMBER 23, 1898

Jemmy's mustache itched. The spirit gum twisted her upper lip into a sneer and smelled like turpentine. Every time she breathed, stiff horse hair snipped from Tiffin's mane brushed her nostrils and tickled her nose unmercifully; but she could do nothing to ease the maddening urge to scratch. If she rubbed hard enough to do any good, she would drag the mustache clean off.

She mumbled one of Mother's favorite wise-saws: "What cannot be changed must be suffered with starch and in silence." She tried to imagine something pleasant, but only conjured a cat coughing up a fur ball.

For the hundredth time she wished she could rewind the clock to the minute before she entered the Butlers' tent. Jemmy and Dorothea pretending to be the Butlers? *Laughable. But to laugh would admit to myself how outlandish this whole idea must be.*

Best think about something else. Jemmy smoothed down her mustache with two fingers. *This is getting to be a habit — dressing in men's clothes. If I'm not careful, I may like going corsetless too well to go back to being a girl.*

She muttered a little prayer to wish Annie luck in her expedition to find Aunt Tilly and Burnie. Failure of Jemmy and Dorothea to report to the Koock home by dinnertime would have sent Aunt Tilly into a tizzy. Jemmy had no doubt she would marshal all resources known to man or matron to find her missing charges.

Dorothea had written notes falsely promising to meet the family by the Wild West ticket office. Jean Max was to take the notes to the house and transport Aunt Tilly and Burnie to the fairgrounds. Afterward, he was to deliver descriptions of how both were dressed to Annie Oakley in the ready tent, the place where the acts finalized their gear just before going on.

Once the two spectators arrived, Annie would waylay them and give them passes. She would promise the pair that Dorothea and Jemmy would soon join them in the mayor's box. Jemmy crossed her fingers in hopes the assassin could be discovered in time to make Annie's pledge come true.

Surely the entire troupe along with city and county law enforcement would nab the criminal in short order. If they failed, Jemmy prayed neither Burnie nor Aunt Tilly would grow too impatient when she and Dorothea failed to appear.

Jemmy had to put aside those worries. Frank dictated instructions so fast, she could barely read her own scrawls. She tried to focus her mind on the paper. She simply had to memorize what to do and when to do what.

Her lack of prowess with bullets now seemed a godsend, even if she felt more than a little guilty. She had left Dorothea to bear the brunt of the McBustle culprit-catching plan. Dorothea faced the near-impossible challenge of replacing the incomparable. No one in the world could match the astonishing talent of Annie Oakley, but Jemmy had set Dorothea the task of doing exactly that.

She sneaked a glance at her hostess. With eyes closed, Dorothea raised her head from time to time. She moved her lips in silence as she memorized the simplified shooting tricks Annie had given her. She pored over the scrap of paper like a hungry waif over Thanksgiving turkey.

Jemmy's own paper shook all the more

324

when she saw Dorothea's remain rock steady. Her admiration for the lady of the droopy nose grew with each hour she spent in her company.

For better or worse, the two women had become partners. They soon would face a ten-minute test of their mettle. Jemmy wondered whether her legs would hold her when she led the cart horse into place. Her feet felt like sponges dangling from the twice-turned up cuffs of her borrowed black britches.

She was no stranger to performing in front of an audience. She had been on stage in recitals and plays. True, those crowds numbered a good bit fewer than ten thousand. In her high school days she'd had weeks of rehearsal — not the hour and a half the Butlers had spent preparing a pair of novices to imitate the most famous shooting team in the world.

Jemmy's role called for her to toss glass balls to exactly the right height. *What if my nerves cause me to throw too high or too low or to chuck the balls the wrong way altogether?*

Getting Dorothea and herself into this mess was her own stupid fault. She remembered her silly words. Her own lips boasted eighteen-year-old Jemima McBustle had the key to solving the Butlers' life-and-death problem. *How could my tongue be so reckless?* The insane plan now seemed to be the product of her uncontrollable mouth — with no benefit of brain involved.

She tried to calm herself. The shooting charade was to be the last resort. If the scheme worked, she and Dorothea wouldn't have to go through with the performance. Jemmy's plan gave hundreds of people nearly two hours to roam the stands and find the assassin. Please — all you lucky stars in the heavens — please let two hours be enough time.

Jemmy and Dorothea would pretend to be the Butlers in the opening parade. Afterward, they would hide in the ready tent. Meanwhile Sheriff Williams's and Police Chief Prentice's men could watch for thieves and other criminals.

If the assassin still had not appeared after all other acts, just one last-ditch effort remained. Dorothea would perform in Annie's place — at least until the crowd began booing. When the hissing started, the real Butlers would emerge from the audience and shoo away the impostors.

Jemmy thought convincing Annie and Frank to accept this outrageous plan would be much more difficult than it turned out to be. The Butlers agreed after only a few minutes' argument.

Frank looked ashamed when he consented. With a start, Jemmy realized the cause. He would sacrifice Dorothea or Jemmy or any human in the world if it meant sparing his little Missy.

She envied such devotion. *Will I ever inspire even a tenth as much devotion in a handsome, dashing man like Frank Butler?*

Jemmy thought Annie had agreed for a different reason entirely — partly to appease Frank, but mostly because she was convinced the shooter had no intention of killing her. She said the shooter's ability was unmistakable. Such uncanny skill proved the shots came from a professional and were warnings only. As for injuring Little Elk, she had no explanation. She just said, "Sometimes, even I miscalculate."

Jemmy became more and more jittery as the decisive hour approached. A few minutes before eight came the words, "Mount up."

Jemmy's butterflies became great flopping toads poisoning her stomach. Her chest muscles squeezed her heart to the point of misery. The horse she was to ride loomed three feet taller than it seemed minutes earlier. Her muscles tensed so painfully she had to pull her left leg up to the stirrup with both hands. She clambered on and looked down from a height that made her dizzy.

Of course Jemmy had ridden on the backs of horses before. Auntie Dee had provided her with equestrian lessons so she could have all the advantages of the St. Louis heiresses who were Jemmy's classmates at prestigious Mary Institute. The lessons didn't help much since they were all sidesaddle lessons — and those horses were trained never to achieve a faster pace than a politely bone-rattling canter.

Jemmy had a teeny bit of experience riding astride, but her lack of ability to control the animal she rode was exceeded only by her lack of ability to remain seated on any animal's back.

The opening fanfare ended in applause for the appearance of Johnny Baker's head through the canvas at the far end of the arena. Jemmy's heart throbbed until she feared she'd fall off the horse and be trampled.

The crucial moment arrived. Roustabouts loosed sandbag counterweights to part the canvas. Dread struck her like a gust of hot wind. She became convinced she would fall off the moment spotlights blazed down on her. Hemmed in both left and right, she had no choice but to move with the crowd.

With shouts and whistles, hundreds of Rough Riders and horses surged forward for the Grand Parade. Jemmy could do nothing more constructive than hang on to the pommel and try not to throw up.

Fortunately, Frank's horse knew what to do. Jemmy gave the big gelding his freedom. Frank would have waved his hat, but the crowd would have to do without that touch of theatricality. Jemmy's head was covered by a length of black cloth which she didn't dare disturb. Her bright hair tumbling down would betray the whole plan.

The horde swept twice around the arena before coming to formation in front of the center boxes. Johnny Baker introduced politicians and celebrities beginning with Governor Lon Vest Stephens and his pretty wife from the state capitol in Jefferson City, a three-hour train ride away. He ended with Lillian Smith, who took a bow and received a nice round of applause.

Sweeney's Cowboy Band struck up "The Star-Spangled Banner." The spotlight hit the American flag. The song ended with punctuation in the form of a cannon blast from the Spanish-American War veterans. The whole troupe swept out whooping and firing pistols loaded with blank cartridges.

Jemmy stopped outside the tent to wait for a roustabout to take Frank's horse. On rubbery legs, she walked to the canvas and peeked through gaps at the next act.

Substituting in Annie's usual place as second on the bill were the cowgirls of the Grand Equestrian Entrée. They raced around barrels in figure eights, then performed daredevil stunts while galloping at full speed in front of the stands. The girls left the arena in fine style. They stood atop their horses in special leather loops while flags and banners streamed behind them.

Jemmy paced beside the canvas flaps as a dozen Mexican vaqueros, Indians, and cowboys trotted past for the quarter-mile races in the third act. Jemmy knew peeking through the canvas was not her assigned post; so she left, albeit reluctantly, for the place where she belonged. One fact penetrated her consciousness as she moved in the direction of the ready tent. The ground in front of the entrance, which had been so full of thundering life, was now deserted.

Where had they all gone? Everyone from the troupe who could be spared was in the stands, yes; but where were police Chief Prentice's men? Where were Deputy Futcher and the others from the sheriff's office?

Jemmy changed direction in midstride.

She walked across the hoof-marked ground to the ticket wagons. *Surely some people are inside toting up the evening's receipts.* The ticket windows had been shuttered, so she walked to the back of the wagon. As she raised her hand to knock on the door, a familiar voice stopped her.

"Damn me. If it isn't the big-city reporter all done up in men's clothes. Not very lady-like. I wonder how little brother would feel about kissing a girl with a woolly worm on her lip."

Jemmy turned around to see Duke, big as life and twice as ugly. He held a revolver — but this time he wasn't drunk. She could think of nothing better to say than, "You're missing the show. It's inside the arena."

He arched his eyebrows. "You're mistaken. The real show is out here."

His snarl turned into something akin to a smile. "For once you can do me a service. I must admit your being helpful will make a nice change from the bother you usually cause."

In mock obedience, Jemmy clasped her hands and dipped her head the way floor managers do at Barr's Department Store. "What service do you require, Master Marmaduke?"

Suggesting he was a child by calling him

"Master Marmaduke" instead of "Mr. Koock" may not have been the wisest course.

He pursed his lips in a scowl. "Do what you obviously planned. Go ahead. Knock on the door — and be sure they let you in."

"I had no plan to go in. I wanted to ask where the police went."

"If you're expecting help from the law, be prepared for a long wait. The police and the sheriff's men are at the Katy shops foiling an attempted break-in."

Jemmy saw the light. "You cooked up a break-in at the rail yards to draw the lawmen off — a what do you call it? A distraction. The real thievery is here. Am I right?"

"Damn me. You're not as stupid as most girls. Go on. Knock — and make sure they open the door."

"If I don't?"

"I'll shoot you. In fact, I'd take pleasure in it."

"They'd never open the door then."

A second voice she recognized chimed in. "Maybe not, but we have ways of persuading them to open." It was the skinny robber — the actual skinny robber from her trip into town. In the light spill from the show's gigantic spotlights, she could see dark bruise patches on his face from the beating he took on the train. He carried an ax in each hand.

Duke's voice took an impatient edge. "Damn me. We've talked long enough. Tell them to open the door."

Jemmy knocked. A voice from inside said, "Who's out there?"

"Miss McBustle. Mr. Butler told you about me. May I come in?"

"What fer?"

"Something is wrong out here. I want you to come and see."

"Can't you tell me?"

"It's better if you see for yourself."

"Nope. Can't come out. Can't open the door. Colonel's orders."

Jemmy shrugged her shoulders in Duke's direction. "I told you they wouldn't open up."

Duke chuckled as he aimed his pistol at her leg. "Bet they will when you start screaming."

Jemmy's mind raced to find something to do — some way to escape. She made up her mind to jump off the steps on the dark side of the wagon. She didn't get the chance.

Before she could gather her muscles for the leap, she hit the ground. She landed hard — on the lighted side of the wagon — on the wrong side.

A gunshot confirmed it. She was dying.

Somehow it wasn't at all as she had imagined.

Strange, I feel no pain, just a great boulder weight on top of my chest. It won't let me breathe. In seconds more I'll be gone.

Her eyelids fluttered and she felt herself slipping away. She expected her all-too-short life to race before her eyes. It didn't.

All at once, the weight lifted. It took her a few seconds to recognize the cause of her near suffocation. When her vision cleared, she saw him — Burnie Koock. In a flash she understood what had happened. Burnie launched himself from the dark and hit her in a flying tackle. Both landed on the ground — with her on the bottom. Her head felt like a balloon leaking air.

Burnie's hand pulled her to her feet. "Nothing to fear now, Miss McBustle. When you and my stepmother didn't join us, Aunt Tilly and I came looking for you. She batted down Duke's gun and he ran off along with another fellow."

As she quick-stepped toward them, Aunt Tilly's voice shrilled, "Jemima Gormlaith McBustle, is that you? What on earth are you doing out here letting boys shoot at you and throw you to the ground?"

Burnie swatted feebly at the dust on Jemmy's coattails.

Auntie stuck her pince-nez on her nose and fairly screeched, "In men's clothes? I am more appalled than I can express. You will resume your proper wardrobe and station immediately."

While seeking the words to convince Aunt Tilly her demand was impossible, Jemmy raised her arms. She gasped in horror at what she saw. The backs of her hands were sticky with clots of darkening blood. She looked at them dumbstruck, then began to search for the cause.

Burnie took her hands in his. "Please, Miss McBustle, don't be alarmed. It's not your blood. It's mine." He crumpled to the ground. The wounded boy apologized for his ungentlemanly action. "It would seem my legs will no longer hold me. I'm sorry to make such a spectacle of myself."

She looked down in amazement. "Did Duke shoot you?"

"I couldn't let him shoot you, now could I?"

She barely recognized the wispy voice coming from her own mouth. "Aunt Tilly, Burnie's brother shot him."

"Truly, young man. Where is your wound? Let me see it."

"You mustn't trouble yourself, ma'am. It's

in a place where I couldn't allow you to look."

"Indeed." Aunt Tilly raised her head to avoid any hint of a presumptuous glance in Burnie's direction. With her cane, she poked Jemmy's chin up. "Mustn't stare, my girl."

To Burnie she said, "I quite understand your reluctance to have me attend you. Perhaps you might not deem amiss some advice."

"I'd welcome your advice, Miss Snodderly."

"You may call me Aunt Tilly. I trust your handkerchief is clean. Can you reach it?"

"Yes ma'am."

"Can you tie it around your injured limb above the wound?"

"Yes, ma'am. Yes, Aunt Tilly."

"The tourniquet should reduce the bleeding. Loosen it every few minutes. I'll tell you when." She inspected her watch and uttered a cheerful, "Well, we must get you the proper medical attention in short order."

Burnie offered, "The Katy hospital is not nearby. Perhaps you'd be kind enough to find help. I don't believe I can walk so far."

"Lie still, young man. I will see to everything."

With the silver head of her cane, Aunt Tilly pounded on the door of the ticket office and received the same answer Jemmy had. They would not come out or let anyone in. She pounded again and insisted. "We have an injured man who requires immediate medical attention. Surely you don't plan to just let him die."

"Dying would be his plan, not mine. Got nothing to do with me."

Aunt Tilly pounded again. "Are you quite sure you won't give the young man succor?"

"I've got my orders."

"You're forcing me to take sterner measures."

Then Aunt Tilly did an amazing thing. She picked up both axes and handed one to Jemmy, then led her around to the ticket windows in the front. Aunt Tilly hoisted her ax to her shoulder and sent a mighty blow through a pair of shutters.

Aunt Tilly cocked her head expectantly in Jemmy's direction. "You needn't be surprised, my dear. I've had the pleasure of wielding an ax in the service of sobriety with Mrs. Carrie Nation." The pair of unlikely lumberjacks hacked through the shutters and sills.

When the glass shattered, the folks inside reconsidered. They came outside armed and ready to confiscate the axes. A trio of men in sleeve garters took a few minutes to grasp what they saw. Oddly dressed Jemmy, oddly upright old maid, and oddly merry wounded boy flummoxed them. The ticket men stared for at least two minutes before they offered to help.

They hitched horses to the ticket wagon and placed Burnie atop burlap sacks on the floor inside. With ramrod-straight back, Aunt Tilly seated herself on the safe.

Burnie held out a hand toward Jemmy. "I'd be obliged if you'd take my hand."

Jemmy felt like a traitor to refuse. After all, Burnie had taken a bullet for her. He probably saved her life. She promised herself to do something nice for him, but that would have to wait.

"I only wish I could go with you. Aunt Tilly says, and rightly so, I must change clothes. I'm sure she'll see you get the best of care. I promise to visit you as soon as I can."

Aunt Tilly agreed. "Lilburn, my boy, Miss Jemima will be along soon — and properly dressed for a hospital call. I'm sure her presence will ease your discomfort. If she were to come with us now, she would add embarrassment for her inappropriate garb to the pain she has already caused you."

As the wagon rolled out of sight, Jemmy picked up the revolver Duke had stolen. The gun was something of an antique. Dorothea had called it a Civil War relic — an 1860 light Colt — whatever that meant.

Jemmy knew enough to place a bulletless chamber under the firing pin. Lessons from Annie were already paying off.

She dusted the pistol off and tried to twirl it around her finger as she had seen some of the vaqueros do. She twirled it all right — right off her finger and back into the dust. Fortunately no one was watching.

She dusted the gun off again and stuck it in the pocket of Frank Butler's second-best frock coat. It promptly fell into the dust. For a third time she dusted it off. This time she tucked it securely inside an inner pocket.

It banged against her leg as she turned toward the ready tent. She stopped noticing the gun as she concentrated on what to tell Dorothea. Should she say anything at all? The scene had been so sordid. Duke had tried to shoot Jemmy and ended up shooting his brother instead.

Uglier still, Jemmy had lied and sent Aunt Tilly off to the hospital to nursemaid Burnie. One thing she could be thankful for — Aunt Tilly must have been too distressed by Jemmy's masculine attire to question Dorothea's whereabouts.

Jemmy had no intention whatever of telling his stepmother the boy had been shot. Well, there it was. She had to face another nasty truth about herself. "The plan" mattered more to her than her friend's feelings. Dorothea would probably never forgive her, especially not if she knew Jemmy's real reason for keeping her friend in the dark.

The story was still out there. The robbers were still out there. The assassin was still out there, and Hal was still missing. This was not the time to give up or give in. This was no time to mess with a plan — a plan that, however improbable, might yet work.

CHAPTER TWENTY-ONE:

THE WILD WEST FAIRGROUNDS
SEDALIA
FRIDAY EVENING, SEPTEMBER 23, 1898

As the saying goes, the show must go on. And it did. On and on and on — steamrolling Jemmy's hopes into flat despair. Her belief in "the plan" crashed a thousand times or more.

Look what I've done. I've set hundreds of people off on a snipe hunt. When this is over and no assassin is in jail, Annie and Frank — all the show people — will tell me things are all right. Sweet words to my face, but behind my back they'll call me anything but nice. They'll kick themselves for listening to a silly girl and vow never to be taken in again by any would-be newspaperwoman.

And what have I done to the Koocks? Sent Burnie away with a false promise. He was bleeding — maybe dying — from a bullet meant for me. And Dorothea. I gave her the impossible job of pretending to be Annie Oakley.

What else did I go and do? I went out of my

way not to tell her Burnie had been shot —
Burnie, her stepson. Why did I do such a
heartless thing? To be kind? To spare her feel-
ings? No, I did it because my plan would fail
without her. What kind of a villainess am I?

Jemmy bemoaned her bad deeds as she
waited for the assassin to appear. Her
anxiety grew as the show acts performed
one by one. She ticked them off on her
program — Pony Express ride, bucking
horses, burro races, war dances, steer lasso-
ing, Rough Riders from around the world.
Before the buffalo chase and stagecoach
rescue, Johnny Baker took the colonel's
place as Custer at the Battle of the Little
Bighorn.

Jemmy prayed to hear the all-clear signal.
Whoever caught the assassin would wave a
bandana to a roustabout on the arena floor.
That man would relay the signal to Mr.
Bailey in the lighting room atop the grandstand. Bailey would shift his spotlight to the
band.

When the light hit the bandleader,
Sweeney would strike up a chorus of "Hot
Time in the Old Town" on his cornet. The
song would signal everyone to relax —
problem solved. She had not heard those
longed-for horn toots.

At length, no more acts preened in the

ready tent. Jemmy and Dorothea were alone except for Marm Whittaker, camp nurse and mother hen. Marm's well-intentioned mothering missed the mark. Events addled the poor woman's wits. She didn't understand that Dorothea planned to shoot in Annie's stead.

Marm patted Dorothea's hand, "Don't worry. Annie Oakley can shoot a fly a mile off."

Guilty conscience made Jemmy envy Marm's innocence. She felt small and insignificant as the day she walked through the heavy oak doors of prestigious Mary Institute. She was once again the poor girl whose mother ran a boardinghouse — enrolled only through the largesse of a rich aunt.

Somehow she had managed to find backbone enough to compete with the richest, snobbiest girls in St. Louis.

And here she was again. These portals were canvas and the choice had been her own, but the dread felt exactly the same. With a knot around her stomach and a vague premonition of evil, she sat up straight in the pony cart as the arena flaps parted. The moment of truth had arrived.

Dorothea blew her a kiss for luck, then skipped into the arena amidst a raucous stomping and cheering. Jemmy's spirits rose. With a deep breath, she smacked the reins on the pony's rump.

She pushed panic aside with a positive thought. *Miss Jemima McBustle had worked hard and done well at "Mary I" — exceedingly well for a boardinghouse daughter sponging off the charity of her rich aunt and uncle. Jemmy had performed brilliantly, or at least passably, in finery borrowed from Auntie Dee.*

She simply had to do it again with "finery" provided from Frank Butler.

Assailed by the smells of oiled leather and horse urine, Jemmy drove the prop cart to its proper spot and managed to stop — mostly because the pony knew what to do. She set the brake, then hopped out. She took the wooden crate filled with glass balls to her mark while Dorothea waved and blew kisses toward the grandstand.

In the blinding spotlights, the crowd became a vast dark mass of noise spewing disembodied shouts. But somewhere in that faceless clump of humanity lurked evil.

Jemmy quashed the thought. *I must have all my concentration focused on the here and now.*

Their routine started with easy tricks. She threw up a single glass ball that gleamed iridescent green in the white light until

Dorothea blew it out of existence. Dorothea imitated the Oakley back-kick of triumph. Applause from the audience lacked enthusiasm. Jemmy threw up two balls and Dorothea popped both into smithereens — to more polite applause.

Jemmy was about to sail three more balls into the air, but her hand stopped as if clamped in an unseen vise. A new person skipped into the arena. Jemmy stood riveted to the ground staring squarely at a second Annie Oakley.

Jemmy felt relief at the quick rescue, but at the same time wondered why Annie should be coming out so soon. Dorothea had hit every target. The crowd had not turned against the pretenders, at least not yet. Sweeney's band had not played the all-clear tune. The assassin had not been caught. *Why was Annie taking over?*

Then she looked more closely. The girl wasn't Annie. In fact, the girl wasn't even a girl. A realization struck her mute with surprise. Dorothea wasn't the only person pretending to be Annie Oakley. The skinny train robber was acting the selfsame charade.

The costume looked real enough. *Had the skinny bank robber raided Annie's wardrobe? If he did, he must not have examined himself in a mirror.* On a fellow more than a foot taller than Annie, the clothes produced odd results. The shirt front was at least three inches too scant to tuck into the skirt.

Embroidered leggings didn't come up far enough over Boy-Annie's knobby knees to meet the leather skirt. His astonishing and scandalous amount of skinny white thigh drew catcalls. The crowd gasped at the effrontery — nudity in a family show? What was the world coming to?

Then a storm of unlikely events collided around Jemmy. In an eyeblink, a matronly woman in lavender appeared from who-knows-where. She commenced poking at the naked thighs of Boy-Annie with a hat pin.

As if Dorothea-Annie and Boy-Annie weren't Annies enough, a third Annie materialized from out of nowhere. Annie number three, a pudgy Annie, pointed a pistol straight at Dorothea's head.

Jemmy regained control and came to point like an Irish setter after a duck. She lunged toward her hostess to knock Dorothea to the ground. At the same instant a shot rang out. In the hush that followed, Jemmy could hear a thud as Pudgy-Annie dropped her pistol. The woman turned on her heel and ran. Yet another Annie chased after the Annie who shot at Dorothea.

Annie number four emerged from behind the settler's cabin in the middle of the arena. She was none other than the real Annie Oakley — the genuine article sprinting at top speed.

Pandemonium erupted. Hundreds of Rough Riders raced after the Annies. The exit of the thundering horde left the arena devoid of action except for just two people — Jemmy and Dorothea.

Dorothea pulled her rescuer to her feet with a hug. She smudged the dust on Jemmy's cheek with a kiss. "Jemmy, you're a heroine."

"The tackle was a little trick I learned from Burnie."

"I'll never forget you saved my life."

"Don't mention it. Burnie saved my life. I saved yours. I'd say we're even."

Dorothea looked puzzled. "All the same, the bullet meant for me could have hit you."

As the pair of pretend-Butlers stumbled off the field, Johnny Baker galloped into the arena with a big grin on his face. He stopped in front of the governor's box and waved his hat while his horse bowed low as if the previous excitement had been staged for the pleasure of the audience. The crowd exploded in noise. Johnny was a real trouper and used to improvising.

In the newspaper articles she wrote later, Jemmy sorted out events in this fashion. When Boy-Annie — scantily dressed — set foot inside the arena, Lulu Cody sailed down the steps of the governor's box. She marched majestically toward Dorothea-Annie and Boy-Annie, the skinny train robber with exposed thighs. An escort formed by Lillian Smith and the magician from Lillian's vaudeville show trailed in her wake.

Next came a third Annie Oakley impostor, Pudgy-Annie. At least this one was female. But her plumpness and swarthy skin — so unlike slim, fair-complexioned Annie — betrayed her. After a long stare, Jemmy recognized the Indian maiden. This was the woman from the fakir's wagon — the same woman who'd spoken with Deputy Futcher in the Pettis County Jail. And she was aiming a pistol dead-center at the back of Dorothea's head.

The unexpected appearance of a magician, two well-dressed ladies in lavender, and four Annie Oakleys on the arena grass startled the Wild West troupe into action. They left their watching posts in the stands and threw themselves on the field. Soon hundreds of people were running toward the commotion near the main tent flaps.

They needn't have bothered.

Lulu and her entourage met the challenge. Jemmy helped a little. She used the flying tackle so recently learned from Burnie to bring Dorothea to ground and out of harm's way.

Lillian Smith grabbed Dorothea-Annie's rifle from the ground and neatly blew the pistol out of the hands of Pudgy-Annie before the woman could fire. Lillian proved her skill, a very good thing indeed. Pudgy-Annie produced a second pistol and leveled it at Dorothea for another try.

Dorothea and Jemmy were still scrambling on the ground when Lillian Smith blasted the second gun out of the impostor's hand as neatly as she had the first.

Bested at every turn, Pudgy-Annie lit out toward the exit. The real Annie Oakley, who could run a hundred yards in thirteen seconds, blazed out of hiding and crossed the arena in hot pursuit.

Meanwhile, Lulu demanded obedience from the Boy-Annie of the indecent skirt with her hatpin. His yowlps added to the general confusion.

Who would think more surprise could be possible after all these singular events? But there it was. The magician had another trick to pull out of his hat — a Pinkerton badge.

As the Wild West troupe closed in on the melee, he peeled off his mustache and held his badge aloft.

When the Wild West staff Pinkertons recognized a fellow Pinkerton, they escorted Boy-Annie out of the arena and into the cook tent. Dorothea and Jemmy — still in borrowed clothes — tagged along.

Speedy as Annie Oakley was, she couldn't outrace a horse. Pudgy-Annie had one waiting. It was just as well. Real-Annie and Frank had a shooting act to do, but not before they vouched for Dorothea and Jemmy to Police Chief Prentice. At last, the law had arrived to demand answers.

The chief said, "Attempted robbery of the Katy office, Annie Oakleys pointing guns and shooting at each other. I've never seen the like." He turned to the Pinkertons. "What's going on here?"

The Pinkerton-magician suggested, "Perhaps Mrs. Cody should start by explaining why she's here tonight."

Lulu said, "I have lived in a state of alarm for more than a month. I feared someone was trying to bring ruin to the Wild West." She dropped her head, "At first, I thought someone was trying to kill me. My husband and I, along with Mr. Baker, were exploring a cave near Hannibal. You know, the one

Mark Twain wrote about in *Tom Sawyer*. While we were inside the cave, a gunshot wounded me."

She pushed up her sleeve to show a bright pink scar. "As you can see, the wound is not bad, but enough to give considerable fright. I must admit, I even entertained the possibility Mr. Cody himself might want me out of the way."

Police Chief Prentice sounded appalled to hear the great hero Buffalo Bill might do such a deed. "Surely you are not implying your husband would do you harm."

Lulu held up her hands and brushed them back and forth to erase the picture from the air. "I no longer think so, Chief Prentice. However, I went to the Pinkertons for that very reason.

"I changed my mind when I received two Pinkerton telegrams. Agency reports made me understand other evils plague the Wild West," Lulu said quietly. "I want my husband to live, Chief Prentice. I may wish he would stay home with greater fidelity, but whatever threatens him, threatens me."

She raised her head, "Unfortunately, the Pinkertons were unable to do much because the recent attacks seemed random. It occurred to me that someone might be targeting the show itself. I came down here to see personally — after persuading Mr. Cody not to perform on this particular Friday."

Chief Prentice did not sound entirely convinced. "Now we know why you and the Pinkerton came. Miss Smith, why did you come to Sedalia?"

"Mr. Butler caused quite a stir at my theater. When I had an unexpected day off, I came to see the Wild West. I treasure my reputation with people in the theatrical world. I wanted to clear my good name with the Rough Riders — my friends — people I've admired and respected for more than a decade.

"I discovered the magician was a Pinkerton pretending to be a fellow actor in my company. I thought Butler sent him to spy on me. I confronted him. He said we might be able to help each other. He was right."

She nodded toward Dorothea. "I saved her life twice. Before you ask, I knew she was too tall and shapely to be Annie. And yes, I would have also saved Annie Oakley."

"Now we come to the pair of you." Chief Prentice's head turned to Dorothea and Jemmy. "If this whole affair had not involved gunplay, I'd laugh hard enough to bust my galluses at the sight of you."

He yanked off Jemmy's mustache and examined it. "A slip of a girl with rolled-up trousers and a horsetail mustache pretending to be Frank Butler? What's that black thing on your head?"

Jemmy unpinned the black cloth. Loosened from the turban, Jemmy's auburn tresses tumbled down and stuck in clumps to the spirit gum left on her lip. She tried to pull the hair off, but only a strand at a time would come loose. People snickered — the ones who didn't laugh out loud. Jemmy's nose itched so unmercifully she wished one of the Annies had shot it off. But she was not about to give anyone the satisfaction of seeing her scratch.

Jemmy was still trying to extricate her lip from her hair as Chief Prentice turned to Dorothea with a sad shake of his head. "Mrs. Koock, respected member of the community and organizer of last week's ice cream social at the First Methodist Church, I never expected to see you like this — showing your legs — shooting on exhibition like a common entertainer — pretending to be Annie Oakley."

He shook his finger at her. "Does your husband know what you're up to?"

From the back of the tent boomed a familiar voice. "Mrs. Koock has my full permission and encouragement to undertake anything she believes she can accomplish." Obadiah Koock strode toward the front of the tent.

Bright red rivulets of blood oozed down his forehead and spread in garish tentacles down his right cheek. Marm Whittaker hustled off for the first aid box. Dorothea paled and put her hands to her face.

She ran to her husband and insisted he sit on a bench. Obadiah said, "A bit of trouble at the rail yards. You needn't worry. Scalp wounds look more damaging than they are because they bleed more." He smiled when he said it, though, and took her hand. "I wish I could have been here to see you shoot. I heard you hit every target."

Shyly, Dorothea nodded to affirm her prowess.

The tent flaps opened again to the noise and chatter of the Rough Riders returning from their night's performance.

Chief Prentice was not happy to see them. "Get those people out of here. I'm conducting a police investigation. Leave before I stick every single one of you in jail for obstructing justice."

Johnny Baker refused to let anyone enter except the Butlers. He raised his hands and yelled to the noisy mob of performers. "You know what the colonel would have us do. Go to your own tents or the ready tent."

A voice protested, "Ain't no sandwiches and lemonade at the ready tent."

Marm Whittaker helped shoo them out. "Ain't no sandwiches here, either. We ain't been able to make none. Reckon you'll have to do without this one time."

After the crowd cleared, Police Chief Prentice sounded even more impatient. "If you please, Mrs. Koock. Why are you and this other female pretending to be the Butlers?"

With her hair almost under control, Jemmy piped up, "It was my idea. After someone shot at the true Annie Oakley this afternoon, I convinced the Butlers to let Dorothea and me take their place while they searched for the shootist. But surely you know as much already. We sent word."

"I received no word. I would never have countenanced such a hare-brained scheme. I'm shocked the Butlers and Mr. Baker took it seriously."

Jemmy picked spirit gum off her lip and snapped back at him. "A convenient absence, to be sure. Nary a one of your men tried to stop the attempted robbery of the ticket wagons."

"I'd spend my time better by arresting you than I would by answering your impertinence. However, I have nothing to hide from anyone. Let me make the facts perfectly clear. I always station men at big events to keep the wagons from tangling up and blocking the streets, but only before and after the performance. I had no idea anything was amiss during the show."

"But surely Deputy Futcher warned . . ." She didn't get the whole sentence finished before two other pairs of boots came striding into the tent. The boots carried familiar faces. Deputy Futcher shoved before him a pouting boy, a stout boy with a bad case of acne.

The deputy said, "I caught this Koock boy trying to rob the ticket wagon." He pointed to the skinny boy with the bare thighs, one of the Annie Oakley impersonators. "That there is his partner. I've come to take them off your hands."

Chief Prentice bristled at the interruption. "Hold on, Deputy. I have a few questions for the young — I started to say 'man,' in the skirt." He smirked. " 'Man' doesn't seem the right word, and it's for sure his skirt doesn't quite cover the subject."

Chief Prentice looked around for a laugh or a chuckle. When none came, he sent a sour stare in the direction of Boy-Annie. "Where did you find such a ridiculous get-up?"

The boy stared at Futcher long enough to make Futcher impatient. The deputy boomed out, "Well, go on. Tell the chief. And I want you to tell him the truth, hear?"

Boy-Annie of the scandalous thighs said, "I pinched the clothes from Annie Oakley's tent."

Chief Prentice asked, "Why on earth did you go into the arena dressed like the star of the show? Surely you didn't expect to fool anyone into believing you to be Annie Oakley."

Boy-Annie looked at Futcher. The young man's chin sagged to his chest. "I was supposed to cause a ruckus. Make noise and upset things so nobody would pay attention to the goings-on outside."

Chief Prentice said, "It's a good thing to confess right up front, young man. The court will take your cooperation into account. The only other thing I need from you is the names of the people who were in on the robbery with you."

Futcher burst in with, "That's easy, Chief." He turned to the boy. "You were in cahoots with the Koock boy. He was the ringleader. Go on, tell the chief."

Chief Prentice lost his temper at the deputy's interference. "I asked the boy, not you. Let him answer for himself."

The boy nodded toward the deputy. "It's what he said. Duke told me what to do and I done it best I could."

Futcher moved to grab Boy-Annie. "You come with me and no monkey business or I'll give you what for."

The whole incident struck a false note with Jemmy, though she couldn't quite put her finger on the reason. Still, she had to do something. As often happened when she needed it most, a good lie sprang to her lips. "Chief Prentice, Deputy Futcher was the one who promised to inform you about our plan. I'd be interested in knowing why he didn't tell you."

"No one told me to tell Chief Prentice nothing." Futcher edged Duke and Boy-Annie backward toward the tent entrance.

Jemmy managed to think of a genuine flaw in the deputy's story. "Ask Mr. Futcher why the Annie who got away, the one who shot at Dorothea, was in his jail cell yesterday — and the door wasn't even locked."

Futcher dropped his hold on both boys and took off running with the Pinkerton-magician hard after. Duke froze like a treed possum. Mr. Koock nabbed him with ease. As for Boy-Annie, Lillian Smith twisted his arm behind him while Lulu warned him with a scowl and a raised hatpin.

Chief Prentice motioned for Lulu to back away. To Boy-Annie he said, "I'm through mollycoddling you. I will get real answers, true answers to my questions or I'll turn Mrs. Cody loose with her hatpin."

He pulled Boy-Annie away from Lillian Smith and shoved him down on a bench. The chief stuck his face up to the boy's nose. The skinny robber cowered until his back pressed against the table edge. Prentice hissed, "Now talk."

Boy-Annie's words came out in a flood. "Futcher got up a gang of boy robbers because he said we'd think robbing folks was a lark — said we'd be famous like Cole Younger and his brothers or the James boys. I didn't think it was much fun after we got thrown off the train on Tuesday. But once Futcher gets hold of a fellow, he won't let go.

"I figured I'd run away, but I needed money. I said I'd help rob the ticket wagons. I was gonna use my share to get as far away from Futcher as the railroad system would take me." He nodded in Jemmy's direction. "I would have done it, too, but that girl with the red hair keeps getting in the way."

Lulu had questions, too. "How were you planning to make money from shooting Little Elk?"

The boy looked blank. "I don't know nothing 'bout shooting no elk."

She waved her hatpin at him.

He protested, "It's true. We never shot at nobody in the Wild West Show — not ever. I don't know nothing about no shooting."

Frank asked, "Where were you Tuesday night when Little Elk was wounded?"

"Here in town at Doctor Overstreet's office. We were some beat up, I can tell you." His voice cracked. "Why don't you get yourself throwed off a train? Then you'd know what a real beating feels like."

Chief Prentice backed away so Boy-Annie could sit up. "Easy enough to check his alibi. Dr. Overstreet is the mayor of Sedalia."

He turned to Duke. "What do you have to say for yourself, young man?"

Duke said nothing until Mr. Koock boxed his ears. "Tuesday night we were all at the doctor's office on Ohio Street."

Chief Prentice stroked his chin. "Let me get straight who was at Overstreet's — Young Marmaduke Koock, Deputy Futcher, this fake Annie Oakley with the short skirt here, and who else?"

"Two other boys."

"Nobody else?"

"No."

Lulu shook her head. "So we haven't caught the person who has been terrorizing the Wild West."

Chief Prentice said, "Apparently we haven't, but you may be sure we'll apprehend Futcher and the other two boys. I have pointed questions for them and for Sheriff Williams, too, as a matter of fact."

To Obadiah, Chief Prentice said, "We'll have to take your boy, Mr. Koock. Needless to say, I'm sorry it's necessary."

"I understand, Chief Prentice. You must do what you must do."

Chief Prentice collected Duke and the Boy-Annie skinny robber. As he shoved them toward the tent opening, Jemmy hit her forehead with the heel of her hand.

She spun Boy-Annie around and fairly screamed at him. "What have you done with Hal?"

He jerked his head back to look over his shoulder. Not until he spied Lulu returning her hatpin to her hat a comfortable distance away did he answer. "I haven't done nothing with nobody named Hal — never met him."

Jemmy stomped the ground, narrowly missing Boy-Annie's toe. She whirled to Duke, grabbed the shoulder of his jacket, and shrieked in his ear. "I know you did something with Hal. He found out what you've been up to so you took him off somewhere." Duke's expression was blank as a plaster wall.

Mr. Koock said, "If you know the whereabouts of Miss McBustle's photographer, you must confess it. Your cooperation will give me some small reason to permit you what aid I can. I trust you would appreciate my help in settling the difficulties you've made for yourself."

Duke said, "I haven't seen Dwyer since the night he dragged me out of the Maple Leaf Club."

"Your actions have given your stepmother and me nothing but pain and disappointment. I blame myself for not seeing the truth sooner. You had every possible advantage any parents could give. It simply never occurred to me that a child of mine would become a criminal." Obadiah looked squarely at his eldest son. "On pain of disownment if I should discover you know anything at all about Mr. Dwyer, do you swear to the truth of your statement?"

"Yes, sir. I do."

The mass of people left Jemmy standing dejectedly as they filed out of the tent. Even the Koocks seemed too distracted — Obadiah by Duke's predicament and Dorothea by Obadiah's bleeding scalp — to notice they were leaving Jemmy behind and alone. She couldn't have explained why she didn't trail after them, what unfinished business held her back.

In the deafening silence, she looked down at Frank Butler's boots. She vented her frustration with a kick to a clump of grass and watched as dust settled to turn the black toes brown.

A new presence in the tent sent a shudder through her shoulders. Whether fear or anticipation, she could not tell.

From the back of the tent came a voice Jemmy had heard before. "I know where Hal is."

Chapter Twenty-Two

Jemmy saw a skinny fellow of the same size and shape as the skinny train robber who pretended to be Annie Oakley. *This can't be the same boy. Chief Prentice hustled Boy-Annie off to jail.*

By the bruise on this fellow's chin, she knew he had to be the man Hal slugged at the Maple Leaf Club. The same man had dragged her into an alley by the Coffee Cup Café — John who-smells-like-apples John. This was a completely different man, not the train robber. This was the ragtime music lover.

She wanted to run but felt compelled to stay no matter how many alarm bells rang in her head. The pair stood alone in the cavernous tent. Her legs ached to carry her out front to Dorothea — to the safe haven of Obadiah's protection. She stood straight and still as a fencepost.

John spoke louder. "Didn't you hear me?

I said I know the whereabouts of the man you're searching for, that photographer fellow."

"Why didn't you bring him with you?"

"He's being held prisoner."

"Why would anyone want to imprison Hal?"

"He poked his camera where it wasn't wanted."

"Is he all right?"

"As all right as anybody tied up more than a day is apt to be. He was alive when last I saw him."

"When was that?"

"Three or four hours ago."

"Come on. We have to catch Chief Prentice before he takes his prisoners to jail." She started jogging toward the front of the tent.

He raised his voice. "I think not."

Jemmy stopped short and spun back to face him. "Why not?"

"If police came around, the people who tied up your photographer would harm him."

"What makes you think they haven't hurt him already?"

"Maybe they have."

"Then why am I talking to you?" She turned on her heel, but stopped short. "We

365

have to let Chief Prentice handle this."

"Can't. Bringing in police would put your friend in danger."

Jemmy started for the exit. "I am going after Chief Prentice. He'll know what to do."

"What could you tell him? You don't know where to find your pal."

In her excitement at recognizing the skinny robber's double, she had forgotten one crucial bit of information — her own ignorance. She called over her shoulder, "So, would you be so kind as to tell me where Hal is?"

"No. But I'll take you there."

Jemmy knew she should be afraid. She could hear Aunt Tilly saying that no man would try to entice a sweet young thing away from her protectors unless he had something sinister in mind. Yet she found herself more drawn to this man than afraid of him. "What can a girl like me accomplish the police couldn't?"

He moved closer to her and spoke in the same sweet tones he had used to persuade her to come with him down a dark alley by a Main Street saloon to listen to ragtime music. "Get Hal to cooperate. Our best chance to get him away free and safe is to use stealth."

As Jemmy turned toward him, the scent

of warm apples addled her reason. At length, she pulled her wits together enough to point at John's bruised chin. "Why would you want to save Hal? I saw the two of you together. He belted you in the stomach, cracked your jaw, and knocked you out cold."

"That's exactly why he wouldn't trust me — that and the fact that I've been pretending to be one of the bad guys. He trusts you, doesn't he?"

"You avoided my question. Why do you want to help Hal?"

"I don't want him on my conscience. If I bust in with guns blazing, your friend is apt to get killed. Know this. I get paid whether he stays in one piece or not, but I want him to come out alive."

"Paid? Who pays you to pretend to be a crook?"

"I work for the Pinkerton Agency. Mrs. Cody hired me to find out who shot at her in a cave near Hannibal — and to get evidence that would stand up in court. She intends to have justice. She wants to prosecute the person or persons who have been terrorizing the Wild West."

"Mrs. Cody didn't hire you. She hired some magician fellow."

"He's a Pinkerton, too. Perhaps Colonel

Cody or someone else hired him. I don't know. I've been spying on behalf of Mrs. Cody for some time — though I've never had the pleasure of meeting my employer."

"Why should I believe any of what you're telling me?"

He produced a folded paper and a badge with a staring Pinkerton Eye and the Pinkerton motto, "We Never Sleep."

"Does this convince you?"

The paper looked like a genuine license signed by Robert and William Pinkerton. But what if it were forged or stolen?

At least the paper did tell her something she longed to know — his real name. Jemmy stared at the name until it became black blurs on white paper. "Mr. Dollarhide, I don't know . . ."

Jemmy clasped her hands together to keep them from trembling. Whether from excitement at seeing him or fear of what he wanted her to do, she could not tell. In her heart, she knew she would have to take the risk.

Pulse racing, she inhaled a deep breath. "Where do I fit in your 'stealth' plan?"

"I think you can sneak him away before his captors know he's gone. Then, I will do my job."

"Just what would that job be?"

"Make up your mind. We have to free him tonight. I mean to capture the murderers. Yes, I called them 'murderers.' I mean to take them prisoner before they leave town — which they plan to do in the morning."

"What will they do with Hal if you don't catch them before morning?"

"I honestly don't know, but they've killed before. I don't think they'd let Hal live — not considering all he knows."

"So why haven't they killed him already?"

"He's their ace in the hole. If they need to, they can use him as hostage."

Jemmy's courage faltered. "I have to speak to the Koocks."

"They would get in the way." John heaved a sigh. "I can't wait. Make up your mind. We have only one hour, two at the most." He paused for her answer. When she gave none, he turned to leave.

Over his shoulder he called, "A real journalist would walk barefoot through broken glass for a story like this."

Jemmy wavered until he reached the back of the tent. "Wait, I'll come."

Her thoughts jumbled as she trotted toward him. *What am I letting myself in for? What else can I do? Hal wouldn't be missing now but for me. I can't just leave him in trouble. More than once Hal has come to my rescue.*

John pulled up a tent wall high enough for them to crawl under. The pair slipped out into a damp chill. The blackness seemed all wrong. Was it only minutes earlier the big carbon arc spotlights spilled enough rays outside the arena to see by?

Her eyes had not adjusted to the dark when John handed her the reins of a smallish horse. She couldn't make out its color in the inky night, but the tang of Watkins liniment from the horse's bandaged knee crinkled her nose. She shivered and wished she had a shawl.

The heavy Colt in her inner pocket banged her leg as she mounted. She took comfort from its presence. It might come in handy.

Jemmy wanted to know how John planned to free Hal. When she opened her mouth, he shushed her. "No talking. We don't want anyone to notice us."

Jemmy chafed to know why John Dollarhide would care whether they were recognized. He gave her no voice and no choice. All she could do was follow his dark shadow.

The twosome avoided well-lighted places in favor of residential streets and alleys. But even when they crossed brick thoroughfares, the horses' shoes made soft clops instead of clacking noises. *John must have muffled the hooves.*

They plodded along without talking as they traveled east, then north past the Katy station. At the Washington Street viaduct by the Missouri Pacific signal yard, they turned west along the tracks. John motioned for her to dismount. She followed his example and tied her horse to a bridge strut. Smoke on a breeze from a distant wood fire made her shiver.

Jemmy felt her muscles tense. Her night vision cleared. Shapes of buildings loomed against the night sky in stark relief. She could even read white lettering on brick walls over loading docks.

Her muscles ached with tension as she placed each foot carefully so as not to dislodge telltale cinders. The pair slithered along buildings as they edged to the back of Blocher's Feed Store.

No piano music filled the night air with ragged rhythm from its upstairs tenant. The Maple Leaf Club had disgorged its last patrons. Not a single light remained to tell of the evening's gaiety. Only the echo of laughter of prostitutes from Main Street's Battle Row offered a hollow suggestion of life in the dark stillness.

John pointed to a canvas-covered wagon as he whispered, "Hal — in there." Jemmy recognized it as the medicine show wagon she had seen in front of the Pettis County Jail, the one with the stage where John Dollarhide had pretended to be an Indian fakir — and where a pudgy woman played the role of an Indian princess braiding her hair. Jemmy's face flushed hot in the chilly air as she realized how fearsome the people inside the wagon really were. In there — with Hal all tied up — was the plump dark woman who tried to shoot Dorothea twice.

Jemmy burned to know why. *Why would the woman want to harm Dorothea — or Annie Oakley, if she mistook Dorothea for the great markswoman?* "Why —" came to her tongue.

"Ssh." John Dollarhide cut off her question. He put his hand over her mouth to demand her silence. Jemmy's heart beat faster as he pulled her toward the wagon. Leaving the security of solid brick walls made Jemmy lightheaded. She felt as if she were being pushed too high in a swing.

The seconds felt like hours as she bent her knees and crept to the rear of the wagon. Jemmy nearly passed out when her foot sliding in loose gravel made a grating sound followed by a long splushing sound. John's hand locked hers in an iron grip while the pair listened for any sound from inside. Nothing changed. His grasp loosened and they oozed forward again.

When they reached the back of the wagon, John pressed the hilt of a Bowie knife into her hand. Panic surged up her spine. *Am I supposed to use this? Does he expect me to kill somebody?*

Don't be stupid, Jemmy. He gave me the

knife to free Hal — to cut ropes.

John knelt to offer his knee as a step. *This is it — the moment of action. Hal's life is in my hands — and so is my own.*

She took John's outstretched hand to steady herself as she perched her right foot on the ledge and pushed herself up. She shut her eyes and tried to imagine her next move. Never once did she let herself wonder why a brave Pinkerton should be goading a girl into heroics instead of performing those heroics himself.

She clung to the canvas and fumbled for the support rod, then raised her left foot by inches until it cleared the drop gate. She eased one boot into the wagon until her toes found firm footing. *So far, so good.*

From the front of the wagon some fifteen feet away came loud snoring. With one leg dangling off the back of the wagon, she peered inside. Even though her eyes had grown accustomed to the dark, she couldn't see Hal. When something moved at her foot, she nearly fell backward out of the wagon. Terror robbed her voice. She couldn't even scream.

Get ahold of yourself. It was just a dog, or maybe . . . She pulled her other leg inside the wagon and knelt down. Her foot had found not a dog, but Hal trussed up like a roast chicken. Behind his back, his feet had been tied to his hands in what had to be a most uncomfortable backward cradle.

So far, so good. Finding Hal had been simpler than she dared hope. She bent to his face with a finger to her lips. His nod proved he recognized her. She held the Bowie knife up so he could understand what she meant to do. She eased the knife under the rope that tied his hands to his legs and began sawing. When she severed the last strand, he straightened with a clomp.

His whole body commenced to shake like a dog coming out of a pond. She held down his legs to stop the thumping of his brogans on the wooden wagon bed.

A stab of pity brought tears to Jemmy's eyes. She realized Hal couldn't move on his own. He had been tied so long his muscles refused to work.

With no better option, she sat on his legs to keep them still and rubbed his back until it began to spasm. She stifled a nervous giggle when she imagined Aunt Tilly's reaction. *What would the Simon Legree of chaperones do if she could see Jemmy massaging a man's back — and the man no relation whatsoever?*

So far, so good. After a few minutes, Hal's spasms calmed. She began sawing through his hand ropes. *Just a little climb down from the wagon. I think we'll be able to get away. I shouldn't have doubted. John Dollarhide knows his business.*

If Jemmy were more superstitious, she would not have congratulated John and herself so soon. An unexpected twitch from Hal's hand flicked Jemmy's. The Bowie knife dropped to the wagon floor with a rattle and clank.

The snoring stopped.

Chapter Twenty-Four:

Jemmy's hands searched for the knife in the sawdust of the wagon floor. A woman's voice purred from the front of the wagon. "I wondered when someone would come to rescue your . . . What exactly is he? Your sweetheart? Your fi-on-see? Your fancy man?"

Jemmy froze. *Perhaps if I stay put, she'll go back to sleep.* Even as she hoped for a miracle, she knew none was to be.

The voice drawled on. "Not handsome enough for a fancy man, is he? But of course, some men don't need good looks. Some men have other qualities — if you know what I mean."

Jemmy found her voice as she rose. "He's an excellent photographer, if you know what I mean — and my bodyguard."

The voice chortled, "I hope he's better at taking photographs than he is at guarding bodies. He can't even guard the homely body he walks around in."

Jemmy willed herself to pretend a bravery she did not feel. She knew full well Hal was still tied hand and foot at the back of the wagon, but the woman didn't. "Go out back, Hal. The Pinkertons are waiting. I'll just stay here and continue this fascinating conversation while you show them you're all right."

Keep her talking. Talking is my best hope — after all, it worked once before — well — almost worked once before. If I can keep her talking long enough, maybe Hal's strength will return. Maybe he can find the knife and free his hands. What I must do is sound like a reporter. I can. I am a reporter.

She adopted a matter-of-fact tone. "I'm a journalist, you know. I write for the St. Louis *Illuminator.* Why don't you tell me why you had Hal wrapped up like a birthday present? I'm eager to hear your side of the story. I want to give you fair treatment in my article."

Silence reigned.

So far, not so good.

The voice drawled louder. "My dear, you're not going to write an article about me or about anyone else — not ever again."

More talk, more talk.

From the front of the wagon came bumps

378

and rustles of the kind people make while getting dressed.

Bluff. That's it.

Scraping noises of shoes on pine boards told Jemmy the woman was standing.

Bluff — bluff and stall.

Jemmy kept the stream of words flowing. "Hal, tell the officers I'd appreciate a few minutes before they come in. Say I'm trying to get the criminals to give themselves up."

Another convenient lie popped to her lips. "I don't think I'm in real danger — not with all the Pinkertons and police Chief Prentice's men surrounding the wagon. I'll stay here and get the story."

Hal lay quiet as a dead slug in a saucer of beer. "On second thought, Hal. Let's stay a bit longer. Perhaps our hostess would like to apologize before we go. You deserve at least that much."

The scrape of a match on a striker nearly caused Jemmy's knees to buckle. A man's mellow baritone offered, "Let me throw some light on the subject."

The panacea peddler lit a lantern to reveal a woman holding a pistol pointed squarely at Jemmy's chest. "Still think you're not in danger?"

The woman kept her eyes on Jemmy as she gave orders. "Scalager, take a walk outside. Search all the way up to the buildings, mind. I don't want any more surprises tonight."

Scalager grumbled, but did as he was told.

Jemmy couldn't tell which surprised her more, a woman giving orders or a man obeying them.

The woman peered toward the gloom where Hal lay. "Doesn't appear your man, fancy or plain, will be telling tales to the police." For the first time she seemed to notice John was not asleep in the wagon. "Where's Dollarhide? I might have known he'd be somewhere else when I need him."

"I'm right here." John climbed in the back of the wagon and stepped over Hal.

"What were you doing out there?"

"Something I know you wanted done — brought this nosy girl to you, and don't worry. No policemen outside."

Jemmy inhaled a whiff of sulfured air and apples. *I should have known a man who drags a girl down an alley has to be bad. Fooled again after I promised myself never to be led down the primrose path by a sweet-talking man.*

The woman damned John with faint praise. "Tricked her, did you? That's the most enterprising thing you've done since we took you on. Most of the time you're nowhere to be found when anything important comes up. Still, what makes you think bringing her here is a good idea?"

"The ugly red-haired fellow isn't worth much. He's church-mouse poor. But this one — her family is well-heeled. They'd pay a pretty penny to get her back."

"Since when have we been in the kidnap-and-ransom business?"

"Another enterprise I've been considering. Do you think I joined this snake oil show because I like smearing my face with walnut juice? It's about time I made some money."

"If we take her hostage, what do you plan to do with him?"

"Take him along."

Scalager returned with his all-clear report. "Nobody out there. Nobody at all."

The woman scratched the back of her neck and yawned. "Why should we feed and watch two hostages?"

"Do you know the story of Medea?"

"Can't say I do."

John nodded at the fakir. "Scalager here knows all about Greek myths, don't you Scalager?"

"I understand what you mean."

Scalager turned to the woman. "The princess Medea ran away with Jason on the

Argo after he stole her father's most prized possession. To steal the golden fleece, she killed her own brother and threw pieces of him into the sea. Fishing the bits of his son from the water slowed Aeetes down. Jason and Medea were able to escape."

Jemmy shivered. *How could anyone be so cruel? And how stupid have I been to trust John? Heavens in a handbag, do they mean to butcher Hal and throw pieces of him on the road? Maybe I'm the one they plan to chop up. Heavens in a handbag!*

The woman gave a wicked chuckle. "A devilish idea, Dollarhide. I'll think on it."

John motioned toward Jemmy. "I'll tie her up."

Jemmy protested as he yanked her hands behind her back. "Do you have to be so rough?"

Mustn't think about the rope rubbing my wrists raw. Keep her talking. Got to keep her talking.

"Before you go cutting anyone in pieces, Hal and I would both appreciate knowing why you've been using the Wild West for target practice."

"Can't think why I should trouble."

"Why not?" The sting of John's betrayal hurt more than rope gnawing her wrists. Jemmy tried to control the quaver in her voice. "Mr. Scalager told you we don't have any Pinkertons or police. With Hal and me tied up, what could you be afraid of?"

The woman snapped back, "I'm not afraid of anything. I simply don't see why I should bother."

"If you're going to ransom me or maybe kill me, couldn't you at least satisfy my curiosity? I've never met anyone like you."

"What do you mean?"

"Well, obviously you call the shots around here. You give orders to Scalager. If the sign outside tells the truth, he ought to be giving you orders because he owns this wagon. You scold Dollarhide like he's a little boy. Why do they obey you?"

Scalager defended himself. "I don't have to listen to that in my own —"

John's words rushed out at the same time. "Are you going to let her talk about me like — ?"

The woman barked, "Quiet. Do you want the police to come 'round because we're disturbing the peace?"

The men fell silent.

The woman paused and tilted her head. "Nobody's sleepin' for the rest of the night. We can't get the mules from the livery stable until sunup without causing suspicion. I might take a notion to tell you a thing or two since we're all awake till dawn. Come up here where I can see you."

Jemmy's feet felt like wagon axles in Frank Butler's too-large boots. They made a fearsome racket as she dragged them over the jumble of cook pots and harness on the floor. She shuffled slowly to the midpoint of the wagon. She might not have managed at all but for John's hand on the back of her neck driving her forward. She wanted to scream. *Don't you dare put your hand near my mouth again. This time I'd bite it and hang on like a bulldog.*

Jemmy's brain caromed from anger at John to anger at Scalager's woman to sheer terror for the desperate fix she was in. *Fight down these stupid thoughts. Think — think.*

Scalager's woman sat down, leaned back on her elbow, and lit a cigar from the lamp. Her voice dripped with mock sincerity. "I'll tell you my sad tale, my tale of woe. You see I planned to marry one of Captain Bogardus's sons. I didn't much care which one. I loved shooting, and I was ready to marry any one of the three who would put me in the Wild West show and make me a star. I'd even have married old man Bogardus himself."

Jemmy's fingers picked at the ropes as she tried to listen with her good ear and half of

384

her mind. *If only I could come up with a way to put out the lamp. It's too far away to kick.*

"I was well on my way, or so I thought. But then everything went wrong. When my Bogardus boy found out the only reason I wanted to marry him was so he could make me a star, he quit me cold and poisoned his brothers against me, too. Seems the only thing the whole family wanted from females was for them to produce little Bogarduses and keep the home fires burning."

There . . . one hand free. If I could get the other hand . . . If I could get the other hand loose? Then what? Put out the lamp somehow?

She looked around for something to throw at the lamp when a nerve sizzled inside her head. Her bad ear clattered and whined as if a locust flew in. Woozy and off-balance, she barely kept herself from falling as she stumbled another step forward.

Her brain wouldn't operate. All of a sudden the tension of the last two days caved in on her. Every anxious moment over Hal's disappearance, the futility of every effort to find him, the restless energy lost in two sleepless nights brought her to the brink of collapse. She lost the ability to sort through events — to plan — to act.

I have to hang onto something.

As she forced her mind to concentrate, the weight lifted, but only a little — from a thousand-pound cow sitting on her head to a nine-hundred-pound cow sitting on her head.

My hands are free. Finding the meaning behind that knowledge took what seemed hours to comprehend. Somehow her hands had worked at the knots on their own, with no direction from her head. She was free but had not the least notion of what to do with her freedom.

She held the rope loosely behind her as she tried to listen to the woman's words. The effort drained her. Her exhausted body refused to move. Her weary brain clung to a thin thread of thought. *Maybe I could throw the rope at the gun . . . and probably get shot . . . maybe at the lantern . . .*

The woman's voice became more animated. Jemmy could almost make sense of it. "What's worse, the Bogardus family would have been useless to me because they dropped out of show business. While I tried to marry a Bogardus, two women stole my spot in the Wild West right out from under me."

So, the woman thinks she can shoot. That must be important somehow . . . but how?

"One good thing happened. Annie Oakley got Lillian Smith fired without my turning a finger. One down — one to go."

Something rang false in the woman's story. Jemmy managed to spurt out a sensible sentence. "But Lillian hasn't been with the show in years. Why did you wait so long to go after Annie?"

"Discouragement. Pure discouragement. I gave up. I'd probably still be hunting wolves for bounty in Colorado if God had not spoken. He sent me a railroad excursion flyer. Colonel Cody's show at the Trans-Mississippi Exposition in Omaha, summer 1898. They even gave the big star his own day, Buffalo Bill Cody Day, the thirty-first of August. I knew it was a sign. How else would an excursion flyer come to me high up in the wilds of the Rocky Mountains?

"Don't you see? I had no choice but to go. That paper gave me the fever all over again. I saw how worthless I'd become because I failed to follow my destiny. I swore to myself I'd find a way to get on the show bill by the thirty-first of August."

Jemmy realized the woman must be touched in the head. "Why were you so sure you were born to be in Buffalo Bill's show?"

"Fate sent me Scalager in Hannibal." She launched an imaginary kiss in his direction. "By pure act of providence we joined up together. Cody brings in big crowds, lots of people to sell panaceas to. Scalager likes to hit town right before the Wild West."

Despite the haze in her head, the name "Hannibal" struck a chord in Jemmy's memory. "Mrs. Cody said someone shot at her in the cave near Hannibal. Did you do it?"

"The trip to the cave didn't work out quite the way I wanted."

She nodded toward the Frank Butler clothes Jemmy wore. "I see you like to dress in men's clothes, too. I dressed like a man and pretended to guide the three of them, the Codys and Johnny Baker, through the cave.

"I sneaked off and hid — planned to shoot Johnny B. I figured the Wild West needed two marksmen — two markswomen would be even better. I thought replacing Baker might be easier than replacing Annie Oakley. Glad I didn't put a bullet in Baker, though. He's the only one can fill in for Cody for so much as a single night."

Jemmy tried to keep her knees from buckling. "And the Indian — were you aiming to kill Colonel Cody when you shot Little Elk?"

"I don't much care for your tone. I was not trying to kill anybody, certainly not the colonel. The show would fold without Buffalo Bill. I was trying to wound Annie Oakley. If she couldn't shoot for a while, the colonel would need a substitute."

"You say you planned to be in the show by August thirty-first. You missed your target. It's late September."

The woman shrugged her shoulders. "I told you my timetable. Fate's calendar seems inclined to teach me patience."

In desperation, Jemmy tried an insult. "Too bad Fate didn't give you patience — not to mention a better timetable and much better aim."

"Keep your opinions to yourself. My aim is good enough to end your sass right this minute."

Knowing she'd hit a sore spot cleared the fog from Jemmy's brain. "Sorry, I didn't mean to offend. But you just admitted you were shooting at Mr. Baker but hit Mrs. Cody. You were aiming for Annie Oakley when you shot Little Elk. Mrs. Butler was sure wrong about you."

"What did Annie Oakley say about me?"

"When you put an extra dot on the "i" in Annie, she said you had to be a great shot, but you couldn't scare her into missing a performance."

"Fate guided my hand."

"Do you think I believe you? You were aiming for Annie and missed."

"How would you know what I was aiming at?"

"You talk big, but inside you know you're not worthy of cleaning horse manure off Annie's boots."

"Shut your smart mouth right now."

Jemmy felt more words gushing out and was powerless to stop them even if she'd wanted to. "Did you ever consider your talent, or lack of it, might be the cause of your many failures?"

The woman cocked her pistol with a loud clack and settled her voice to a low menace.

"I won't be discouraged. Not again. I'll be in the Wild West or kill trying. It's my destiny."

The woman had finished her story. The silence afterward sent a rush of panic up Jemmy's throat when she could think of nothing to say. *More talk. Keep her talking. Say something!*

Much to her own surprise, Jemmy's mouth obliged. "How amazing you are. No matter how impossible the goal, you won't let yourself be disheartened. No wonder these men take orders from you."

The woman cocked her head as if she didn't quite follow the shift in conversation.

Jemmy rushed on. "You went to a great deal of trouble to sideline Johnny Baker and failed. You set your sights on Buffalo Bill Day in Omaha and failed. You shot at Annie in her tent today and missed. Then tonight you tried twice to shoot Dorothea dressed up as Annie Oakley. You not only failed to shoot her, you weren't even shooting at the right person."

"Why you little . . ."

"Not much of a shot are you?"

The woman gurgled in her throat and started to move toward Jemmy.

A man's voice outside the wagon interrupted what promised to be a long tirade or a quick bullet. "Mr. Scalager, sir, I wonder if anything is wrong. I saw your light and thought I might be able to help."

Scalager mouthed the name "Scott Joplin — the piano player at the Maple Leaf Club." Aloud he said, "No, nothing is wrong, Perfessor. We're trying to get an early start. Nothing more than that."

The voice neared the front of the wagon. "Do you have sickness? I could fetch a doctor."

Scalager clambered out over the front seat. "I'll be right out, Perfessor Joplin."

No sooner had he finished those words than a shot rang out — *bam.* Jemmy jumped. The lamp glass exploded and snuffed the flame. The wagon pitched into darkness.

I'll not have a better moment to escape. If only I can . . . Jemmy took a deep breath and held it. She plunged forward with the vague hope of knocking away the woman's gun.

Before she took a step, John shoved her against the side canvas. She tumbled over a trunk and banged her head on the side of the wagon bed.

Betrayed, bruised, and all but helpless, she pulled herself upright behind the trunk in hopes bullets coming her way would bury themselves in the wood and leather instead of her own tender flesh.

For some moments her mind couldn't grasp the events which came next. She heard scuffling noises.

As she peered over the trunk, she saw a shape that must have been John Dollarhide lunge at the woman. The pair of them fell to the wagon bed with a whump.

Another shot came — this one from inside the wagon. John yelped. Not until then did Jemmy remember the pistol she had tucked in the inner pocket of Frank's frock coat. *What good does having a gun do? I can't see which one is John and which one is the woman. I don't even remember whether there's a bullet ready to fire.*

She pulled the gun from her pocket with a trembling hand. The warmth of the wooden grip comforted her but didn't keep her hands from shaking.

As she edged closer, she could see a pair of black rolling shapes and thought she could make out the woman's head. Suddenly, Jemmy knew what to do. She hoisted the Colt by the barrel and thwacked it down on what she hoped was the woman's cranium. She missed her target. She didn't hit John, but she didn't hit the woman, either.

The blow smashed into a crate of Sagwa Elixir. The gun butt slammed through a half dozen bottles and left Jemmy's hand stuck in the splintered orange wood box. Noxious fumes of whiskey, turpentine, and something like rotten turnips made Jemmy's eyes water.

She backed away from the stench with the crate still stuck on her arm and her hand still firmly attached to the Colt. *No way am I letting go of that gun barrel.*

She tried to rid herself of the crate with a mighty shake of her arm. At last fortune smiled. The broken crate and unbroken elixir bottles flew off Jemmy's hand and hit the woman's head full force. She slumped motionless as glass shattered around her.

Jemmy crunched through broken medicine bottles to grab the woman's limp arms. She untied the rope still dangling from her own wrist. It came in handy for binding the woman's hands behind her. Scalager's woman was not going to cause more trouble any time soon.

The back wagon gate dropped with a bang. A light appeared with a familiar face behind it — Dorothea Koock, still dressed as Annie Oakley. "Jemmy, Mr. Dwyer, are you all right?"

Jemmy sang out, "Never better."

Hal made some sounds through his gag until Dorothea removed it. He offered a feeble, "I'll be okay as soon as I stop shaking."

Jemmy scooped up as much un-Sagwa-ed bedding as she could find. Dorothea bundled Hal in wool blankets and chafed his hands to bring back his circulation.

Jemmy remembered Dollarhide's outcry and returned to the front of the wagon.

John pressed his blue bandana to his shoulder. He acted cheerful despite his wound. He called back to Dorothea, "Are you the one? Did you shoot out the lamp right through the canvas?"

Dorothea said, "Yes, I got off a lucky shot. Of course, Mr. Joplin deserves much credit as well. Without his help in getting Scalager out of the wagon so he and Obadiah could subdue him . . . Well, our chance of success would not have been half so good."

Jemmy tied the bandana in a knot. "Did you follow us? We didn't hear a thing, did we, John?"

"I knew they were behind us. I figured they were tagging along to keep you out of trouble."

Dorothea piped in. "Naturally we couldn't allow you to come to harm. We understood why you left with this gentleman. We saw you slip under the tent with him."

Dorothea rubbed Hal's hands to bring back circulation. "When we went back to find you, we figured out what must have happened. We followed from a distance because Mr. Koock said we mustn't scare away the one man who could lead us to Mr. Dwyer."

John gave a little grunt of pain before he said, "We thank you, all three of you — Mr. and Mrs. Koock and Mr. Joplin — don't we Miss Jemima? You saved our lives."

"John — if 'John' is your real name — I'm still not entirely sure you're one of the good guys."

"Chief Prentice can verify I'm a Pinkerton with the Kansas City Office. Would that and the word of the agency's branch manager convince you?"

"I suppose."

A lantern appeared over the front seat of the wagon. The face appeared as little more than two winking white marbles with deep brown centers, but the hand on the lamp gleamed the color of polished mahogany through elegantly slim fingers. Scott Joplin said, "Is everything all right in here?"

John answered. "If the offer to get a doctor still stands, I'd be much obliged."

Jemmy added, "He's been shot, but the bullet didn't damage his mouth."

"I'll bring the doctor back directly — and the police, too." The lantern winked away.

The appearance of Scalager at the back of the wagon startled Jemmy until she saw Obadiah bend the panacea peddler over the rear wagon gate and force the man's face down on the wagon bed.

Hal applauded as loudly as his stiff hands would permit. "So you caught him, Mr. Koock. It would make me feel better if you'd let me tie him up the way he tied me up. My fingers are prickling, but I think I have enough use of them to tie a few knots."

Obadiah waved him permission, "Be my guest."

As Hal trussed Scalager, Obadiah beamed admiration at Dorothea. "You make a fine Annie Oakley. Put out the lantern light in one shot — and through canvas!"

Jemmy couldn't resist a final gloat at Scalager's woman's expense. "The only job in Buffalo Bill's Wild West that would-be shootist woman is fit for is mucking out stalls. Replace Annie Oakley or Johnny Baker? She must be a madwoman as well as a rotten shot."

The Sedalia mayor, Dr. Overstreet, spirited John Dollarhide off to the Katy hospital. Hal, Jemmy, Scott Joplin, and the Koocks delivered Scalager and the woman to the police station in the wee hours of Saturday morning. The quintet drank coffee that could have passed for kerosene while they wrote sworn statements of the night's events.

The sun was up by the time they walked out the door. The energizing smell of morning dew refreshed Jemmy's face.

Hal shook Scott Joplin's hand. "I hope you will come perform in St. Louis. I was mighty taken with your music."

Jemmy added, "Your piano playing amazed me. You sound like an entire orchestra."

Obadiah shook hands with the musician. "I don't know how we could have managed to free Mr. Dwyer without you, Mr. Joplin.

If I can be of help to you in some way, please don't hesitate to call on me."

Scott nodded. "I'm honored to be able to help. The event itself was reward enough. It gave me an idea for a ragtime title, 'Something Doing.' Maybe I'll find an honest publisher who will give me a royalties contract instead of making me sell my songs outright. Someday I might get 'Something Doing' published — in F major, I think — for the Scalagers, the major fakirs." He smiled as he tipped his hat to the ladies and took his leave.

Obadiah looked thoughtful as he turned to Dorothea, "I know an honest music dealer right here in town, John Stark. Perhaps he knows an honest publisher."

Jemmy turned back to read the sign announcing the building on Second Street as home to the Sedalia Police. She shook her head in bewilderment. "Those criminals had some gall. The wagon where Scalager and the woman held Hal prisoner stands only five blocks from the police station."

With one hand Obadiah steadied Dorothea's elbow as she mounted her horse. With the back of his free hand, he covered a yawn. "I can't remember a more exhausting day in my entire life. I'll send word to the Katy shops I won't be in at all."

400

He motioned to Hal to hand Jemmy up on the other Koock saddle horse as he stuck his foot in the stirrup to climb on behind Dorothea. "We can ride double back home. It's not far."

Hal backed away. "I have to get my camera — all my gear from the wagon."

"Don't fret yourself. I'll send Jean Max with the cart."

"I have to go to the arena." Hal hung his head. "If I don't get some pictures, my boss will fire me."

"You could hardly take pictures while you were tied up. Surely he wouldn't expect you to do the impossible."

"Mr. Koock, sir, you don't understand. Mr. Hamm must not find out outlaws tied me up. I'm supposed to be a bodyguard and a photographer. How can I tell him I got myself hobbled like a calf for branding? What's worse, I didn't take pictures, either."

Jemmy added under her breath, "And instead of rescuing a damsel in distress, the damsel rescued you."

Obadiah seemed to appreciate Hal's problem, even if Jemmy didn't. "What do you say, Miss McBustle? If you choose to write the whole story exactly as it happened, Mr. Dwyer won't be able to hide the facts from his boss or anyone else."

This moral dilemma twisted Jemmy's brain pretzelwise. She had never taken an oath to tell the whole truth, but journalists — true journalists — lived by a code. The unwritten laws allowed them to exaggerate and sensationalize. But true newspapermen viewed the out-and-out lie as a crime punishable by excommunication from the ranks of the elite.

On the other hand, she owed Hal. He had helped her out of some tough scrapes. Yes, he was a pain, but a replacement — if Hamm would hire one at all — could be even worse.

If Mother didn't believe Jemmy had proper protection, she would insist Jemmy stop working at the *Illuminator.* Jemmy couldn't stand the thought of failing as a stunt reporter. *What would I do? Hire on as clerk at Barr's Department store? Marry a rich old codger with nothing better to do than complain about his gout?*

Hal reminded her of a sad-eyed bloodhound that had lost its power of smell. She could no more resist his begging look than she could leave him in the clutches of kidnappers.

She made up her mind, but she didn't speak right away. Base motives popped into her head. She tried to quash them. Still, she couldn't suppress a shamefully devious thought.

Not only would Hal owe her on a scale he could probably never repay, but if he should ever get out of line, she had the means to gain his cooperation. Saving him from the Scalager woman was as good as a nose ring in a bull. She could twist it any time she wanted and cause him unendurable pain.

With gracious condescension she offered, "Of course. I wouldn't wish Hal to lose his job. Let's get a few hours of sleep, then go to the fairgrounds."

Obadiah threw cold water on her idea. "I doubt you would find anyone there later today. The Wild West is playing the town of Joplin, Missouri, tonight. Their train leaves at seven-seventeen. I know, because they're taking the Katy line."

Dorothea offered, "We have plenty of time. I suggest we borrow the Pinkerton fellow's horses, collect Mr. Dwyer's gear, and go straight to the Wild West. I expect we'll catch the performers at breakfast."

Obadiah grinned. "The campgrounds it is — if Miss McBustle agrees."

Jemmy felt a tiredness so overwhelming she feared falling asleep before they traveled a single block. She refused to let it stop her, but gamely mounted the little mare she had

403

ridden the night before. "Lead the way."

Dorothea added, "On the way home, we can drop by the Katy Hospital and see how Lilburn and the other injured fellow are doing. We can ask the Pinkerton man what we should do with his two horses."

The time had come for Jemmy to confess. "About my not telling you when Aunt Tilly took Burnie to the hospital —"

Dorothea said, "I wish you had trusted me enough to tell me, but I understand why you kept silent. Mr. Koock's telephone call to the hospital reassured us Lilburn will be fine. That's the main thing."

The fairgrounds hummed with action as the four rode up to Annie's tent. The Butlers were enraptured by the story of Hal's release. They applauded the capture of Scalager and the woman who had been plaguing the Wild West. The famous couple wore broad smiles as they posed for Hal's endless picture-taking.

Members of the cast were only too happy to don costumes and even war paint. Hal could not have commanded more eagerness to please if he were President McKinley. Johnny Baker personally wrote ten passes for each of them to the governor's box at any future show. He apologized again and again because the colonel was not on hand to reward them properly. "I know the colonel will honor you in a manner befitting the heroes who saved the Wild West star attraction and the ticket money, too."

Annie insisted Dorothea and Jemmy keep the togs they'd worn when they played Frank and herself — along with a promise to send proper rewards as soon as she got home to Maryland.

Not until late morning did the four arrive at the Katy Hospital. The Sisters of the Incarnate Word did not welcome visitors who arrived outside of regular visiting hours. When they saw Katy boss Obadiah Koock himself had come to see his son, they relented. The sisters did insist each of the two injured men would have only one visitor at a time.

The four settled on an order: Hal would see John while Obadiah visited Burnie, then the men would switch. Afterward the ladies would take the men's places. Dorothea had to prod Jemmy awake when Hal returned.

As she passed Mr. Koock, she noted his blinking eyes and red nose. They betrayed the tough businessman's tender feelings for his son.

Exhausted, Jemmy plodded behind a tiny nun in a snowy wimple to the far end of the men's dormitory. She sat in a chair recently vacated by Mr. Koock.

She steeled herself for what she had to do. She knew she should be pouring out her gratitude to John and Burnie. Both fellows had been shot to save Jemmy — voluntarily, too. But as she sat down by Burnie's bed, she now asked for still more sacrifice. "I wonder whether you might do me a great favor."

His face lit up. "Anything. Just ask."

"Be my hero, a second time."

"I'd like nothing better, but I don't understand."

"I want to write the story this way. You saved me from robbers at the ticket wagon just as you most valiantly did. But then the assassins who were trying to ruin the Wild West kidnapped you and tied you up in a wagon. Of course it was Mr. Dwyer they actually tied up, but he would lose his job if our boss found out. You wouldn't want Hal to be fired, would you?"

He looked doubtful. "Why would anyone kidnap me?"

"Because the Scalagers know your family has money and that I'd come for you. They needed money. They wanted to hold me hostage because they thought my family would pay a big ransom. Two hostages from families with money would be worth even more, don't you think?"

His eyes opened wide and started blinking; but he said nothing.

Jemmy hurried on. "Naturally, I brought your parents to help. They captured the crooks and rescued me. They're extraordinary people — so brave — so clever. Anything you want to know about last night, ask them."

Burnie grabbed her hand as she tried to stand. "Don't go, please. I agree to the favor you want. Don't I deserve a favor in return?"

Jemmy sat down. "Ask away."

"Wait for me."

Jemmy didn't follow. "Wait for you to . . . ?"

"Turn fifteen. It's less than two years away."

Jemmy thought she knew why, but she needed to make sure. "What happens when you are fifteen?"

"I can marry without my father's consent."

Jemmy tried to let him down easy. "I know you want to marry me now, but two years is a long time. I doubt you'll feel the same way then."

"But I will. You may count on it."

She removed his hand from hers and patted it. "I can't promise to marry you. Most particularly, I would never marry you without your father's consent. I'm sure he has great plans for you that do not include marrying when you are only fifteen years old."

"He wants me to go to the University of Missouri in Columbia. He says I'll learn the wisdom of the ages and make good contacts."

"I'm sure he's right. You must know I would never do anything to displease your parents. They saved my life last night."

"I'll have lots of time to talk them into it. They like you. I know they do. Will you wait? Please tell me you will."

"I have no plans to marry anyone, none at all. I can tell you no more."

He covered her hand with his and bit his lip. "Will you at least promise not to marry without speaking to me first?"

He sighed with such longing she had not the heart to refuse him. "I promise."

He fell back against his pillows and released her hand. "Thank you. I'll make myself worthy of you. I'll swear as much on my mother's grave." Burnie looked so pitifully earnest, so eager for a kind word from her — like a cute beagle yearning for a pat on the head for bringing its master a dead toad. She felt a sudden and completely inappropriate urge to laugh. She managed to suppress it, barely.

She smiled to herself as she walked toward John's cot. As if the two could read each other's minds, Jemmy and Dorothea crossed paths at the center of the ward as they exchanged places.

Jemmy slipped into a chair by John's bed. "Thank you for saving my life."

"And thank you right back. Scalager's woman stopped battling right quick when you bashed her over the head with the crate of elixir. How did you ever think of it?"

Jemmy tried not to wince when John patted her battered hand. She didn't want to disappoint this brave man. She was not about to tell him she beaned the woman purely by accident. Jemmy was only trying to shake the smashed crate off her arm without letting go of her pistol.

She said, "We made a good team — the two of us — along with Scott Joplin and the Koocks."

"You're too modest. I don't know how long I could have kept up the fight after Scalager's woman shot me in the shoulder."

Jemmy's smile turned thoughtful as she leaned toward him. "Tell me something. Why did you persuade me to get out of the carriage that night in the alley by the Maple

Leaf Club? Was I window dressing for some Pinkerton plan or —"

"Did you think I had something nefarious in mind?"

"No, I don't think you had evil intentions. Truly, I didn't then and I don't now. I just want to understand. Why did you defend Duke and me?"

He answered lightly. "My chivalric nature, I guess."

"So it wasn't personal."

John sobered. "It couldn't have been more personal."

"Yes?"

"I'm trying to decide whether to tell you the real reason." He grimaced as he flexed the swollen fingers sticking out of his muslin sling. "I have a lonely job. Undercover work is hard. I have to cozy up to crooks I despise and romance women who would poison my beer if they discovered I am a spy. Most of the time I find myself in places no self-respecting bum would go, much less a true lady."

He looked up at her. "But Wednesday night — just three days ago — I saw a lovely face, the freshest face I've seen in months. I wanted to pretend, if only for a little while, that I was just a young man from town who had a right to listen to music with a pretty girl."

His words brought tears to her eyes. He brushed away one that fell to her cheek. "No tears for me. I chose my line of work, and I'm good at it. This is the first time I've ever been shot."

With a jolt, Jemmy remembered the duties of a hospital visitor. "And I haven't even asked how your shoulder is. All I've talked about is how I feel. You must think me a heartless, selfish girl."

"I think you're a brave girl who has a good head on her shoulders. The kind of girl I'd pick over a frail empty-headed lass any day."

Jemmy teared still more. "You're too generous. It was on account of me you got shot."

"Don't be silly. Risk goes with the job — and with good pay and expenses and bonuses, too."

Jemmy fumbled for her hanky with her free hand. John lifted the other to his lips and kissed it, then sank back in his pillows. "Maybe we'll find ourselves putting crooks out of business again sometime. When I'm in St. Louis, I'll look you up at the *Illuminator* — if you don't get too famous, that is — Mac."

Jemmy dabbed her eyes as she nodded.

She felt an overwhelming warmth to know he recalled even the phony name she gave herself. "You remembered."

"A girl named 'Mac' is hard to forget."

She leaned toward him and inhaled the sweet clean smell of apples and shaving cream. She took her leave with a chaste kiss to his forehead.

She didn't see him dab his eyes as she left. Her own eyes clouded by tears, she stumbled through the ward. Thank heaven in a handbag, Aunt Tilly didn't see the kiss. *Auntie would make me suffer for such a vulgar display.*

Back at the Koock home, the four crime foilers took to their beds. They left clear instructions not to be disturbed until the following day by anything less important than a large earthquake or a small tornado.

Jemmy would have relished the chance to sleep until she couldn't sleep any more, but Aunt Tilly's displeasure would be too high a price to pay. All four rose for breakfast, church, and a dutiful Sunday dinner with Parson Polkinghome and his family as the Koocks' guests.

Jemmy spent Monday writing articles while Hal tinkered with smelly chemicals and glass photographic plates. Monday night's farewell dinner showcased the new, very efficient butler. By then, Fanny and Sissy were firmly under the thumb of the new nanny, who had been chosen by Aunt Tilly to resemble herself as much as possible.

Obadiah not only attended, he played the true host. He told jolly stories and complimented Dorothea on everything from the food to her perfume.

Aunt Tilly seemed satisfied with her handiwork at the Koock household. Still, Jemmy had a premonition of the tongue-lashing she was apt to receive from the stern dame on the train ride home.

Jemmy would have liked another late-night gabfest with Dorothea, but the chat between friends was not to be. Obadiah and wife had become all but inseparable.

The train ride home was as unpleasant as Jemmy expected. The official explanation of where Hal, Jemmy, and the Koocks had been Friday after the show failed to satisfy. Aunt Tilly knew it to be false. After all, she had been at Burnie's bedside in the Katy Hospital through the entire night.

Aunt Tilly was too polite to give brash girls like Jemmy their comeuppance while they were houseguests. Ordinarily she would not air dirty linen in so public a place as a train. However, she couldn't contain her disgust. "I am shocked! A girl under my own personal charge showed off the shape of her legs in men's pantaloons. What cheek!"

For once, a lie was slow to come to Jemmy's lips. Hal rescued her. "It was the Pinkerton fellow. He persuaded Mrs. Koock and Miss McBustle to help him with his case."

"The very idea. I shall write to the Pinkerton Agency and seek the dismissal of anyone who would have such little regard for the fair sex. Jemima so young and Dorothea a mother — the very idea — appalling. What's this fellow's name?"

Jemmy stammered. "I-I-I never found out his name."

Hal rubbed his chin as if he were in deep thought. "Wasn't it Phineas? Yes, I feel certain it was Phineas T. Munrab."

Jemmy bit her lip to keep from laughing at "Barnum" spelled backward. She adopted a pose of innocence. "Was it? You found out more about him than I did."

"Maybe Hamm will make a reporter out of me and a bodyguard out of you."

Aunt Tilly gave each one "The Look" until both busied themselves with their private thoughts for the rest of the ride back to St. Louis.

Jemmy focused her thoughts on two famous women she'd seen in action. They were alike in bravery. Louisa Cody didn't need a firearm to bring criminals to justice. Her hatpin was weapon enough. Annie Oakley was the world's greatest shot, but she didn't put a deadly bullet into her target criminal. She simply chased the Annie imposter on foot.

Of course, the two were also different as a brass ring from a bathtub ring. Annie Oakley earned her fame by endless hours of practice. Louisa Cody's fame radiated from her bigger-than-life husband.

But Louisa's life only looked plush and easy on the surface. It didn't take Sherlock Holmes to see the woman's misery. Jemmy thought she must be desperate, to travel from Nebraska to Kansas City to have a showdown with her roving husband and end up protecting him instead.

Choosing between these two as the better role model for herself posed no great problem. She vowed to herself to become the best reporter St. Louis ever saw — no matter how long the hours or how painful the sacrifice.

Of course, Jemmy envied one more thing about Annie. She and Frank were completely devoted to each other. Someday

Jemmy might be lucky in love, too. At least, seeing Annie and Frank together made her believe some man might come to love her even if she happened to be headstrong and willful. Well, she could hope for such a miracle.

Jemmy placed new trophies in her souvenir strongbox. She touched the smooth barrel of the Smith & Wesson revolver that she had liberated from the robbers on the train.

She never fired the revolver. She had found a use for it though. The gun butt had come in right handy for coshing a crate to smithereens — and the crate for coshing Scalager's woman's head into the land of the unconscious.

John's blue bandana was a souvenir less lethal. For a week she wore it tucked into her chemise next to her heart. When it ceased to smell like apples, she laundered it and put it away. She chose to forget one detail — that she had used the bandana to stop Duke's drunken mouth.

Still every time she bit into an apple, she wondered whether John Dollarhide would really turn up at the newspaper office in St. Louis to see her as he had promised. On occasion she woke dreaming of him. His words echoed in her heart. ". . . the kind of girl I'd pick over a frail empty-headed lass any day."

Several weeks after she returned home she received a package from Annie Oakley — a complete sharpshooter suit of clothes — hat with a star, boots, pale buckskin skirt, and bolero with fringes. Most gorgeous of all was a pair of embroidered leggings even more elegant than the ones Annie had worn in Sedalia.

Annie explained the meanings of her symbols — oak leaves for bravery, red clover for hard work, and yellow iris for friendship.

Bravery, hard work, friendship — Jemmy was touched. The great Annie Oakley saw wonderful qualities in her and considered the would-be stunt reporter a friend.

Jemmy's mementos from her adventures would no longer fit in the tin strongbox. She had to squeeze the Frank Butler and Annie Oakley costumes into her hope chest.

As she smoothed the buckskin inside tissue paper, she wondered whether she'd need the linens she'd suffered so many needle pricks to make. Would she ever use those embroidered pillowcases or crocheted doilies? Would she ever have a home of her own — a husband?

Her wistful thoughts bumped up against reality. She'd quashed her hopes of marrying a likely fellow of her own age. Her outlandish behavior was more than enough to blacklist her. The grand dames of St. Louis didn't suffer unconventional females to go unpunished. The crop of men wealthy enough and independent enough to thumb their noses at society matrons would be far older and far more likely to rule young wives with stern face and cement fist. Jemmy shuddered at the thought.

Maybe she'd rent an apartment over Annette's Millinery on Olive Street. Of course, she'd have to make herself a success as a journalist first. So far, she'd managed to stay one step ahead of her editor. But Suetonius Hamm would like nothing better than to personally escort her out the door.

Aloud she said, "So, Mr. Hamm, I've delivered on my promise. I write stories people love to read." *As long as I sell papers, he can't fire me — probably.*

On the same day, Jemmy received a letter from Dorothea. She ignored it until she'd admired Annie Oakley's gift and carefully packed it away for safekeeping.

Why didn't I open my friend's letter first? Why did Annie's fill me with more excitement? She had to admit it was snobbery. *Annie is a celebrity. Dorothea is merely a friend.*

She traced the shape of the *claddagh* round her neck with her thumb — friendship, love, loyalty. She felt a little ashamed when she compared it with another symbol, a sapphire star and moon on a golden chain. These bejeweled souvenirs had very nearly cost her everything she held dear. *I should pick the claddagh — friendship over fame.*

As a child with no pen pals, Jemmy had never looked forward to mail delivery until she began corresponding with Dorothea. Reading day-by-day reports of events in Sedalia became a highlight of Jemmy's week.

Chief Prentice deferred Hal's abduction case. He asked the prosecuting attorney not to file charges until after Jackson County had its due. He sent Scalager and the woman to Kansas City to stand trial for shooting Little Elk.

The chief avoided Duke's case with equal dexterity. He approved the Koocks' plan to send young Marmaduke off to Wentworth Military Academy.

Duke fared a little better than the other boys in the gang. Without well-heeled parents, they found themselves hustled off to the Missouri Industrial School for Boys at Boonville.

Mr. Koock tried to drill into Duke's

unwilling brain the need to mend his evil ways. If he should be sent down for academic failure or bad behavior, he would find himself packed off to Seattle to work in Smoot's Hardware Store.

Elsinore Smoot had gone west to Seattle to sell miner's tools to folks heading for the Klondike in '97. Elsie Smoot was married to Sophie Snodderly Smoot, sister to Auntie Dee and Aunt Tilly. Shuffling unruly boys off to relatives in the wilderness was the last, desperate hope of a respectable family wishing to avoid scandal. Of course, they hoped to tame the lad, too. Even if the tribulations of the wilds killed the lad or caused him to run away, at least the family problem solved itself.

Deputy Sheriff Futcher turned out to be the criminal mastermind behind the train robbery. He finagled boys into doing the dirty work while he specialized in creating diversions.

Some of his diversions worked better than others. He had sent Sheriff Williams to the far reaches of the county on rumors of places where the robbers "holed up." Of course, Sheriff Williams was always just a little too late to catch any miscreants.

It was Futcher who had created the scuffle that gave Obadiah his bashing at the Katy shops. The deputy had Mr. Koock sidelined in order to give Duke Koock and the skinny robber from the train a clear field to steal ticket money from the Wild West.

One crisp day in late fall, Jemmy tore into a letter from Sedalia.

My Dear Friend Jemmy,

I thought you should know the fellow who calls himself John Dollarhide is not a private investigator. The Kansas City manager swore no such person ever worked for the Pinkerton Agency. Why he was with the Scalager show or why he helped you and Hal is a great mystery. We may never know what really happened or why. I wanted to warn you in case you should ever see him again.

Your loving friend,
Dorothea.

Jemmy cursed her own gullibility. *That confidence man had me convinced he was a hero. I should have known anyone so mysterious had to be two-faced.*

Deeper reflection turned her anger to sadness. *He must be good somewhere deep inside. After all, he did save me — well, almost — I think. Perhaps.*

She sighed as she returned to Dorothea's letter.

PS. Dearest Jemmy, wish me luck. Thanks to your help I found the courage to do what I have longed to do. Tonight I am going to wear my Little Egypt costume and dance for Obadiah.

Jemmy brushed a tear from her cheek as a thought struck her. She had a friend, a real friend. Dorothea was not like those mindless girls from school. They deserted Jemmy when she had to nurse her grandmother through months of illness. Those self-absorbed girls were always too busy with dances and picnics to visit when she needed them most.

Dorothea not only shared secrets with Jemmy, she understood Jemmy's need for independence. Jemmy now had one friend who accepted Jemmy's thumbing her nose at society's traditions, one friend who never scolded Jemmy's bad temper or thoughtlessness or lies.

Dorothea risked her dignity and her life for no better reason than Jemmy wished it. When Jemmy was in trouble, Dorothea came to the rescue. No one had ever done more — not even Jemmy's own bodyguard.

Jemmy found herself contemplating love and friendship. She felt permanent and unconditional love from her mother. But mother-daughter love comes with rules. Mothers expect obedience. A friend does not. *As for a man one might take an interest in? Those waters would have to remain uncharted.*

How is a body to tell which is lasting reality and which is fleeting pretense?

Dorothea embraced Jemmy just as she was — imagination, nimble tongue, willfulness — the whole A-to-Z alphabet of contradictions that made up Jemima McBustle. Jemmy cherished her first genuine adult friend. She thought of Dorothea's sweet face, and didn't even recall she had once compared Dorothea's long droopy nose to a peeled turnip.

Jemmy started to reread the note but was interrupted by her sister Miranda. "I wouldn't be in your shoes if they were top of the line at Brown Company."

"What do you mean?"

"Visitors await you in the parlor."

Jemmy scowled with impatience. "Well?"

"Well what?"

"Well who are they?"

"You'll see."

Jemmy patted loose strands of hair back

in place, then walked down two flights to the parlor and slid open the pocket doors.

Sipping tea in regal state were two Snodderly sisters. Auntie Dee glittered resplendent in dark brown serge with matching hat crowned by pheasant feathers and a pair of stuffed bobwhite quail.

Aunt Tilly looked even more severe than usual as she set aside her silver-headed walking stick and tugged at the fingers of her black kid gloves. "My dear, I bring you splendid news. Your Uncle Erwin and your Aunt Delilah have most generously decided to sponsor your grand tour of Europe."

She took a genteel sip of tea without making even a teensy slurping noise. "Their offer quite overwhelms me, as I'm sure it does you. The Erwin McBustles promise to provide proper traveling clothes and spending money as well as the usual expenses for transport, hotels, and the like."

Aunt Tilly set her teacup back in its saucer and added a splash of milk. "I believe April would be the appropriate month for departure. The Atlantic crossing is not nearly so rough in late spring. Naturally, I will be your companion."

Jemmy tried not to look as stunned as she felt. "Auntie Dee, I'm speechless. When did you decide?"

Auntie Dee nodded toward Tilly. "My sister convinced me a trip abroad would do your cousin Duncan a world of good after his difficulties in the Spanish-American War, and for me, too. You must know how I've worried about my son since he returned from Cuba. Why shouldn't you come along as well? Paying for two more is scarcely an added burden. We'll have a foursome for whist.

"I might add that we'll be able to examine an entirely new crop of young gentlemen there. You'll be introduced to fellows who know nothing about those recent events in St. Louis that might make you seem less than ideal as a bride to our local swains."

Jemmy's ability to lie deserted her. She could think of nothing better than "How very generous of you, Auntie Dee."

Jemmy had once envied the rich girls at Mary Institute who expected to go on grand tours the way poor girls expect farina for breakfast. Since her father died, she didn't dare imagine she would find herself sailing across the ocean. She had given up hope of seeing those romantic locations she had read about in Mark Twain's *Innocents Abroad.*

Going to Europe with wild cousin Duncan would no doubt be an education. Going to Europe with Auntie Dee would have good moments and bad. Both would make interesting travel companions.

Then reality hit. Aunt Tilly was to be Jemmy's personal companion. Aunt Tilly would hem her in and criticize her every move. Going to Europe with the Caligula of chaperones was just plain unthinkable. *Heavens in a handbag. How am I ever going to get out of going to Europe with Aunt Tilly?*

ABOUT THE AUTHOR

Fedora Amis has won numerous awards, including Outstanding Teacher of Speech in Missouri, membership in three halls of fame — state and national speech organizations and her own high school alma mater. Her nonfiction publications include books on speaking and logic and educational magazine articles. She won the Mayhaven Fiction Award for her Victorian whodunit, *Jack the Ripper in St. Louis,* and performs as real historical people and imagined characters from the 1800s. Fedora loves live theater, travel, plants, and cooking. She has one son, Skimmer, who partners Fedora in writing science fiction, fantasy, and magical realism.

"Why do I write? I love words — always have — reading them, writing them. I even like looking them up in the dictionary."

The employees of Thorndike Press hope you have enjoyed this Large Print book. All our Thorndike, Wheeler, and Kennebec Large Print titles are designed for easy reading, and all our books are made to last. Other Thorndike Press Large Print books are available at your library, through selected bookstores, or directly from us.

For information about titles, please call:
  (800) 223-1244

or visit our Web site at:
  http://gale.cengage.com/thorndike

To share your comments, please write:
  Publisher
  Thorndike Press
  10 Water St., Suite 310
  Waterville, ME 04901